Beat Not The Bones

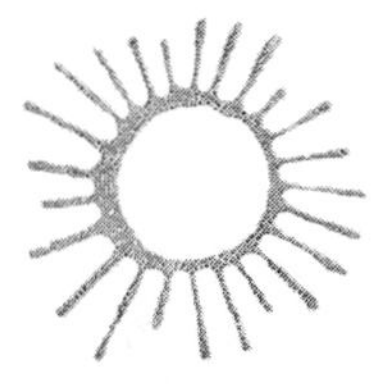

Beat Not The Bones

CHARLOTTE JAY

First published in Great Britain by Collins, London in 1952 and in the United States of America by Harper, New York in 1953

Published by
Soho Press, Inc.
853 Broadway
New York NY 10003

Library of Congress Cataloging-in-Publication Data

Jay, Charlotte, 1919–
Beat not the bones / Charlotte Jay.
p. cm.
ISBN 1–56947–047–2
PR9619.3.J36B4 1995
823—dc20
95–18476
CIP

Manufactured in the United States of America
10 9 8 7 6 5 4 3 2 1

For Julian Halls

The sweet war-man is dead and rotten;
Sweet chucks, beat not the bones of the buried
Love's Labour's Lost

Beat Not The Bones

It is said of a young man in a popular song that he has the moon in his pocket. Alfred Jobe had two moons in his. Sickle moons. Witches' moons. Mr Jobe stroked them lovingly with his fingertips as he walked up the wharf on his way to the town.

No one but a prophet would think of fear and death on such a morning. The little island town of Marapai glittered in the pristine sunlight of the Pacific seas. The south-east wind was lulling off into the two doldrum months that preceded the change of season and now only lightly tossed the grey fringes of the casuarina trees and flapped faded green blinds back and forth on bungalow verandahs. The grass skirts of the Papuan girls fluttered about their calves, and the harbour was dotted with the tilted, wedge-shaped sails of fishing canoes.

But though Marapai looked on this morning feckless and gay, she had her sinister side. Fear and death were no strangers here. The older inhabitants remembered days when they were commonplace, and were never particularly surprised when Marapai displayed again her old, cruel and terrifying nature. Such behaviour was expected of her, for though she was light-hearted, she was also savage. The arrangement by which a collection of white men had gathered here to undertake the taming and development of this wild land had not always worked. There was something now of the white man (unfortunately, some said) in the young Papuan who deserted village life, donned shirt and shorts, played hillbilly tunes on his guitar and gambled into the small hours of the morning. But there appeared to be other sinister and contrary forces at work that led in a very different direction. Frequently it was the white man who was won round.

He found himself developing tastes and traits he had known nothing of. A latent nature within him stirred and took command. People who had known him down south would barely recognise him, for he instinctively realised the futility of following rules of conduct that had come into being in lands where flowers were small and dim, birds were drab and seas were cold. Some worked out satisfactory substitutes for the discarded life, and some ran amok.

Certainly what happened – beginning that morning with Mr Jobe and his sickle moons – did not greatly astonish the inhabitants of Marapai. They agreed it was shocking, monstrous, terrible. But they could believe it and understand how it came about, for they were always expecting something like this from the country they lived in. The people south when they heard the truth – or that part of the truth that was made known – were incredulous. They could not accept such events. They were partly right. What happened could not have happened anywhere else.

To Alfred Jobe, Marapai had particular charms. He had just spent four months in the jungle and this primitive little town with its fifteen hundred whites was the big city, Sydney, London, New York – civilisation. Here there were cold beer and picture shows and white women, and he greeted it with all the fervour of his robust spirit. Good old Marapai! Good old Marapai! But pictures, women and beer must wait. He had more important things to do.

He had reached the end of the jetty, paused and looked around the customs sheds. There were no white people to be seen. A police boy stood aimlessly in the centre of the road, and half a dozen locals were squatting down in the shade of one of the sheds. One of them scratched in his enormous mop of hair with a long, pronged comb.

Jobe called out to the police boy, 'Hey! You! You black bastard! Come here when I tell you!'

The boy was not black, he was brown, with a handsome, Malay-type face. He moved forward hesitantly.

What a lot of bloody useless savages! A man might be murdered, he might be robbed and they'd just stand and stare. Jobe swallowed his rage. His instinctive reaction with natives was to hit them. He had been born too late and belonged to an earlier, less disciplined age. Now there was a law against striking natives. You weren't allowed to hit them at all. It was scandalous the way things were going. But he must keep his head, he told himself. He must play his cards carefully. There must be no trouble in Marapai.

'Government office. House paper. Where they put 'im now? Same place?' 'House paper' was the pidgin term for 'office', but this Papuan either did not understand or was struck dumb. He stared and looked blank.

Jobe swore at him and walked glumly on past the customs sheds. He had not been back to Marapai since the war and noted here and there signs of devastation. Bombed houses had not been cleared up and the wharf was still littered with heaps of rusty junk. Then he remembered that the government offices had all gone up in smoke, which in his opinion was the best thing that could happen to them. He hoped that his record had gone up in smoke too.

There were still a lot of Papuans about, and they were more westernised. The men wore coloured cotton ramis, or shorts and shirts; only the women had kept to their traditional grass skirts. There were more than ever, mobs of them. It seemed a pity that more hadn't been killed. Seemed all wrong that a lot of decent white men should die and leave these senseless niggers wandering around the place.

He started off down the port road that led out of the town to the other side of the harbour where the administration offices had been before the war. It was reasonable to assume that they would be rebuilt on the same site. The road dropped down to the beach where half a dozen canoes had been dragged up on the sand. The smell of burning copra drifted towards him. He sniffed and spat, then hailed a jeep, but it rattled past him. A few minutes later a car drew up behind him and a white policeman leaned out and said, 'Want a lift?'

Instinctively, Mr Jobe recoiled. He felt caught, discovered there in the middle of the road without a house or tree to dodge behind. His hand closed protectively over the treasure in his pocket. Then he squared his shoulders, beamed and stepped forward. 'Government offices round this way?'

'Yes, I can drop you off.'

Jobe got in and the jeep moved off. 'Place has shot up,' he said, looking around him. 'I haven't been back since the war. It's spread out quite a bit. And the place is crawling with kanakas.' He leaned over to spit but thought better of it.

'On the contrary,' said the sub-inspector. 'The population is decreasing.'

'You don't say?' He started to whistle and jangled the contents of his pocket. His spirits lifted. Hear that, my friend? You think that's money, but it's not. You'd be surprised if you knew what that was! Thinks it's money, the silly dumb cop. Thinks it's a bunch of keys.

'This fella Nyall,' he said, 'that's the bloke I've got to see. What's he like?'

'The director of Survey?'

'Yeah. What sort of a bloke is he? Give you a fair deal?'

'He's well thought of,' said the sub-inspector shortly.

They were out of the town by now, still driving along by the water's edge. A bend in the road revealed a group of white buildings dotted about under coconut palms.

'Is that the new government show?' asked Jobe, pointing.

'That's it.'

He started to laugh. 'Gawd! Look at it, will you. You'd think they were running Australia instead of a few thousand dirty niggers.' He stopped laughing and started to feel angry. It always made him angry when he thought of native education, hospitals, the rebuilding of native villages and all the other wild schemes that had ruined the country and squandered the taxpayer's money. Mr Jobe was not a taxpayer, but he was sensitive about the taxpayer's money.

The sub-inspector gave him a keen glance. 'Haven't I seen you somewhere before?'

Mr Jobe beamed. His tight, round, baby face was built for affability and his eyes were so deeply set beneath ragged brows few were able to ascertain their vindictive, greedy gleam. 'Not that I can recollect. But you more or less can't help it in this place, can you? Always rubbing up against people some time or another. People you don't want to know, what's more. Ha! Ha!'

Want to drag up the dirt, eh? Well, it won't do you any good. I'm having a chat with the director of Survey, see. All above board, all on the level.

The sub-inspector dropped him at the bottom of the road that led up into the government buildings, and he walked on through the trees, whistling and thinking of Mr Nyall, the director of Survey, and how surprised he would be. The road he followed led into a square, around which the government offices were built. Coconut palms gave way to frangipani trees, which dropped their pink and white, cream and lemon flowers on the peeling tin roofs. Wherever the eye turned, clusters of blossom and green leaf thrust up between the sheds, as poppies sprout out of a battleground.

The Department of Survey operated from a building on the far side of the square. It was made of timber and had an iron roof. The administration staff had more than doubled since the war, and these makeshift buildings were all that were available to house them. The offices were optimistically known as 'temporary', though many of them had acquired the mouldy patina of antiques.

Mr Jobe, who had no appointment, was told to wait, and waited for an hour, sitting on a wooden chair in the general office. He did not mind; he was used to it and anyway he had plenty to think about. Every now and again he smiled to himself, because nobody looked up or took any notice. He thought how they would behave if they knew, and his smile broadened. There he was, sitting among them, quiet as a mouse, and nobody knew, nobody even guessed. The tall, thin fellow with the bright blue eyes had not looked at him again after the first casual glance. Two Papuan clerks rattled away on typewriters. Not that it would mean anything to them. Stupid, *innately* stupid. It was a word he had heard used by a judge, and he thought well of it. He knew it covered much. He began to get angry then, thinking of the innate stupidity of natives and the enormous wages they were earning, typing in offices and ruining the country. Then a young girl with short blonde hair came out of an inner office and said, 'Come this way, please.'

Jobe rose to his feet and followed. His anger evaporated as quickly as it had materialised. Anger had been Jobe's trouble all his life. It spouted up like a geyser. Before he knew where he was he had acted on it, and next moment was looking at his handiwork in bewilderment, wondering what on earth could have provoked him.

The yellow curls of the typist bobbed up and down just before him. He forgot the Papuans and their enormous wages and resisted instead a desire to stretch out his hand and stroke this curly head. He liked curly hair.

The director occupied the southern end of the building, which was partitioned off from the rest by a paper wall. He sat behind a large, littered desk facing a map of the Territory.

Jobe stood in the doorway, summing him up. He was a shrewd man, could hardly help being so. Shrewdness had been the inevitable product of his erratic mode of life. But about

Trevor Nyall he was not sure. He was prepared on almost all counts to approve of him. He had a strong but good-natured face and arresting eyes, but he was too clean. He might have been a dummy in a Sydney shop window. There was no speck or crease in his shirt or white trousers, and he had not taken off his coat and tie, which was absurd. Mr Jobe distrusted cleanliness. It was a sign, for one thing, of education, and everyone knew that education produced dishonest men.

Dishonest, that is, in a big way. No one minded about little dishonesties. But he always felt that men as clean as this were trying to hide behind their well-laundered glory. You were supposed to be impressed and to look at the suit instead of the man.

But he was prepared to overlook this fault in Trevor Nyall. 'Name's Jobe, Mr Nyall. Alfred Jobe,' he said in his most affable manner. 'Just come down the coast from Kairipi.' Kairipi was one of the government stations about three hundred miles along the coast west of Marapai.

Nyall said nothing.

Jobe's affability increased. He became playful. 'Suppose you think I've come to buy land, eh? Start growing copra down the coast, eh? There's an old washed-up plantation fifty miles east of Kairipi. Nuts rotting on the ground. Let them rot. I don't want them.'

'What *do* you want?' said Nyall. 'Let's hear it. I haven't got all day.'

Jobe turned slowly round and pulled up a chair. He was enjoying himself. So you haven't got all day. So you want to be off talking to someone more important than me. Well, there isn't anyone more important than me. You wait!

He settled himself on the edge of the chair, then drew the two moons out of his pocket and put them on the desk between them. They were about six inches long – flat, thin, new moons, with holes punched in their horns. They were made of gold and decorated with a crude design scratched by a sharp instrument.

The director's face was expressionless. Jobe chuckled to himself. He decided he liked Mr Nyall.

Nyall stretched out his hand, picked up the gold ornaments and weighed them in his palm. 'What are they? Neck ornaments?'

Jobe nodded and leaned forward. The little game was over. Now they would get down to business. 'Yeah, they wear them round their necks on a bit of string. Like the pearl shell. You could have knocked me down when I saw them. Never seen anything like them before.'

'There is nothing like them,' said Nyall. 'There is no indigenous metal work in Papua, or at least so we believe. These are Stone Age people. They never got that far.'

This was education, and Mr Jobe brushed it aside. 'There's gold, Mr Nyall,' he began. 'I know where it is.'

'Where?'

Jobe lowered his eyes, though such a precaution was unnecessary. They never gave out anything but a submerged gleam. 'The Bava valley.'

'You want to put in a claim?'

Jobe nodded and slapped the palms of his hands on his knees. 'That's right,' he said. 'That's what it all boils down to, Mr Nyall.' Then his stomach lurched uncomfortably, and he rose to his feet. His voice was truculent and querulous. 'Heh! What's the matter now? I haven't done anything illegal. I found that stuff. There's nothing wrong in that. All fair and above board. Coming to you. That's the law. I'm not breaking the law.'

Nyall had stretched out his hand for the telephone. With the other hand he waved Jobe back in his chair. 'Don't worry. You did quite right. But from what I can see there'll be another department concerned in this.'

'*Another* department,' said Jobe. Even approaching *one* had been against his principles. Another bloody department! And they were going to fiddle around together and ring each other up and write each other letters while he hung around cooling his heels. 'What department?'

'The Department of Cultural Development,' said Nyall coolly. 'It's probable that these neck ornaments have some ceremonial significance. We'll have to find that out before we can consider your claim.'

'Cultural development!' Jobe's face turned scarlet. With a supreme effort he controlled himself. It wasn't Nyall's fault. He was only doing his job. He had to do what he was told. It was the Australian government. They'd ruined the place with their native education and tommy rot. Cultural development was the last straw. Culture was churches and music and theatres. Any fool knew that. And they talked about native culture! Dirty coons. Naked too, except for a bit of leaf and string. It was all very well for the Australians. They'd pushed their natives off into the middle of the desert and abandoned them, or killed them off. And now they sit back and tell us what to do. Native culture!

Nyall was asking for a man called David Warwick. 'Can you come over straight away?' he said.

There was a pause and Jobe heard a faint voice. 'What's it about?'

'I think ...' said Nyall '... not over the phone.'

'Who's this bloke Warwick?' said Jobe when Nyall had hung up. Warwick ... Warwick ... the name rang uncomfortably in his head, but he couldn't place it.

'Haven't you heard of him? He's an anthropologist.'

'Oh,' said Jobe. He might have known. The whole trouble had started with anthropologists.

Nyall waited and Jobe soothed his outraged feelings.

About five minutes later the door opened and Warwick came in. He was a broad-shouldered, thick-set man in his forty-ninth year. He had lived in the Territory most of his life and, like many Territorians, did not look his age. The climate agreed with him. He was strong, active and clear-eyed. His name had meant nothing to Jobe, but actually he was one of the island's aristocrats. He had been born in Marapai, a distinction that not many of the older men could boast of, and here the aristocracy were not those of blue blood or noble occupations but the ones who had lived here longest. This, however, was not the end of his achievements. He had half a dozen books to his credit and a reputation for learning and practical ability. To that minute section of humanity who had any interest in this primitive island, he was a celebrity.

Even Jobe, who had not known his name, recognised him immediately. His heart sank. What rotten luck. What a piece of filthy, rotten luck.

Warwick had not looked at him. He moved into the centre of the room and stood looking at Nyall. He seemed rather ill at ease and said uncertainly, 'Well, Trevor ...'

'This,' said Nyall, waving a hand vaguely, 'is Mr Jobe.'

Jobe came boldly forward with an outstretched hand. It was rotten luck, all right, but there was nothing to do but brazen it out. There was just a chance that this fellow wouldn't recognise him.

Warwick looked straight at him but appeared not to see him at all. He looked vague and worried.

'He's just come back from Kairipi,' said Nyall briskly. 'He's been up the Bava River – hasn't told us yet exactly where. And he brought these back with him.'

Warwick took the two gold moons from his hand. The look of anxiety passed from his face. He turned the moons over and peered at them intently, then said, 'Most interesting.'

'Mr Jobe finds them interesting too,' Nyall said with a faint smile.

Warwick looked up and focused now on Alfred Jobe.

Jobe held his breath. He thought he saw for an instant a faint beam of recognition in Warwick's eyes. 'I suppose he would,' he said.

'Well, come on, Mr Jobe. Let's have your story. I'm afraid you'll have to tell us where these things come from.' Nyall spoke briskly now.

Jobe had hoped he wouldn't have to tell them but saw that

this would be impossible. He squared his shoulders and went over to the map. His finger followed the coastline west from Marapai and mounted inland up the Bava River.

'Here's the river,' he said. 'Bava. Here's Kairipi on the coast. Patrol ends at Maiola. You can take a boat up that far. The district officer goes up every six months from Kairipi. Eola's about here, three miles west along the river.' He tapped his finger on the map.

'Eola,' repeated Nyall.

'Outside patrolled Territory,' said Warwick.

'Eola,' said Jobe again impressively. 'I was having a look around these parts. I've got a boat, been doing a bit of pearling up in the north. I took the boat up the Bava River and in one of the villages I came across one of these ornaments. They said they didn't make them there, and I traced it back to Eola.'

He paused. The two men were silent, their eyes turned intently to his face. He went on. 'Eola's a river village. You know the sort of thing ... twenty or thirty grass huts built on the bank of the river. Big long house in the middle of the place, for the men – no women allowed – you know. Where they do all their hocus-pocus nonsense. Pretty wild people. Only half a dozen of them had ever seen a white man before. One of them had been down to Kairipi. They get a bit of trade stuff through from Maiola. A couple of them had cotton ramis on, and they had some tins of bully beef.'

'Were they at all hostile?' asked Warwick.

Jobe became vague. This was a subject that he did not wish to go into. These government fellows were always worrying whether the locals were hostile. Wouldn't even let you carry a gun. A man would be a fool to go into the jungle without a gun, but it might frighten the poor bloody natives.

'Bit nervy at first, you know,' he said airily. 'Only natural. Not used to white men. Soon got used to me, though. Got quite fond of me after a bit, you might say.'

'And the gold?' said Nyall.

'There's a lot in the village,' said Jobe, dropping his voice to a whisper. 'Some of the old men wear those things round their necks, like pearl shell, you know. I'd say they was beaten out nuggets. And they've got a lot of rough stuff stuck away, and one special bit they make a fuss about that would be worth a few thousand on its own. There must be more of it round the place.'

'Did you look when you were there?' said Warwick.

Jobe shook his head. This far he would not go.

'Why would they value it!' said Nyall, turning to the anthropologist. 'It couldn't have any utilitarian value, and these things are so crudely made they're nothing to look at. The pearl shell is at least ornamental.'

Warwick shrugged his shoulders. 'There might be a hundred reasons, it's hard to say how these things begin. Take those two rocks in the middle of the harbour. They're more or less sacred, or used to be. There's a legend about them. There'd be magic behind this somewhere. Where do they keep the gold?'

'In the long house, or whatever you call it. The big hut in the middle of the village where all the men get together, and dance and eat and howl and God knows what.'

'In the long house!' exclaimed Warwick. 'How on earth did you get in there? I had to wait in a village for three months once before they'd even let me look at it.'

Jobe shifted uneasily. He had not been prepared for these questions. He knew well how taboo the long houses were; in fact it was there that the trouble had started.

'Well, when I first got to the place,' he said, 'I saw some of the old men wearing ornaments like these, and I asked them if they had any more. There was an old bird who'd been to Kairipi and spoke a bit of police motu, and we could more or less understand each other. They was pretty cagey at first and wouldn't say anything, but I managed to break them down. I had some trade goods with me, and I handed them around to sort of sweeten them up. Then one day he took me into the long house and showed me what they had hidden away. Very secret. Very hot, it was. This one big nugget, seems to be the prize piece, was hidden under leaves and feathers.'

'Did they explain why they kept it?' Warwick asked.

'They seemed to think the big bit looked like a crocodile. It was quite rough. They hadn't touched it. But there was a sort of look about it.'

'Would it be a clan totem?' asked Nyall.

'Possibly,' said Warwick. 'Something like that. It probably started with the crocodile. Some sorcerer may have found it and made some sort of magic with it and then gradually the material itself – the gold – would be believed to possess the same properties.' He turned back to Jobe. 'Did you try to take any away?'

Jobe's spirits bubbled up afresh. Everything was going all right. This fellow Warwick hadn't recognised him. And they were interested, they were quite excited about it all. It paid to put your cards on the table. It wasn't such a bad show. They couldn't help it if Australia interfered all the time. 'I tried to buy some with trade goods, but they weren't having any. The old boy sold me one of those ornaments for tobacco. But when the others found out about it they got a bit restive, and I had to hop it. One of them pitched a spear at me.'

He extended for their inspection the underside of his arm. Across the delicate, almost feminine, flesh was scrawled a shallow, red scar.

He saw immediately that he had made a mistake. Warwick looked up at him, faintly narrowed his eyes and glanced across at Nyall. There was a moment's silence in which the only sound was of Jobe's heavy breathing. Then Warwick put the two gold moons carefully on the desk. 'We'll have to talk this over, Mr Jobe, and let you know later on. But ...' he paused '... I don't want to hold out much hope for you.'

Nyall nodded and said nothing.

Jobe, looking from one to the other, thought he detected a faint, identical expression of satisfaction on their faces. 'Oh. Why?' he said loudly.

Warwick did not look at him. His voice was soft and tired. 'From what you've said, Mr Jobe, this gold is obviously of considerable value to the Eolans. The fact that they keep it secreted away in the long house means that it has ceremonial, to them almost sacred, significance. They wouldn't sell it to you, they wouldn't give it to you.' He paused and shrugged his shoulders. 'The fact that you value it for a different reason does not give you a right to it.'

Jobe's face was crimson. Words choked in his throat. For a moment the probable loss of his gold was a secondary consideration. It was this white man talking about native rights that enraged him.

Warwick looked at him sharply. This time his eyes were curious. He's remembering, thought Jobe. It's coming back. He changed his tone, smiled and said sweetly, 'It seems to me that we haven't always been so mighty fussy about the things that natives value.'

Warwick still stared at him. 'That's true,' he said. 'But you're speaking of the past. Exploitation has stopped now; at least, we're doing all in our power to stop it. But there's more to it than that. If you'd found the gold within patrolled territory, we might have had a different answer for you. But these people have no culture contact whatsoever. They don't know our law. When you take their gold, they throw spears at you. The whole enterprise might end in a welter of bloodshed.'

'They've had trade contact,' said Jobe, still smiling. 'They've bartered trade goods from Kairipi. They're very fond of bully beef.'

'A few tins of bully beef could hardly be called culture contact,' Warwick said coldly.

'I thought the policy of this government was to encourage private enterprise,' Jobe bellowed.

Nyall rose to his feet and spoke sternly. 'The policy of this administration is also to protect the Papuans, particularly the unsophisticated people in backward areas.'

'Protect!' said Jobe, cut by the implication of his words. 'Protect! Now, Mr Nyall, I come to you in all good faith. Fair and above board.'

Nyall looked at his watch. 'Come back at three this afternoon when we've had time to think it over. You never know ...' he ended vaguely. 'In the meantime I trust you won't mention this to anyone. We don't like rumours to get around.'

'I'm not such a bloody fool,' said Jobe. He threw a baleful glance at Warwick, bowed respectfully to Nyall and left the room.

They waited till his footsteps had died away, then Warwick said, 'You can't let him go, Trevor.'

Nyall turned away. 'Why?'

'Well, apart form the obvious reasons that I've been trying to explain to Mr Jobe – there's the man himself.'

'I saw you didn't like him.'

'He shouldn't even be here,' said Warwick. 'He would have been deported, but war broke out and things slackened up a bit. He's been gaoled twice – in Rabaul before the war – once for nearly killing a boy, hit him over the head with an oar and nearly beat him to death, and once when he was tried for peddling spirits in a local village. Got away with that on insufficient evidence. He's a really nasty type – makes trouble in the worst way, and there are others like him. They hate the local people, exploit them and teach them bad habits. They should never be allowed near a country like Papua.'

'You seem to know a lot about him. I thought all the Rabaul court records had gone in the war.'

'They have, too. It was bad luck for him he happened to run into me. I gave evidence against him. Obviously he struck trouble in Eola too. He would never have come to us except as a last resort. It's my guess they chased him out and he was scared to go back. So he thought he'd try and get government protection, possibly the help of the district officer and some police boys. Why else would he come here and tie himself up in red tape?'

'Well,' Nyall said. 'That settles it.'

Warwick picked up his hat. 'I must get back.' He glanced at the door and back again at Nyall. He waited, as if for permission to leave.

Nyall said, 'I have a feeling he won't take it lying down.'

At three o'clock that afternoon Warwick was sitting at his desk writing a letter to his wife. He faced out through the open louvres of his office onto a long, open parade ground ending in a belt of coconut palms. The letter he was answering fluttered in the breeze and he picked up a stone adze and put it on top of the paper.

'My dear love,' he had written. 'Your letter arrived this morning. You should not have dismissed your father's nurse without asking me. He is sick and can't know what's best for him. You must consult me about these things. Now you will have far too much to do. I am very angry with you. No, I am not angry – how could I be? But I hate the thought of your taking on too much work. When you come up here you will have nothing to worry about ...'

His pen faltered and he looked for inspiration at a framed snapshot on his desk. For some unexamined reason he found it difficult writing to his wife. The snapshot showed a young woman in her early twenties, wearing slacks and open-necked shirt, who sat, cross-legged, on a lawn, a spaniel puppy in her lap. She was bare-headed and smiled. They had been married for only two months, during his last leave in Australia, but his wife had not been able to leave her father.

The telephone rang. It was on a table behind him. He turned and glanced over his shoulder. His assistant, a man fifteen years his junior, was sitting on the other side of the room, his chair tilted back, feet on the desk. He was pulling the heads off a cluster of frangipani and threading them on a piece of string. The telephone rang again, but he did not move or look up.

Warwick leaned across for the phone, but he hardly heard the voice that said, 'Hello, Mr Warwick please.' His lips bit tight. Something will have to be done about him, he thought. It was awkward, but things could not go on like this.

'Hello. Warwick here.'

'Is that you, David?' It was Trevor Nyall. What now? he wondered. Then he remembered Jobe.

'I thought I'd just ring up and let you know,' Nyall said. 'I think our friend might pay you a visit. He's not in a pretty mood.'

'Oh?' Warwick was barely listening. His eyes were still fixed on the cluster of frangipani and the brown, nimble fingers threading the string. They were narrow, long, smooth, like native hands. He had never liked them.

'He seems to think that the whole thing is your fault,' said Nyall. 'He won't listen. He says I'm a good bloke, and would have given him a fair deal. He thinks you've got your knife into him.'

'He must have recognised me,' said Warwick, attending now.

'I expect so. My guess is he's in the pub now getting a skinful, then he'll come and tell you what he thinks of you.'

'Thanks,' said Warwick and hung up. He turned round. Jobe did not worry him greatly, but the flowers did.

'What's the matter, Tony? Nothing to do?' The garland dropped on the desk. The hands were folded.

'Plenty, but this seems the least destructive. This at least I shall not have to answer for. When our brown brothers ask us for excuses and explanations I shall be able to say, "You've got nothing on me, I only played with flowers ..."'

Warwick was not unsympathetic to the younger man. He was perhaps too clever for the Territory, and it did not do to be too clever here. He was too clear-sighted and saw not only the good but the inevitable evil that was trailed after all that was done. But he needed rounding up. He worked under direction with bad grace.

'We all know it's difficult. We've all made mistakes. Probably it's impossible, but we've got to stick at it. You're neurotic, Tony. Want to pull yourself together,' Warwick said.

'I'm not neurotic. I'm normal. Here it's the happy, successful and untroubled who are neurotic.'

Warwick turned away angrily. Me, I suppose, he thought. He had never allowed Papuan problems to make him feel uncomfortable. It was suicidal to take the show too seriously. He picked up his pen and wrote – not because it could be of any interest to his wife, but to rid himself of irritation – 'an interruption ... words with my difficult assistant. If things weren't so tied up I'd get rid of him. He has a neurotic, jealous nature and doesn't like doing what he's told ...'

He was still writing this letter at 3.45. The office was empty and he sat alone. The rest of the staff had gone home except for one of the clerks who appeared now in the doorway. Sereva was tall and well built. He came from a nearby village and had once been Warwick's houseboy. Warwick had become attached to him, taught him to speak and write English and, after the war, took him into the department. Although he was educated – as far as Papuans could be called so – he was not superficially westernised and had none of the blind regard for anything imported. He did not despise his village customs and preferred to wear a rami rather than shorts and shirt.

He spoke in a soft, whispering voice. 'There is a gentleman to see you, Mr Warwick.'

In the next instant Mr Jobe had blundered past him, thrust out an arm and sent him spinning backwards. 'Get out of my way, you filthy savage!'

Sereva, knocked off his balance and crouching on the floor, rose to his feet.

'If Sereva had a vindictive nature,' said Warwick quietly,

'he could see you in court for that. Are you all right, Sereva?'

The boy nodded. 'Yes, taubada.' He did not glance at Jobe, but quietly left the room.

'Don't you know that it's against the law to strike a Papuan?' Warwick said.

Jobe looked frightened. 'I didn't hit him. Only gave him a sort of friendly shove.' He stood looking red and sheepish in the centre of the room.

'I'm sorry about the gold,' said Warwick. 'It's bad luck, but there you are.'

'Bad luck!' exploded Jobe. 'It's a dirty trick, Mr Warwick, and I'm bloody well not standing for it. This fellow Nyall, he's okay. Everything would have gone along fine if it hadn't been for you.' He smiled and stretched out his hands. 'I ask you, Mr Warwick, is it fair? Throwing up a fella's mistakes at him. Dragging up the past when a fella's trying to be honest?'

'That had nothing to do with it,' said Warwick. 'You don't understand what's involved. If you take gold from these people, you strike at the very roots of their culture, and we don't do that until we're in a position to replace it with something that we consider better. You might just as reasonably ask for permission to plunder the crucifixes from churches.'

Mr Jobe, who believed in God and damnation, was deeply shocked. 'I must say, Mr Warwick,' he said loudly, 'that's not a very Christian thing to say.'

'I'm sorry, Mr Jobe,' said Warwick curtly, 'but that's the way we look at it. You can't have that gold. It belongs to the Eolans.'

'Natives! You only bother about them when it suits you.' The air of ingratiating sweetness had entirely left him. There was a wild gleam in his partly submerged eyes. He lurched towards Warwick and crashed his fist on the desk. 'I'm not standing for it!' he shouted.

'Oh? And what are you going to do about it?'

'Think I'm not good enough for you, you dirty snob! I'll

get around you, Mr bloody Warwick. What about *him*, he'll help me.' He waved an arm at the empty chair, the garland of frangipani still tossed over one of its arms. 'You're not God Almighty in this town, Mr Warwick. Plenty of people don't like you. I only had to spend half an hour in the pub to find that out. You're in debt, up to your neck. And your offsider here would be the first to step on your face.'

'Are you threatening me?' Warwick said quietly.

Jobe's hands fell to his sides. He paused for a moment and wondered if he had committed a punishable offence. One more and he'd be out of the islands, probably forced to earn a living. The thought was a sobering one. He gave Warwick a look intended to be pitiful and said, 'I only want my rights, Mr Warwick. I only want fair play. Came here on the level. It's hard for a man who's trying to forget the past. And it seems to me that you presume a lot when you say that going in and getting the gold will cause trouble. I shouldn't have shown you the spear. That's what comes of being honest.'

'As a matter of fact,' Warwick said, 'I've been thinking that we might go in and have a look.'

Jobe stepped forward. 'You and me?'

'No. You can wait here till I come back. I'll take a surveyor. Quite apart from the gold, I'd like to have a look at these people. From the point of view of material culture they are extraordinary.'

Jobe winced.

'If they don't particularly value their gold and would part with it peaceably, then you might be allowed to do something about it. If not now, perhaps later on. If not, you'll have to forget the whole business.'

The man and woman who occupied the two rear seats of the plane each leaned towards a window and peered down. For a moment their faces wore an almost identical look of longing.

The plane was flying over the coastline. They could see the reefs – long purple bruises under the water – and the bands of brilliant turquoise that marked the sandy shallows around the islands. Rising almost straight up from the sea the hills banked up, some of them naked, others blotched with patches of forest until, as they rose higher, forest entirely took over. It was cloudy ahead.

The woman, Stella Warwick, leaned back in her seat, closed her eyes and gripped her hands in her lap with the dramatic intensity of one who does not know or care if she is watched. Her first glimpse of Papua had moved her. The hostess, thinking she might be ill, moved towards her but paused when her eyes opened. Stella sat now staring before her and the hunger in her face had given way to resolution. Then she leaned towards the window and looked at the land below.

So far she had not felt much curiosity about the country towards which she was being so swiftly propelled. The flight had been a dream. She had no picture of the people in the plane or the places they had flown over. She had not wandered around to look at the two northern Australian towns where they had landed, but had sat in the airways offices, her only feeling being anxiety lest she should be left behind, a fear that always encroached when she travelled alone. Now, for the first time, she experienced vague excitement. Here, unrolling before her, was the strange land she had matched herself against.

The plane, which had continued to follow the coastline over an estuary and past a group of small islands, now turned inland and flew straight for the clouded mountains. A light flashed, telling passengers to fasten their safety belts. Stella fancied she could see houses far to the left crouched around a group of hills.

'Is that Marapai?' she asked the hostess, who was moving past offering the passengers barley sugar.

'Yes, madam,' said the hostess, blasé but indulgent. 'That's Marapai. We're going to land soon. Will your fasten your belt.'

Stella, who had chosen her own fate and did not wish another to intrude prematurely, did as she was told.

The hostess, whose name was Penny Smart, had served as a WAAF during the war and was now, seven years later, a debonair woman with somewhat gnarled sensibilities. The bed of her heart had become of necessity stony, yet she found herself unaccountably touched by the sight of Stella's small, clumsy fingers working on her safety belt. What on earth can she be doing up here? she asked herself as she bent to help. Never been away from home, like a child at its first party.

'Thank you,' said Stella, and lifted her large fanatical eyes.

Disturbed, Penny Smart turned away. No, not a child at her first party. She glanced at the list of passengers that was folded in the pocket of her uniform. She found Stella's name, and a notion of who she might be flashed into her mind, but she dismissed it; this girl was either too young – or too old – and she turned with her barley sugar to the man in the opposite seat.

He was big – not exactly fat, but solid and tight-skinned, which gave him an air of joviality and self-satisfaction, such as men will sometimes wear after a heavy meal. He refused the barley sugar, and Penny Smart passed on up the plane. He folded the paper he had been reading, pushed it under his seat, and looked around him, taking stock. Like Stella, in a particular way, he appeared to have arrived. His eyes travelled along the seats ahead. Stella was the last to suffer his scrutiny.

She leaned her head against the window, gazing down at the land as it rose to meet them. The sea was behind them, and through a gap in the round, golden hills they had made inland and circled over an airstrip. On one side a straight metalled road led to Marapai, on the other, an enormous bulwark of mountains, their summits lost in cloud, marked the limits of the white man's world. Stella's face was quiet and pale. Her short ruffled hair gave her the look of having just woken. In fact she felt desolate and afraid. All that was before her seemed to rise up like vapour from the earth and fold around her. The future she had sought breathed in her face, but it was not as she had wanted it, clean and somehow comforting, but frightening and lonely.

Her eyes turned and sought those of the man beside her. His future promised to be rich and favourable, and he smiled. Poor kid, he thought, she's been sick. He'd been airsick once himself and sympathised with her. Pretty little thing too. He liked curly hair.

She felt his friendliness and smiled. An image of his broad jovial face, with its tight, unlined flesh, downy hair and little eyes beneath protuberant rambling brows, printed itself in her mind.

She turned again to the window. The airstrip, rising, slid away beneath the plane. They bumped on the earth, rose and fell once more. The plane had landed. It coasted a little and stopped before a low, tin-roofed building. A moment later the gangway was brought forward and the door flung open.

Stella did not move. It was not the thought of landing into danger that frightened her but of landing alone. For the first time in her life there was no one to meet her, no one to manage her luggage and drive her to her destination. Small, practical details that had always been seen to by someone else.

'Are you coming now?' It was Penny Smart who spoke, standing with the door open and smiling at her.

The hot, noonday glare burned down on the ground. The tarred airstrip was warm and sticky under her feet. The curiosity and astonishment that are part of the will to live were not so dead in her as she had imagined. She forgot her luggage and the desolation of being alone and looked around her in profound surprise.

Papuans, brown-skinned, with enormous mops of black hair, and blue-skinned, with heads cropped close and peaked like coconuts, were lifting luggage out of the back of the plane and dumping it on to a carrier. Her own countrymen were dressed in white. The little airways shed was lifted up on stilts, as if escaping from the ground. All around her was a landscape so rugged, so blue, green and fantastic as to take her breath away. The fierce, majestic hills seemed hardly real, more like a backdrop for a film. Against this decor, it seemed incongruous and strange that passengers were being greeted by friends and luggage was being carried and checked.

Stella picked up her case and walked across to the office, away from the shining eyes and flushed cheeks of those who had husbands and lovers. She stood in the doorway, looking into a waiting-room filled with people talking and attending to their affairs. What was she to do? How would she get to Marapai? There had always been someone who said, Sit, wait here till I come back, found out when the buses left and filled in forms.

A girl behind a counter saw her white face and dismayed frown, caught her eye and beckoned. There was a form to fill in. Her luggage was being taken off the plane, and a bus left for town in half an hour. She had only to wait. With relief she looked up and smiled at the fair, pretty young clerk who had been attending to her. As she turned away, the clerk said to Penny Smart, who stood beside her lighting a cigarette, 'Is she all right? She looks a bit mad.'

'She's all right,' said Penny Smart, dropping a match on the floor. Her moment of compassion was over. People came, people went, they all had troubles, and you had your own. Those with any guts kept a brave face. Mysteries, however, were another matter. The Territory fed on them and, when it could not find them, invented its own. She bent conspiratorially over the passenger list that was spread open on the desk, and tapped a long, lacquered fingernail over Stella's name. 'Take a look at that! That's an interesting name to be carrying in this country.'

The clerk read the name aloud. 'Nonsense! Why, what would she be doing here?' She looked up and smiled. 'Yes, sir. Can I help you?'

The man who stood in front of her appeared not to hear. He had turned his head and was staring over into the corner of the room, where Stella sat alone, her legs crossed, her overnight bag on the floor at her feet.

Half an hour later the airways bus left for Marapai. Apart from Penny Smart, the clerk and two of the airways male staff, Stella was the only passenger. The man who had sat next to her had disappeared.

The road wound for a mile or so through low hills covered by small, twisted gum trees with flat, frilly leaves. They were not gum trees as Stella knew them. They looked to have gone mad, thrusting out leaf and branch, without reason or design, in all directions. Occasionally they passed Papuans walking barefoot on the side of the road, the women's grass skirts swinging below their knees.

Stella had seen these people before, standing stiffly in illustrations in anthropological books, or in snapshots fixed in a brown album, but these originals, walking loosely along on broad, flat feet, the sun striking coloured lights from their polished skins, were utterly unexpected.

The road mounted and turned. Below them stretched the coast with its scattered islands, green and smooth-backed as lazy whales. The little stunted trees had passed by and tropical vegetation blanketed the hills – trees with huge serrated leaves, the long, bending trunks of coconut palms and creepers tangling tree with tree. To the right on the plain below and straggling up the low hills were the houses of Marapai.

Penny Smart, who sat in front with the clerk, turned to her. 'Do you want to be put off somewhere?' she said.

Stella, attending passionately to the scene ahead, started and looked at her with vacant eyes.

'Do you want to be dropped?'

'Yes, if you don't mind.'

She produced a notebook from her handbag, opened it at the back page, and read, 'Number 16, Port Road.'

'To the mess?' said Penny Smart. 'Are you working for the administration?'

Stella nodded.

'Is anyone meeting you?'

'No,' said Stella. But I am not alone, she told herself. I shall have friends, and enemies. It was on the enemy that her thoughts most lovingly lingered.

They had now reached the outskirts of Marapai and drove along the seafront through a long avenue of casuarina trees. Coconut palms reached out over the water's edge as if yearning for other islands, perhaps the islands of their origin, for they dropped their nuts on the sand, and the sea cast them on many far-off sands. On the other side of the road, bungalows were stilted up among green trees and shrubs with variegated leaves, and there were banana trees with huge, floppy leaves, shredded by the wind.

She looked around her at the people they passed thinking, *He* might be any of these (for she had little information about him and the picture of him that she held in her mind was purely imaginary). He might be sitting in any of these houses, or driving a jeep along this road, not dreaming that today would be different from any other, thinking himself secure, safe.

They had nearly reached the end of the avenue. The driver tooted violently and an old, crippled man hobbled nimbly out of the way of the car. 'Nearly wiped off that savage,' he said, roaring with laughter.

A few moments later they drew up by a long, wooden bungalow with an iron roof.

'That's number 16,' Penny Smart said, and opened the door. The driver saw to her luggage.

Stella looked at her new home without much interest. It needed painting and looked dilapidated. There was a grey, blotched look about the walls, as if they were breaking out here and there into patches of mould. A strip of corrugated-iron had been nailed over one window, and a front step was broken.

She mounted the steps and turned to wave goodbye. There would never again, it seemed to her, be anyone permanently beside her, only odd strangers who filled in forms, carried her suitcases, or saw her into cars. The wheels turned, the dust puffed up, and she was alone once more.

She was confronted now by a short passage and three closed doors. The corridor was bare except for one frayed grass mat. From the door at the far end came the sound of voices. What should she do? Knock? Go in? Wait? Those who had loved her had failed to equip her for this moment – indulging themselves in the enjoyment of her helplessness – and had left her in panic at the sound of voices behind closed doors.

Then the door opened and a man in a long white rami came out, leaving it ajar. She could see into the room beyond. Twenty or thirty young women were sitting at long trestle-tables having lunch. They were served by locals, like the one she had just passed in the hall, who were barefoot and wore only white or coloured ramis. Some of them wore black and yellow bands round their forearms and beads in the pierced lobes of their ears. In the centre of the room stood a woman with grey hair who looked to have authority. Her head flicked back and forth, watching the waiters.

Stella paused, hesitating against the wall. The girls nearest her were eating cold meat and hot tinned peas, which they denounced with ardour, but no one noticed her. Eventually she walked over to the woman in the centre of the room. 'Excuse me,' she said softly, 'I have a room here.'

The woman did not look at her. Her eyes, set between narrow lids which she contracted as if it enabled her to see more keenly, flicked about the room in search of material for correction. 'There are no rooms here,' she said.

'I arrived today,' Stella said. 'By plane. I shall be working for the government. I have a letter.'

'There are no rooms here,' said the woman clearly. 'I ought to know. I'm in charge of the place.' She looked at Stella now. Her manner was so forthright, her words so direct that Stella accepted her statement.

'What shall I do?' The loss of her room seemed a disaster. She'd had little enough, a letter saying that a room was waiting, a pillow for her head. Now she had nothing.

The woman said, 'Of course, I remember, you've been moved. You're in Castle Warwick now.'

'What?' said Stella, flinching.

'Castle Warwick,' said the woman, carefully. She was evidently very nervy. 'Your room went to someone else, and you've been transferred up there.'

'Why is it called Castle Warwick?' said Stella.

The woman stared about the room. Matters, she implied, were piling up that needed her attention. 'Because somebody called Warwick lived there.'

'I won't go there!' said Stella, passionate and terrified. 'I won't go there! My letter says I'm to stay here.'

'There are people,' said the woman, apparently used to this sort of thing, 'who have been waiting for this room for months. Why should you get it when you've only just arrived. You'll like Castle Warwick.'

'You can't force me to go,' cried Stella. 'I have a letter saying I'm to stay here.'

'Your letter,' said the woman tersely, and patience seemed pain to her, 'was written in Australia. This is Papua, and things here are different. Someone has taken your room. You're lucky to have one. At least your house is made of wood. There are men living in native police barracks on the other side of the town. What on earth do you expect of this place?'

She was not unkind, but she was tired of complaints she could not rectify, and the climate made her nervous.

For a moment Stella felt she could go no further. She had been struck down before the fight had started.

Then slowly, mounting out of pain, emerged that servant of life, curiosity. What was it like? There had been those snapshots in the brown album, but how nullifying and misleading the snapshots had been proved to be. There was something in this country, its colours, its trees, its glittering air, its beautiful, silky skinned peoples, that evaded all attempts to capture it in pictures, words or writing.

'How long has it been a government mess?' she said quietly.

'Only a few weeks, since the owner died. It's been open a fortnight. You take the fork by the hotel and follow the right-hand road up the hill. Ask someone, you can't miss it.' She turned towards one of the boys who was walking past with a pile of dishes.

But Stella had conquered the dread in her situation, had discovered in it a kind of joy, and stood her ground. 'What room shall I have?'

'Good heavens,' said the woman, turning and staring at her, 'I don't know. You'll find that out when you get there.'

'I have luggage here.' This woman who had said 'Castle Warwick' twice in the space of a few moments was more important than the shadowy forms that had drifted across her life for the past two months, and she dreaded to let her go.

'Leave it on the verandah. I'll send up some of the boys with it when lunch is over.' And she darted off, making her escape from a girl who struck her as being stupid and odd. They ought to be more careful, she thought, for the twentieth time that week, who they send up to this place. Good solid girls with heads on their shoulders, girls with strong bodies to withstand the climate and the conditions, and strong heads to withstand the men. Not pale, little, tenderly raised creatures like this.

Stella mounted the steps of her future home. It was built back from the road; the land rose sharply so that the garden was terraced and the steps were long and steep. They were bordered on either side by strange, flat-topped trees, reminiscent of trees in Japanese prints, that were breaking out into scarlet blossom and carried long, black pods from last season's flowering.

It was very hot, and Stella, slowly climbing under the thin shade, became aware that she was tired. The brilliant sunlight, splashing on the ground at her feet, dazzled her eyes and made her feel sick and dizzy. She approached the house ahead almost without emotion. As she climbed higher, the garden grew thicker, more ordered, composed mainly of the trees with the scarlet flowers, and other trees with round, smooth branches and clusters of white, scented flowers.

Every now and again she paused and looked around her, but it was to gather strength rather than absorb impressions. As the steps mounted higher she could see, over banks of green and flowering trees, the bleached tin roofs of the town, the wharf where one large steamer was tied up and, directly below, the backyard of the hotel with piles of amber bottles burning in the sun like huge heaps of resin among a tangled mass of rusty junk, metal, machinery, wrecked vehicles and wire.

As she reached the door, all this dropped out of sight and she was left with a clear view down the coast to the final dim islands and misty peninsulas. A faint breeze fluttered the leaves around her and dried the sweat that had broken out on her body. She mounted the steps and looked in through the open door. The sunlight and the feathery shadows of leaves played on the bare floor. At the end of the passage a black and white cat appeared and swayed towards her, lashing its tail.

She felt again dimly that the photographs had misled her. There was something utterly unexpected here, to do with the light and the leaves, and the feeling that she was not inside a house at all. But she was too tired to think about it.

She tried first the door on the right, but the room was occupied. Untidy clothes draped a bed and chair. The bed was unmade, and there were unemptied ashtrays, a bottle of gin and two empty glasses on a table. She tried the door opposite. This room was unoccupied. It was small and bright, and included a bed with a once-blue cotton cover, a floral curtain fixed across one corner, a chest of drawers, a small carved wooden table and a woven grass mat. There were no windows but the top half of the verandah wall opened outwards like a flap and was held in position by a long peg of wood. Coarse wire netting had been nailed over the aperture.

Stella, her head and heart now entirely empty, walked to the bed. An enormous cockroach shot out from under the mat and scuttled across the room. She lay down on the bed and her limbs seemed to fall apart with weariness. In one corner of the ceiling crouched a little grey lizard. She went to sleep feeling obscurely glad that the lizard was there, that she had infinitesimally escaped utter loneliness.

She awoke to the sound of scuffling feet and voices on the verandah outside. She had no idea where she was, and for some moments she could not make out what was happening. The room in which she lay burned in a rosy glow. The grey lizard on the ceiling was now pink, as if lit from within. Three Papuan men were carrying her luggage on to the verandah. She rose, straightened her dress and went out to meet them. A small, brown-skinned man carrying her hat box addressed her incomprehensibly.

In the garden behind him a few flowers blazed like torches in the trees, and his body glowed with red lights as if from the reflection of a fire. The sky was so violently coloured it shocked her. She felt she wanted to dive indoors and hide from something in the garden that threatened her. She was so oppressed by colour she forgot to feel lonely.

She pointed to her room and the three boys took the luggage in, then departed single-file down the steps to the road, flopping from step to step on flat, yellow-soled feet. Their bodies heaved from side to side and the red lights shifted from shoulder to shoulder. The boy who had spoken went last and, as they reached the bottom of the garden, he thrust up a thin arm, dark as a serpent, and plucked a flower. A vague, unbidden emotion stirred within Stella as she watched, but, suspecting in this sensation the threat of further pain, she turned her back on the garden and went inside.

The door on the other side of the passage opened and a young woman appeared, lifted her arms, stretched and yawned. She was tall, dark and in her late twenties. She wore a black dressing-gown embroidered with scarlet dragons. One sleeve was torn, and her black hair fell in heavy, uncombed locks around her shoulders. She looked rather dirty, but this impression might have been imposed on her by a glimpse of the room behind, which remained as Stella had seen it, the bed unmade, the two unwashed glasses and unemptied ash-tray still on the table, and soiled clothes draping the backs of chairs. But looking at her face, Stella felt immediately that she rode clear of her soiled and sordid air, that her dirty brocade slippers and the frayed grandeur of her scarlet monsters were in no way signs of a tarnished personality. Stella thought her beautiful. Her face was dignified and calm. Her long, heavy eyes looked incapable of any expression but a serene gentleness.

'Have you just arrived?' she said, in a smooth, deep voice.

Stella nodded.

She blinked her eyes and said vaguely, 'So they stuck you up here. You were allotted to number 16.'

'Yes,' said Stella. 'But somebody took the room.'

'It's not liked here.' She turned as she spoke, pushing her door further open to look at an electric kettle on the floor. 'It's the rats, the place is over-run with them. It's falling to bits. They should have patched it up before they let us in. It may be all right for a mad anthrop. They're a dippy lot and put up with anything. Still, housing's a problem. Lucky we're not all in tents.'

'Mad anthrop?' said Stella. She looked at the woman eagerly.

'Come in, I'm making tea.' She led the way, and Stella, drawn by the kind look, followed her inside. 'The fellow who used to own this place' – she cleared some clothes off a chair and tossed them on the bed – 'David Warwick. I hadn't heard of him, but that doesn't mean a thing.'

From a shelf behind a curtain she produced two cups, a bottle of milk, a teapot and a tin of biscuits, and found places for them among the ashtray, glasses, and bottle of gin. 'He committed suicide,' she said, staring at the kettle, which was coming to the boil.

Stella stared too, and did not reply. She was as near to happiness as she had been since she left Australia. She forgot the parrot-breasted sky and the hand thrust up to pluck a flower. She lost her sense of alienation and felt that she had come home. 'Why?' she said quietly.

'Debts. Look at this place, falling to bits. It's one of the biggest in town. You can always tell the pre-war houses, they're big and airy, with verandahs. Since the war they put us in boxes, designed for people in snow countries. They think it's progressive.'

'But did he have such debts?'

'It's come out since that he had enormous ones. He borrowed money from his friends. But being a celebrity – a sort of national figure, you know – some of the debts were wiped out, and he just came out clear. He must have been hopeless with money. Just didn't care about it ...'

'I can't understand,' said Stella, 'why a man who didn't care about money would kill himself because he didn't have any.'

The woman flicked a lock of hair out of the tea she was pouring and handed the cup to Stella. 'I entirely agree with you'.

'Do you mean that you don't believe he killed himself?'

'For money? Never.' She spoke with gentle emphasis. 'A lot of other people don't believe it either. It's just said – well – for something to say.'

'Then why?'

The woman stirred her tea. Her lids were lowered, face sombre. 'Some people don't seem to need a reason,' she said. 'Just being here is enough.'

'Oh, that's *not* enough!' said Stella passionately.

The spoon went round and round. The woman's lids were

still lowered. 'Some people aren't right for this place,' she said. 'You need a particular sort of thick skin.' She looked up and a lazy smile touched her eyes. 'Like mine. I can never see anything to complain about. Plenty of sun. I love the sun, and bathing. I love walking round with practically nothing on all day. Some people get jittery.'

'Not *this* one!' cried Stella. 'He'd been here for years.'

'No,' she sipped her tea. If she was surprised at Stella's knowledge, she gave no sign. 'Probably not this one.'

'Then if people don't believe – about the debts I mean – why don't they *do* something?' She leaned forward. The teacup rattled in its saucer. She put it down and clasped her quivering hands.

'What could they do?' She blinked at Stella over the rising steam. 'Why don't you drink your tea?'

'But if they didn't believe it they should find out the truth.'

'The facts are he's dead, and we're in his house. What does the truth matter and when do you ever find it? How far do you go?' She put down the cup and began chipping nail polish off her thumb nail. 'All my life I've lived with people who want to find out the truth – about me, about themselves, about anything. I don't give a stuff about the truth.'

Stella's shining eyes looked straight through the face of the girl before her. 'Truth and justice are the only things that matter.'

'Do you think so?' The woman was inspecting the chip of pink lacquer in the palm of her hand. She had lived the last five years of her life among people who were, or tried to be, intense, and Stella's un-Australian earnestness did not alarm her. 'I don't think they matter so much. When I think at all,' she added, 'which isn't often, so I'm told. I'm a philistine. I'm against knowledge and truth. Most definitely against justice. It would be terrible for the people I like most if we had justice.'

Stella picked up her cup. Her hands had stopped trembling. 'Where was he found?'

'In this house, alone, except for a gecko.'

'Gecko?'

'Those little creatures up there,' she pointed to the ceiling where two lizards clung with their splayed feet. 'Don't be scared of them. They're gentle. There's a saying that a man who has no geckoes in his house is not to be trusted.' She threw Stella a brief, searching glance. 'By the way, my name's Sylvia Hardy.'

'I'm Stella Warwick,' Stella said, not looking at her. She put down her empty cup.

'More tea?' Sylvia said, holding out her hand.

'No, thanks.' Stella stood up and looked at the door, but she felt reluctant to go. Something desperate in her had grappled itself on this chaotic little room and its occupant. 'Do you know this man named Trevor Nyall?'

'Yes, everyone knows him. He's one of the upper-crust.'

'Do you know where he lives?'

'Just up the hill. Where all the big boys live. You follow the road up the hill. It's the third house from the top.'

Stella moved to the door.

'Don't be late for dinner. It's at 6.30, and it's five now,' Sylvia said. 'Is he a friend of yours?'

Stella shook her head. 'Not exactly.' She thought she detected irony and scepticism in Sylvia's eyes. 'I was told he would help me.'

'He'll probably shower you with kindness,' said Sylvia. 'It's his reputation.'

The road mounted steeply and was bordered on either side by houses set back in thick gardens. Some were built like the house she had just left, bungalows with verandahs and walls that opened out like the sides of boxes. Others were more like Australian flats, square and box-like with wire-screened windows. Everywhere the tree with the black pods and feathery leaves was breaking into flower. Two Papuans, walking towards her down the hill, had stuffed clusters of blossom into their thick hair. As she mounted the road the view down the coast behind her cleared and lengthened, but she did not pause to look back. Her feeling of anxiety had returned, and she walked quickly, without looking about her. A lorry passed by, and behind walked a woman in a white cotton dress carrying a tennis racket. She stared at Stella but did not smile.

Soon the road turned sharply and narrowed. The vegetation had thinned and ahead she could see three houses, the last of which appeared to crown the hill. A new house, only as yet a timber shell, stood like a pile of pink bones on the hill above. She paused at the bottom of some steps and looked up.

The house that Sylvia had recommended was blind-eyed – the sun blazed in its verandah windows – and appeared to reject or ignore her.

She went up the steps. The exertion of the climb and the knowledge that she had begun, that this was the first step, made her heart thump and caught at her breath.

She had not, since waking, laid a firm grasp on this strange new land, with its huge leaves and burning flowers, and her presence here was hard to believe in. The garden was not behaving according to laws known to her. The sun had gone from the slopes of the hill, but colours were brighter and denser. Shrubs with red and yellow leaves seemed about to burst into flame. A vine of apricot bougainvillea flowering on the verandah ahead touched her senses like a hand on a raw wound.

It struck her that this country had passed the limits of beauty and richness and dived off into some sort of inferno. She was one of those from whom the tropics drew an immediate and passionate response. To respond with joy at such a time was unthinkable to her; it would have suggested that her sorrow was frail. But she could not deny having responded in some way, and decided, as so many who feared their own passions had decided before her, that the country was evil. The flowers around her might have gorged on blood.

Half way up to the house she met a man walking down the steps towards her. He might have been a house boy for he wore no ornaments or arm bands, only a clean, white cotton rami that fell from his waist to his ankles, and was embroidered on the front fold with a red 'N'. His hair was cropped straight across the top like a thistle.

She spoke to him, hardly expecting to be understood. 'Is this Mr Nyall's house?'

He stood aside, stopped, but said nothing. His eyes, black and so soft as to be like dark, clotted fluid, regarded her without evasion. Then his face broke into a smile. He lifted an arm in a loose, exquisite gesture and waved at the house.

'Mr Nyall, yes sinabada.'

She went on up to the house. As the inferno dropped away behind and the old, familiar world of houses, rooms and verandahs drew nearer, she began to feel nervous. Had she acted correctly? Should she have written or phoned? Would she offend by landing on them like this? She paused at the bottom of the verandah steps and listened.

No sound came from the house – at least there were no guests. She climbed the steps and looked in through the open door. She could see a large, bright room. Actually, it was hardly a room at all: the top half of the outside wall was lifted out and propped open, and sprays of green leaves had found their way in from the bushes outside. Long, gauze curtains falling down over open doorways wafted to and fro in a faint wind. There were rugs on the golden floor and the furniture was made of thick gold bamboo. Stella, caught unawares, thought it the most beautiful room she had ever seen.

A man was kneeling on the floor at the far end of the room, mending the plug of a reading lamp. She paused in the doorway and studied all she could see of him. He was thin, which she had not expected – she had thought of him as large, possibly even fat. His arms were as brown, in this light, as those of the boy she had passed on the road. His hair was black, rather long, and untidy.

He switched on the light, stood up and must have felt her there, for he looked round, still holding a screwdriver in his hand. His face was thin and he looked ill. She had an impression, not of an important man, but of one who avoided importance. He was tall and well built, but stooped, as if he believed that a good physique was a disadvantage and better disguised. He could not have been more than thirty-five and was possibly younger. She had expected someone much older, about the age of David Warwick.

'Mr Nyall!' she said.

'I can't see you. Come in. You're standing against the light.'

'I'm sorry.' She felt rebuffed, that he should have recognised her instantly. She moved forward and he watched her intently. He wore glasses behind which his eyes, already large, were magnified so that they looked enormous. His eyelids were purple, almost black.

'I don't know you,' he said. 'Though your face is familiar.'

'You might have seen a photograph.' She had reached one of the crises of her pilgrimage and felt that for him, too, the moment should be similarly illuminated.

He looked away as if she disturbed him and shook his head. 'I'm sorry.'

'You haven't met me,' she said. 'I'm Stella Warwick.' She waited. It was one of those moments which she thought would offer happiness. There was still a bitter joy in belonging to David Warwick. She had been, after all, his choice, and some trace of his eminence was surely reflected in her.

But he gave her a very curt acknowledgement. '*You* can't be his *wife*!' he said.

'I am.' She resented his incredulity.

He was staring at her, but at the very moment that expression started to flood his face, it became like a mask. He jerked around and turned his back on her. She stared at him, so surprised she did not know how to go on.

After a moment he turned around again. 'What are you doing here?'

'I have come to see you.'

He brushed her remark aside, waving the hand with the screwdriver. 'Here, in this country?'

She saw that something was wrong. 'Where else would I go?' she said. 'This is my home.'

'You've never been here before.'

'I have no other,' she said. 'My father is dead and the house is being sold. Anyway, where else would I go? His friends were here. This was where he lived and worked.'

'Yes,' he muttered, 'that's so.' But he did not look at her, just threw a wild glance about the room. 'You're Australian, aren't you?' he said. 'You must have people in Australia?'

She resented his response, and answered tartly, 'I have no people.'

He looked away again. A faint sound came from his lips. She thought he had said, 'Oh, my God!'

She spoke stiffly now, unwilling to expose to him the more precious motives that had brought her here. 'There was no one, there was nowhere else to go, there was nothing else to do. You sound as if I shouldn't be here. Where else should I be? There's no other place for me.'

'And *this*,' he said harshly, 'isn't possible for you.'

She began to see his behaviour in a new light. Eagerly she moved a little nearer, then restrained herself. 'Why?'

'It's a queer place,' he said vaguely.

'Is it wicked?' she asked. It was only four years since she had left the convent where she had been educated – she was not Catholic but her father had believed a convent training suited a child he hoped would turn out gracious, submissive and 'womanly'. The four years following this had been given over almost exclusively to nursing her father and completing secretarial training. She had had no time or opportunity to formulate any complicated notions of wickedness. Wickedness, she believed, was a quality you recognised in in the faces of disreputable strangers. She had not yet learned to suspect the gentleness of parents or the generosity of friends.

'Not entirely,' he said. 'But any wickedness that there is, is likely to come your way.'

She moved forward again, her eyes sparkling. 'Do you think so? It was dangerous, wasn't it, to come here?'

He looked down at her young, eager face. 'Yes, it was stupid, and dangerous.'

'Thank God! But you will help me, won't you? I've come here for your help.'

'Where are you living?'

'In my husband's house.'

'You're mad! What in God's name are you up to?'

Her voice dropped to a whisper. 'I'm looking for a man called Jobe. Do you know where he is?'

He flung up the hand holding the screwdriver. 'I won't help you. I won't help you in any way. I want nothing to do with you.'

She drew away from him. The fact that he was her husband's friend had held her loyal to the hope that he would help her, but now she felt a rush of anger. She hated him, for having refused to help her, and for some other more terrible reason. She felt that some new obstruction had presented itself. She never wanted to see him again. She wanted to forget his face and everything that he had said and before she left she wanted to wound him. 'I thought you were his friend. I was told that you'd help me. But I can see you're afraid and don't want to implicate yourself.'

He was frowning. 'I've never professed to be your husband's friend,' he said, 'and I'm quite sure he's never claimed *me* as one. I'm beginning to suspect that you're making a mistake.'

'You're not Trevor Nyall.'

'No, I'm not.' He was moving to the door.

She stood watching him, glad that he was not Trevor Nyall. It felt good not to have to change your mind about someone you had theoretically trusted. But best of all it was good to know that David had not been wrong. It would have injured her memory of him to have found that Trevor Nyall had been a false friend.

'Who are you?' she asked, following him out on to the verandah. But he ran down the steps ahead of her. She saw to her surprise that it was almost dark. Stars had broken out in the sky and the fires had left the shrubs and trees. The bougainvillea twining over the verandah was papery and colourless.

'I'll drive you home,' he called back over his shoulder and disappeared round the corner of the house.

She followed him round the drive to the back where a jeep was parked under a large tree. 'I'm not going home,' she said. 'I'm going to see Mr Nyall.'

He opened the door and stood waiting for her to get in. A light switched on in the back of the house, and he turned his head and looked at it anxiously. He slammed the door behind her and hurried round the front of the jeep to the driver's seat. His movements were urgent, almost desperate, as if he wanted to be rid of her as soon as possible. He started up the engine and drove along a short drive at the back of the house and out through a gate. Twice he looked back over his shoulder.

'I am not going home!' she said again. 'I am going to see Mr Nyall!'

He did not answer. She knew that he would not take her there, but it did not occur to her to ask herself why she had consented to drive with him at all. She was conscious now of a strange new exhilaration. Hostility fluttered like passion between them.

'Isn't Mr Nyall's house further up the road?' she said as he turned down the hill. She had known he would turn, but there was a perverse excitement to be had from forcing out of him a declaration of uninterest. She had taken the right path. She had made her first enemy. And since there could be no love, hatred was what she most yearned for.

'I'm not taking you there,' he said. 'I'm taking you to your house.'

'I'm not going home!' she cried. 'I'm going to see Mr Nyall.'

'I don't care. You can do what you like, but I'm not taking you there.'

'Why won't you take me?' she cried. 'Why don't you want me to see Mr Nyall? Are you afraid he'll help me? Is that it? Are you afraid I might find Mr Jobe?'

He made no answer, and his face told her nothing.

They did not speak again till they reached Castle Warwick. She sat beside him with her hands clenched in her lap, fires of anger and excitement slowly dying down within her. He leaned across her and opened the door but did not get out.

She stood on the roadway, closed the door and faced him. 'Thank you for all you've done.'

He looked at her with a quizzical expression, but said nothing.

'I've always known that something was wrong. And you've given me my first proof. Now I shall find the truth,' she said.

'The truth!' He echoed the words, but they broke from his lips like a moan. In the next moment he had gone, the jeep spurting away, raging up the hill.

She was late for dinner. She found the dining-room, a large, airy room opening on to a verandah, on the other side of the house. There were three tables, and two young girls sat at one talking and giggling. The other diners had left and the staff were carrying away the dirty dishes.

She sat by the verandah and looked out over the darkening town. Those who have always known, and suddenly lost, security and comfort, find these evening hours the hardest to endure. Darkness brings with it tenderness. Voices, impatient during the day, are subdued. Stella forgot the man on the hill.

When she had finished dinner it was dark. The town below twinkled with lights and only a pale streak along the horizon remained of the sunset. There was no light in the hall outside her room, and she felt her way with one hand along the wall. She paused outside Sylvia's door and hesitated. The picture she held in her mind of the little room, warm, untidy and musty as a burrow, enticed her. She raised her hand to knock, but the door swung away from her, and a man, evidently in a hurry, lurched out into the passage.

She did not see his face because he collided straight into her. She felt his body quiver. A sound that was almost a scream broke from him, and he stepped, or rather fell, back, and slammed the door in her face.

Philip Washington leaned against the door, pressing his body against it.

'What on earth's the matter?' said Sylvia in her slow voice. She sat on the bed with her legs tucked up beneath a green chiffon skirt, fashionable some years ago, renovated, but still revealing its departed heyday. A cockroach had eaten a hole in the hem, and she scratched it absentmindedly with her fingernail.

'There's a native outside!' He spoke quickly, and his clear, rather high-pitched voice trembled. 'Prowling around outside the door.'

'Don't be absurd,' said Sylvia. 'It's the girl in the opposite room. I heard her close the door.'

'I tell you it was a native! Do you think I don't know one when I see one!' But he had relaxed a little and spoke sharply, not because he was convinced, but because he did not like being contradicted, particularly by Sylvia. 'I can smell one a mile off. You want to be careful about boys prowling round up here. If you aren't careful you'll be raped, lounging around with nothing on all day and flashing your legs about.

'The place is "boy-proofed",' Sylvia said mildly. She knew that when Philip was nervous or upset he would invariably take it out on whoever happened to be near, and took no notice of him. That he was upset was evident. The blood had come back to his face, but it still looked pinched and strained. He did not go out again, but reached for the gin bottle with a hand that trembled. He was, in his calmer moments, a handsome man with a thin, well-featured face and light-grey eyes. He was tall, spare and graceful, and was looked upon by his rather more husky associates as effeminate. This was only partly to do with his appearance. He was interested in native life, particularly native arts, and this was supposed by the average white Marapai male to be queer and slightly indecent.

He sat down in a chair from which Sylvia had removed some but not all of her clothes, slopped a little water into his glass and lifted it unsteadily to his lips.

'You're a pack of nerves, darling,' said Sylvia gently. 'You really ought to take leave.'

'For God's sake, stop telling me I ought to take leave!' he burst out petulantly. 'Of course I ought to be taking leave! Any fool can see that. I tell you I can't get away.' He put down the glass and upset the still unemptied ashtray. 'Really, Sylvia,' he continued coldly, brushing ash from his faultlessly laundered trousers, 'you are a slut. You live like a pig. I don't know how you can bear this squalid mess.'

'I tidied it,' said Sylvia. 'And you don't have to come here. I can't think why you did. You always swore you'd never set foot in this house.'

Washington, realising that if he became more objectionable he would probably have to leave, did not answer, but leaned back and lit a cigarette.

Of course it hadn't been a native, only a girl with a pale face. He could see it now quite clearly. The other figure – of a naked brown man with a face painted white for dancing – had been, as Sylvia had implied, purely imaginary, the figment of wrought-up nerves, a fortuitous banking of lights and shadows. And yet, imagination – he poured the barely diluted gin down his throat – where did it, in this cursed country, begin and end? The longer you stayed the less sure you were where flesh ended and phantom began. That a little brown man with a painted face could project his image over miles of jungle – there was nothing strange about this to a man of imagination. Washington pulled his fingers back through his hair.

This was the house, he remembered, where David Warwick had shot himself. His hands started to tremble again. Oh, my God! I shouldn't have come here. Poor Warwick! Perhaps I'll be the next.

'And speaking of the girl,' said Sylvia, 'she's an odd little thing, looks like a chicken who's come out of the egg a few days too soon. And oddest of all is her name. Have a guess what it is.'

He made an impatient gesture.

'Warwick,' said Sylvia. 'Stella Warwick. Could our ghost have a daughter?'

'He was only married a few months,' said Washington shortly. 'Common enough name.'

'She had an introduction to a very dear friend of yours.'

'Of mine?' He evinced a little more interest.

'Trevor Nyall,' Sylvia said with a faint smile.

Washington did not reply. Six months ago a position as assistant to Nyall had fallen vacant in the department. Washington had applied for it, but his application had been rejected and the position had gone to an older man from the south. Since then Washington had seized on the idea that Nyall was a man who picked the brains of his subordinates but kept them lowly because he could not stand competition. Washington had lost interest in his work. It was, he decided, pointless to work when power from above was always on the look-out to baulk you.

In the tropics decay is as swift and violent as growth. Overnight, mould will bristle up on a hat or shoe; in a few hours a body will rot, in a few weeks a personality will crumble. It was generally said that over the past few months Washington had gone to pieces. He was aware himself of some sort of internal disintegration. He held together just enough to be able to do his work without provoking complaint, for although he hated Nyall, he also feared him.

'That,' said Sylvia, 'made it even odder.'

This attempt on her part to involve the girl across the passage with David Warwick annoyed him. Such a circumstance would be one more intolerable quirk to an already intolerable situation. He answered sullenly, 'Nyall has a million acquaintances. *Doing* things for people, *little* things that don't matter, putting people under a sense of obligation ... that's life to a man like him. And Warwick ... it's a common name.'

'I wouldn't say so.'

'*Women*,' Washington said acidly, 'must always be making situations. They can't see two people having lunch together without packing them off to bed. They must always be clamped on to someone else like limpets.'

Sylvia leaned forward and replenished his glass. She had worked, after she left school in Sydney, as an artist's model and was used to exhibitions of temperament. The artistic nature was, she believed, strange, unaccountable, and unpredictable. And it was to be admired and respected - all who laid claim to it had told her so. She, knowing herself to be ordinary, had never tried to be otherwise. She had lived most of her life with those who loved, or professed to love, painting, music, poetry, but had failed to cultivate in herself any interest in these various obsessions. She knew all the jargon but had never contracted the fever. You were born with it, she believed, you came into the world with the print of Apollo's lips on your forehead. To these artists, these men of imagination, all reverence was due, all aberrations of behaviour permissible, all forgiven. For the past seven years she had dedicated her life to looking after them. She had lived with three artists who had all seen in her the image of their loved, lost or treacherously remarried mothers. Finally, when the last one left her, she fled in despair to a land where men, she had been told, were made of more solid stuff, only to find her heart drifting back to the artistic temperament, back to Philip Washington.

He was, it was true, hardly an artist in the correct sense of the word. His achievements in the creative line were confined to esoteric little poems, the distressing callowness of which, Sylvia – awed by an impressive profusion of Papuan place names – failed to recognise. There were, however, fresh ideas and fresh enthusiasms. Not ballet, but native dancing, not Picasso, but Sepik masks, not continental cooking, but strange, exotic, indigestible concoctions of taro and yam. The old familiar traits were there, rising like the ghosts of her former lovers through the bizarre vestments that twelve years of tropical living had imposed – the warm, but so transient affections, the sharp, lively, cruel tongue, the hysterical heights and depths of pleasure and despair.

'Here,' she said gently, 'have another drink.' For he was calmer, and therefore, she supposed, must be happier, when half drunk. He patted her hand, relenting. 'Dear little slut.'

'I think this place upsets you,' she said kindly. 'Perhaps you shouldn't have come here. It's only lusty wenches like me that don't mind lying down with dead men.'

This pleased him. He was proud of his sensitivity, though of late it had troubled him. 'Where else can I go?' he said sulkily. 'You are, in spite of being stupid, about the only sane human being in this incredible town.'

Sylvia smiled and blinked. Constant wounding had never toughened her, and almost every word he spoke conjured some painful response. But no flicker of pain showed in her face. 'You used to be happy enough to ask people home,' she said.

'The place is falling to pieces,' he said bitterly. 'It's infested with cockroaches. I can hardly sleep at night. They stamp about in the thatch like elephants. And Rei's such a fool he can't even make a cup of tea.'

'I told you that you'd regret sacking those two Kerema boys,' Sylvia said. 'At least that dirty old devil, the tall one, was a good cook.'

'I don't regret it,' he cried childishly. 'Don't present me with your silly regrets. Only fools regret. I regret nothing!'

He did not mean to hurt her. He believed her for the most part incapable of intense feeling and incapable of understanding half of what he said. It relieved his feelings to have someone to lash out at. But looking up into her untroubled face, he yearned momentarily for her calm, uncomplicated view of things. He stood up, went across to her and, sinking down at her feet, buried his head in her lap. Sylvia stroked his head and smiled. She could put up with his tantrums for they nearly always ended in this.

She reminded Washington not of his mother but of his sister, who was ten years older than he was, and had looked after him throughout his childhood and adolescence. She was a plain woman with an unselfish nature and a twisted foot, who lived in Melbourne and made 'artistic' pottery.

It had been his ambition to live with her in a house on the hill among the administration's most distinguished servants. Though he despised the successful, he yearned for success and wished to cut a figure in the world. But seven years lived extravagantly on a low salary had seen little advancement of these plans. He had no money to build a house of his own and the government would not provide. Housing was difficult, and the names on priority waiting lists had a way of shifting in favour of high salaries. It was argued by the housing department that he at least had a roof over his head, even if only thatch infested with geckoes and cockroaches, and boards beneath his feet, rotten with white ants as they were. He was one of the fortunate, they informed him. Most of the single men lived in an unspeakably frightful mess and almost went off their heads with noise and discomfort.

But for a few years he had been fairly happy. He loved the tropics and his house, until it began falling to pieces. He had usually two Papuan servants and sometimes as many as five, and had formed friendly and sometimes passionate attachments to all of them. They had kept him poor but had amused him. There had always been the hope of promotion and, with it, a house. Six months ago, these hopes had vanished. The higher position in the department had gone to someone else. His house was falling to pieces. His clothes were patched, the stores were demanding payment. His sister was still making pottery and had stopped asking for further news of housing in her letters. The government obviously could not provide and he certainly could not build. People had found him difficult and decided that he was not, after all, so terribly entertaining. If Washington had been offered a job down south he would have gratefully taken it.

Now, like a frightened puppy, he buried his nose deeper into the folds of Sylvia's skirt. She stroked his head.

'I can't sleep,' he said, his voice muffled in her dress. 'If I could only sleep. I haven't slept for weeks.'

'You must take something,' she soothed him.

'People prowl around at night. I know they do. I hear them walking around. Somebody came into my house last night.'

'Nonsense,' she murmured, stroking his hair.

'I tell you somebody was there,' he insisted. 'I was lying with my eyes closed – not asleep, I never sleep these days. It was a native, I could smell him. I could see him.'

'Perhaps it was Rei,' said Sylvia.

'I asked him and he said he hadn't been there. Anyway, do you think I wouldn't recognise Rei?'

'Well, he'd lie about it, wouldn't he? If he felt you were accusing him. Or if he'd been in, sneaking after a cigarette or something.'

'*It wasn't Rei!*' he almost shouted at her. 'Perhaps it was one of those damned Keremas, and up to no good too.' He did not believe that it might have been a Kerema, but this was all he dared to say. Actually, until speaking about it, he had not been sure about the native at all. Had it been a man? Or just a patch of moonlight? It was only thinking that made it grow more solid. And the smell was something he had not made up. He had smelt it then, as he had smelt it out in the passage half an hour ago. It never left him. He carried that odour round with him. He felt he would never lose it as long as he lived.

'What could they be up to?' Sylvia said calmly.

He laughed wildly. 'Getting their own back because I threw them out. Probably trying a bit of purri purri or something.'

'Sorcery!' She lifted her eyebrows and smiled. 'Nonsense, I expect you imagined the whole thing.' Anticipating another outburst, she reached for the only cure she knew and poured him another glass of gin.

'Here, drink this, darling. You're nervy. You don't get enough sleep.'

'How can I get enough sleep,' he complained, 'if damn natives wander round my house all night.'

But the gin was having its effect, and he was beginning to feel happier. He began to stroke Sylvia's thighs. She loved him, dear silly, stupid Sylvia. And his sister loved him. And Rei at least was loyal to him, even though he was a bad cook and couldn't be relied upon to keep the dogs away. Soon he would buy land and build his house, and they could all go to the devil. He would snap his fingers at the lot of them. He would snap his fingers at Trevor Nyall, because he would have his house, and people would respect him and come to his dinner parties and be astonished by the magnificence of his hospitality. He knew a particular way of serving pawpaw. He would import a Chinese cook – the immigration authorities, having been lavishly entertained, would not raise objections. He began to work out the menu for his first dinner party and drew up a list of guests. Trevor Nyall, he decided, would not be invited.

It was 11.30 when he left Sylvia. The jeep was waiting pulled up by the side of the road, but Rei was nowhere to be seen. Washington, a little unsteady on his feet, but fairly clear-headed, looked up and down the road and whistled. The houses farther up the hill were still lit up, and from somewhere above him came the sound of Papuan voices, but the road was empty.

The wind had dropped and only a light breeze soughed through the fringes of the casuarina trees. He could smell the scent of frangipani. He paused, enjoying the cool night air. Then he remembered Rei and tooted the horn furiously.

The darkness ahead broke and a vague form appeared, moving hesitantly towards him. It was a police boy. Washington could see his belt shining in the darkness. 'Oh, go away!' he said impatiently.

He tooted again, sat down in the front seat and lit a cigarette. Down the side of the opposite hill a loose white blob was moving towards him. It was all that could be first be seen of Rei, his white rami flapping. He arrived breathless. He had evidently been making a night of it. He was chewing betelnut, wore a hibiscus flower in his hair and had knotted round his neck one of Washington's new dishcloths. Under his arm he carried a guitar decorated with strips of coloured paper.

'Where have you been?'

'Boyhouse,' Rei said, smiling broadly.

'Whose boyhouse?'

Rei pointed with a vague, sweeping gesture that took in most of the hill.

'What taubada's boyhouse?' said Washington. The feeling of well-being that Sylvia's body had imparted was already drifting away. He felt suddenly suspicious of Rei, though he did not know why. What had he been doing? Who had he been talking to? He feared ... he did not know what ...

Rei did not answer. His smile had died. His face had become stupid and still, but his eyes seemed to grow larger and brighter. Washington, who could read these signs, knew he was nervous and might now say anything.

'Have you been with any strange boys, any bad boys?' he asked more gently.

'No, taubada.' There was no way on earth of telling what might be going on behind those lustrous eyes, staring now so steadily into his own.

'All right. Get in and let's go home.' They had probably

just been gambling. They would naturally not like being questioned. When Rei started up the engine and the jeep moved down the hill, Washington said, hoping to soothe the boy's ruffled nerves, 'Sing to me Rei. What was that song you were playing up there?'

'I no sing, taubada.'

'Why not?'

'Sore head,' said Rei, chewing again.

Washington looked away. They were passing along the dock side. A cargo ship was tied up against the jetty. It was still lit up and the lights from its ports tossed and broke as the water lifted and fell. There was no unloading that night and the jetty was deserted. Only one solitary native squatted on the edge of the wharf, his black, fuzzy head silhouetted like a flower against the sky.

Even Rei had changed, thought Washington. He had always been a fool, but a gay one. He was always happy. He would bring his friends up to the boyhouse and play his guitar and sing for hours on end – local songs, hillbilly songs, Samoan dances learned from the early Polynesian missionaries.

But now he only sang with his own people, making Washington feel a stranger. He went about solemnly, and quietly, in a manner altogether foreign to his nature. He had ceased to be childlike and had become enigmatic. Sometimes Washington felt he was hiding secrets.

All of them, thought Washington – retreating further from the comfort of Sylvia's caresses – including Rei, had turned against him. And he had been their friend. They had come to him with their troubles – a piece of old sheet for a sail, iron to patch a roof, a rusty knife, a letter to be written to a friend. He had made speeches at their weddings. But now they no longer came and there was nobody to sing to him. Rei, who wandered around looking enigmatic and doing things more efficiently than usual, was the only one left. He felt the whole brown race had smelt him out and no longer trusted him – conspired to shun him, perhaps, God knows, even more than this. He suppressed a shudder.

The road wound round the edge of the water. The tide was out, leaving a few yards of pebbly beach, and half a dozen native men with flashlights were fishing in the shallows. He could see the vague, shadowy outlines of their bodies. The road turned and led back past a long row of buildings towards the hills. A wild hillside with only one path threading over its crest loomed ahead. The road turned again and finished in a group of tumbledown iron sheds that had once been army stores.

'There's no light,' said Washington, standing up and peering through the trunks of half a dozen coconut palms. 'I told you to leave a light.'

'No light,' reiterated Rei, and they both stared at the black smudge on the hill ahead that was Washington's house.

'Well, you bloody well go up and light it and come back with my torch.'

Rei, who did not like the dark any more than Washington, rolled his eyes.

'*Go on*! Hurry up ! I don't want to wait here all night!'

Rei clambered out of the jeep and started slowly up the path. The darkness swallowed his head, shoulders, arms and legs, and left only his white rami floating away like a moth into the gloom. He started to sing.

Why does he sing now? thought Philip. To keep spirits away? What spirit is he afraid of here? Or did he, without knowing why, sense that there was no peace in that decrepit little hut?

The white moth of Rei's rami had disappeared but his voice could still be heard, chanting away up the hill. Washington lit a cigarette. In the tangled rubble of the sheds something moved. A door scraped and a piece of tin fell with a clatter to the ground.

'Damn that boy!' he said aloud. He was beginning to feel nervous again and jerked violently as a flying fox stirred in a pawpaw tree. The leaves scraped and rustled with a papery sound, then the big, shadowy bat flopped out of the leaves, its heavy wings beating the sky. His skin had started to prickle. He stared at the path ahead. *What was that boy doing?* He tooted furiously on the horn, and in the next moment a light showed in his house. He caught a glimpse of Rei moving across the front door and then the point of torchlight moving towards him down the hill. He watched it pick out the path in a long, narrow beam. He heard Rei call out, 'Wow! Wow!'

Across the beam of torchlight raced a thin, black dog. Washington sucked his breath between his teeth and clenched his hands in a spasm of rage. For a moment he could not move, then he flung open the door of the jeep and scrambled out on to the road. 'Hold that dog!' he screamed. 'Throw the light on that dog!'

The light bobbed up and down wildly, but the dog was almost down to the sheds. Washington clawed about on the ground and picked up a handful of stones. He threw them with wild, inaccurate fury. There was a rattle of struck tin and a faint yelp. The dog, headed off, was streaking his way. He kicked at it as it passed, but it was a gesture of fury rather than an attack, for the dog was at least five feet away. He cursed it savagely and threw another stone, this time taking careful aim. His mind was full of brutal images. He saw his boot crack the dog's skull, he saw a pointed flint pierce its eye. He heard its scream of agony. But it had gone, unscathed.

Rei was advancing slowly towards him.

'Where was he?' he said. It was agony not to shout, to speak quietly and reasonably, not to frighten Rei.

'Under the house, taubada.'

'Under the house!' In spite of his efforts, his voice rose. 'What was it doing?'

'Nothing, taubada. Kaikai.'

'Eating? What was it eating?'

'Bone, taubada.'

'A bone! What bone?'

Rei looked nervously away. 'Nothing, taubada. Taubada's kaikai. Bone long taubada's kaikai. 'E take 'im long frying pan.'

Fear drained out of Washington's body, leaving a feeling of nausea and weakness. 'Oh!' He remembered a chop bone lying in a frying pan outside the back door. He started to walk up the hill.

At about three next morning he woke. It was still and cool. Dawn had not yet come, but the sky outside his window was light and empty waiting for the sun. The leaves of pawpaw trees spread out like hands against the sky. Three glow-worms winked palely in the thatch above his head, their lights blinking on and off like the beating of tiny hearts. For a moment he lay in peace, as he had done in the old days before there was anything to fear, looking at the glow-worms and the pawpaw leaves. Then, remembering where he was, his naked body grew tense beneath the sheet. He lifted the mosquito net and his eyes, wide and wary, began their careful examination of the room. His gaze started at the foot of the bed and slowly moved across to the opposite wall. There were many objects which in this eerie hour looked odd and out of place. His raincoat hooked up on a nail over the front door showed no fold or crease, and might have been the dark, humped shape of a waiting man. But it was a phantom that he had faced before, that he had spoken to in fact on a previous evening and flashed his torch upon. Tonight he passed it by, and his gaze moved on across the wall. Here a boar's tusk glimmered like a disembodied smile. Three lime gourds set on a shelf had the stark, bone foreheads of human skulls. Tapa cloth rustled like the dry, whispering tread of rats. The only other sound was the faint tinny rattle of a bundle of bamboo jews' harps hanging on the opposite wall.

Not until his eyes had reached the door did he see it. It was standing in the doorway, blocking out what he should have been able to see behind – the hillside, the banana trees, the corner of the boyhouse. None of this was visible, only above its head a few pale stars. It was a man. A little man, a native. He was not Rei or for that matter any houseboy, for he wore no rami. As soon as Washington saw him, he could smell him too. The whole room stank with the odour of his flesh. Native flesh, unwashed, primitive native flesh. Not the sweet, musty odour of the coastal people who washed and swam in the sea, but the rank stench of a primitive inland man who rubbed pig fat on his skin.

Panic seized him. His hand shot out, his fingers clawed the first thing they touched, which was the half-empty rum bottle on the table beside his bed, and he flung it at the open door. The bottle struck the side of the door and rolled down the steps to the ground outside. The shadow had gone. It seemed not to step aside but to fade away, leaving clear the sky with its pricking stars, the hillside and the long floppy leaves of the banana trees. There was no sound but the faint drip, drip of the spilt rum, the tinkle of the jews' harps and the dry, husky flap of the tapa cloth.

Sobbing with terror, Washington lay as if chained to his bed.

At 8.30 the next morning the phone rang on Washington's desk. He let it ring for a few moments, then lifted the receiver and said sulkily, 'You're late.'

'I'm sorry, darling,' said Sylvia, who phoned him every morning at 8.15. 'I've only just arrived. I've been round at Staff, looking after a lost lamb. Has anyone come into your office during the past few minutes?'

There was a pause while he looked around. 'Only a girl.'

'A thin girl with short hair, looking frightened?'

'I wouldn't say frightened. She's talking to Finch.'

'She's the girl you bumped into last night,' said Sylvia. 'An extraordinary creature. She's only just arrived and had to report at Staff this morning. But she was scared to go alone, so I had to go with her.' Then she said, with a certain note of self-satisfaction, 'She's not Warwick's daughter, she's his wife.'

There was no answer from Washington and she went on. 'What do you suppose she's doing here? It's odd, isn't it? She's so terribly young. I feel sorry for her and yet I wish she wasn't here. She seems unbalanced, makes me shiver. I have an odd feeling about her ...'

'How do you know who she is?' said Washington. His voice sounded far away for his head was turned away from the phone.

'Oh, I know. From things she says. And she's working for your department. She wanted to get into Cultural Affairs where her husband used to be, but Nyall's secretary's on leave, and they've put her in there, relieving. She was upset about not going into CA, but when she heard about Nyall ... Hello! Hello! Are you there?'

'Yes, I'm here. I've got to go now.'

'You haven't told me how you are. Are you all right?'

'Rotten. I've got a bout of fever coming on, I think. Didn't sleep last night.'

'Darling, you should be home in bed.'

'I might go home too. I've been thinking about it.'

'I'll come up and cook for you. Poor darling ... Philip!'

But he had hung up.

Trevor Nyall entered the Department of Survey at ten. Stella, sitting in his office at the far end of the building, heard voices outside saying, 'Good morning, Mr Nyall,' and a man's voice heartily replying, 'Good morning, good morning.'

She waited, staring at the typewriter on the table before her. But he did not immediately appear. On the big, empty desk in the corner a loose sheet of paper lifted in the air, drifted down and settled on the floor. She did not move to pick it up, but sat, waiting, her hands gripped in her lap.

The door flung open and a gust of wind swept down the length of the building. The paper soared and dived at the window. A file flapped over on the desk and a jam tin tipped water and frangipani flowers on the floor.

The man who had entered shut the door behind him and bent to pick up the paper. It was quite a task because he was tall and broad and his face, when he straightened, was beaded with sweat. It was a handsome, arresting face. His hair was thick and iron grey, his skin yellow tan, his eyes brilliant and youthful. He had an air, not exactly of complaisance, but of satisfaction. You would think, to look at him, that he had found life to his liking, that he had not been baulked, frustrated or put down, and had managed to make his way in the world without damage either to his conscience or his desires.

Stella had never seen a photograph of him, and she put down his familiarity to the fact that he was so exactly as she had imagined him. He glanced across at her, smiled and said, 'Good morning.' His smile was charming. It isn't everyone, she told herself, her heart warming towards him, who would smile at his typist, and she thought of the man on the hill who had not smiled.

'I'll pick them up,' she said.

'Thanks, it's rather a way down for me.' His voice was strong and hearty. Stella, bending down beside him to collect the scattered flowers, was beginning to tingle with excitement. He exhaled an air of vigour and optimism that had already infected her. He would help her.

'You must be my new secretary.'

She stood up. 'I am Stella Warwick,' she said.

His heavy, dark lids lifted. His hands, which had been held clasped together on the desk, broke apart and lay there, fingers curled, palms upward. 'No,' he said softly and shook his head.

He sat and stared at her, then he rose and walked around the desk towards her. He took her hands and, looking down at her, said, 'Oh, you poor girl. What are you doing here?'

Stella's eyes filled with tears. She was happy. She had found a friend. He would look after her, tell her what to do and how to do it.

'What are you doing here?' he repeated, still holding her hands.

'I came to see you. I wanted your help.' She fixed on him the wide, dependent, childlike gaze that had so endeared her to her father and her husband.

'Of course I'll help you. I'll do anything I can for you.'

'I came to find out why my husband was murdered.'

He did not start or flinch but gazed steadily back into her dilated, shining eyes. Then he pulled up a chair and made her sit down. He walked to the door, opened it, looked outside, shut it and turned back. He stopped in front of her, looked down at her and slowly shook his head. 'Stella,' he said, 'your husband was not murdered. He committed suicide.'

'No, you're wrong, Mr Nyall. He was murdered.'

'Now, don't think that I'm surprised that you should think so,' he said, smiling down at her. 'You don't like the idea of suicide, do you? You think that it's dishonourable and you know that David was not a dishonourable man.'

Stella felt his words did not do justice to what she felt and moved to interrupt him, but he held up his hand and went on, speaking in the gentle, explanatory tone with which people were prone to address her and which reminded her now of her husband. 'But this isn't a romantic fabrication. This is true.'

He beat his fist on the palm of his hand. 'It will be hard for you to understand. This isn't Australia, Stella. People here behave differently. We are none of us in this country normal, balanced human beings.'

She looked at him gravely. She felt she had never seen anyone so normal and balanced. 'Everyone says that David had debts,' she began. 'I know he was extravagant and he hardly left anything. But debts ...' She paused. 'He didn't *care* about money.'

He shook his head at her indulgently. 'How simple it sounds to you. He was a gambler. He borrowed a great deal of money from his friends.'

'I see no *reason*,' she insisted, 'why you should think he killed himself.'

'If you stayed here for a month or so,' he said, 'you'd see reason enough.' He spoke slowly now, emphasising each word with a movement of the hand. 'This place is heartbreaking, Stella. Just *heartbreaking*. We have before us an insurmountable problem.' He had turned away and was pacing the room, speaking now in an expansive way as if addressing a larger audience. 'This is a young, savage, uncultivated land, full of people who are amongst the most primitive in the world. I wonder if you understand what that means. We must not only teach them from scratch our western ideas of law and religion, we must drag them, as it were, in a few years, over aeons of time. And so much that we have done has been wrong. It's not always been our fault; the problem is immense. And frequently this country attracts the people who just want to make money. They make it impossible for us.' His eyes returned to Stella's face. 'To those of us, Stella, who feel strongly about all this, the past few years have been heartbreaking. Think of this country as a young child whom we are trying to turn into a respectable adult. People like David have in mind a bright, strong youth, with all our knowledge and none of our corruptions, but what does he find himself producing? A cheap, shoddy waster, who isn't an adult and isn't a child. A sort of sly, seedy ten year old, who isn't even happy. It's terrible.'

Stella did not understand. 'Are you now telling me that gambling and owing money to his friends had nothing to do with David's death?'

'There are many ways of committing suicide' – Trevor tapped a cigarette on a silver case – 'and here you find them all. Sometimes it's drink, sometimes it's gambling, sometimes it's just general moral disintegration.' He paused. 'I'm more distressed than I can say that you've got this idea in your head. Believe me, it's best to let the whole thing lie. You'll only injure David's reputation.' His face cleared and he smiled at her. 'You must come and stay with us and we'll show you some of the country. You can have fun here, sailing, golf ... Who knows, you might meet someone here, you're young ...' he ended optimistically.

Stella contained her anger. 'It isn't true,' she said, 'what you said about David.'

A faint frown appeared between Trevor Nyall's brows. The corners of his mouth drooped.

'You see, David wrote to my father.'

'What!' he said sharply.

'He knew he was going to be murdered, and he wrote

and told my father. He might even have told him who the murderer was.'

Nyall's face had entirely altered. His lips were tight and thin, his eyes had lost their softness.

Stella's heart lifted at these signs of firmness and strength. Now he'll help me, she thought.

'What do you mean? Did you see the letter?'

'I've told you. Only part of it.'

'Did your father tell you what it said?'

'No,' she said, 'he couldn't tell me.'

Stella had not heard from her husband for three weeks. He had written to her the day before he left on the trip to Eola and warned her that there might be no word from him for some time. But by the end of a month she had looked forward to news. The postman, like most postmen in suburban streets, had taken an interest in the almost daily correspondence he had been delivering, and rarely failed to pass remarks about the devotion of husbands and the compensations of separation. He had been so concerned over the sudden cessation of letters that she had found it necessary to explain to him that David was away. One morning at about ten o'clock she was returning home from the shops at the end of the street, and met him finishing his round. He had just slammed the gate of a house about twelve doors down from her own. He swung his leg over his bicycle, but seeing her, dismounted again and smiled.

'He's back, Mrs Warwick,' he called.

'A letter for me?'

'Not for you, for your father.'

Stella ran up the front steps of the house, calling her father's name. Since his recovery he had spent his mornings sitting in a room on the east side of the house, which caught the morning sun. She flung open the door of this room. 'You've had a letter, Daddy! How is he? Is he back?'

The high back of her father's chair was turned to the

door. A fire was going, for though it was spring and the plum blossoms outside the window were already falling, the air was sharp, and there had been heavy morning frosts. The room was filled with sun, but the silence chilled her. The flames of the fire were weak and pale, as they are in morning sunlight. 'Daddy.'

His hand moved and dropped listlessly down the arm of the chair. She moved across the room and round in front of him. She thought he might be asleep, but he was staring into the fire. Stella did not at first notice the grey pallor of his skin and the loose folds of his cheeks, as if life were already leaving his flesh to sag and crumble. She looked at the table beside him, and there was the envelope with its green air mail stamp and familiar writing. But the envelope was empty.

'Daddy, David ...' she looked at him. His eyes were still fixed on the fire. She forgot the letter, saw the shrivelled horror in his face. It struck her that his eyes were trapped forever on some point in the fire from which he could never again break free.

'Daddy, what's the matter?'

'I'm not well.'

She looked around her wildly, feeling helpless and terrified. 'What can I do?'

His eyes still fixed on the fire, he raised a hand and groped in the air. She bent over him and his fingers struck her face, fumbling on her cheeks and lips, as clumsy as the hands of a baby.

'Is that you, Stella?'

He did not turn his head. 'My poor little daughter,' he said. 'You are all alone. Murder! Murder!' Tears started into his eyes, and his fingers, groping up her face, closed over a lock of her hair and dragged her head towards him.

She pulled back but his fingers had locked in death. The last of his life poured into that clutching, desperate grasp. And when she jerked her head away strands of her torn hair were still clutched in his hand.

The phone was on the windowledge by the side of the fireplace. Her father sat staring into the fire, his eyes wide and unblinking; his hand, still holding the torn strands of hair, dropped slowly to his knee. His mouth was setting into a tight, twisted line. One side of his face was quivering, the other was rigidly, terribly still. She could not bear to look at him. His jaw dropped and closed again to lock into its final immovable lines.

Trevor Nyall had walked over to the open louvres and was looking out into the harsh sunlight. She sat waiting. 'I know everything about the gold, Eola, Jobe. He wrote and told me everything. How Jobe threatened him ...'

'Threatened him!' Nyall turned around.

'He said that David was standing in his way, that he would get the gold in spite of him ...'

'David should never have told you about this. This matter was highly confidential. If all administration employees confided in their wives ....!'

She shrank away from his accusing eyes. 'I know. He told me not to mention it. But I must find Jobe. Don't you see? He *killed* David. There is no other explanation. He must have seen him when he returned. David was afraid and wrote to my father ...' Her eager voice rose. 'I must find Jobe!' She shivered as you might when you speak of someone you secretly love.

'Please,' he said, 'speak quietly.'

Her voice quivered shrilly. 'I don't care who hears me!'

'You *must*. You don't know what harm you may be doing.'

'I'm sorry,' she said humbly.

He looked down at her hands that writhed and clenched in her lap. 'It's all right,' he said.

'I must find him,' she said, softly but passionately. 'If I didn't have this to do I would die.' She shivered, remembering the evenings closing in, over no one, nothing.

'My poor child,' he said, looking down at her gently. 'You've made such a grand game of this and how will you take what I'm going to say? Mr Jobe has left the Territory. He left straight after David's death.'

Stella stared up at him. She felt cold.

'He was told of David's decision,' said Nyall, pacing again back and forth in front of his desk. 'Which in case you don't know, was a refusal of the claim. Apparently he expected it. A few days later I found he'd gone, left for Sydney.'

'He could be back,' said Stella. 'He could have gone away until the affair died down, and then come back. Perhaps he's here now. Perhaps he's in Eola!' She clenched her fists. The blood had come back to her face.

'*Why* would he kill David?' Nyall said, with a little hopeless laugh.

'I don't know,' she cried. 'Perhaps for revenge, perhaps because he was angry. Perhaps because no one else but David would remember Eola and he could then go and get the gold without anyone knowing. Perhaps he will put in a new claim that will go through. David had an assistant...' She paused as Nyall looked up sharply, and then rushed on, interpreting his keen glance as some kind of approval. 'Perhaps Jobe and he had come to some agreement. This assistant hated David. David said he was jealous of him. Jobe might be back. There are only two ways of coming into this country. We could find out if he's back by checking with the airways and the shipping people.'

'Stella,' Nyall broke in. 'Two words of a dying and delirious old man, and you come to this! Go *back* to Australia. This is morbid and unhealthy! It's madness. What *good* will it do you?'

'I don't expect good,' she said. 'I expect the very worst.'

He saw in her face unreasoning emotion. '*Well*, now.' He smiled and patted her shoulder. 'You've made up your mind. We can't let you go off on your own now, can we? I'm your friend. I must help.'

She looked up at him gratefully, her moment of passion and exultation over. She felt tired and very young.

'I'll tell you what we'll do,' he went on. 'We'll go to the shipping people and the airways, and we'll find out if Mr Jobe has returned. If he has, I'll help to find him. If he hasn't, you're to forget about murder and try your best not to grieve for David. Will you shake on that?'

She looked down at the hand he offered. She was not happy about the bargain, but her strength had gone, and he was at that moment so like David himself, spoke so strangely in David's own indulgent phrases, that she took his hand. 'Yes, I'll do that,' she said. 'If he's not here, I won't worry you any more.'

He picked up his hat from the table. 'We'll try the airways first.'

The airways office was a little maisonnette building in the main street next to the hotel. Nyall drew up his car at the same time as a bus bringing passengers in from the airstrip, and they waited for a few moments while luggage was carried into the office and transit passengers drifted off towards the hotel.

'That's the store down there,' Nyall said, pointing to a low building on the right. 'Not bad either considering the isolation of this place. See these fellows? They're from down the coast. Never have one of those boys for a houseboy.'

Three tall, slim, young men were walking down the footpath towards them. They wore red ramis, and around their throats necklaces of dogs' teeth and thin strands of coloured beads knotted into tight collars that hung down to their belts and swayed to and fro as they walked. Their hair was uncut and stuck about with flowers. They did not smile or look to right or left but stalked past slowly with an air of truculent arrogance.

'Most unpleasant people in the Territory,' said Nyall. 'Steal anything. Can't trust them. When you need a laundry boy you'd better come up and see my wife. We'll look after you, take you around a bit.'

'I'm not interested in the country,' said Stella. 'I just came to find Jobe.'

He smiled and patted her knee. 'Of course, of course. And now we'll go and see if he's back. You stay here.' He was out of the car and had closed the door behind him. 'I'll go and ask.' He smiled at her again, turned and crossed the footpath. A fat Papuan woman with coloured, paper bows in her hair drew back to let him pass.

Stella waited till he had gone up the steps and then got out and followed him. She stood in the doorway and watched. A young man in white uniform was weighing luggage. Behind him, sitting on the edge of a table, was the air hostess. She was smoking and dabbing polish on her nails. She looked up and tried to catch Stella's eye. But Stella, leaning in the doorway staring at Trevor Nyall's wide, white back, was praying. Let him be there. Let him be back! If he wasn't there ... it didn't bear thinking of. There would be nothing.

Trevor Nyall leaned forward. She heard his voice murmuring and the girl on the other side of the desk started turning the pages of a thick book in front. 'I seem to remember the name ...'

Nyall moved his heavy body and leaned on the counter. Stella could see the girl's bent, curly head. She turned the pages slowly, then raised her hand and straightened the collar of her white uniform. She's not looking for his name, Stella thought desperately. She's thinking of her uniform and how nice she looks, wondering if her collar is creased. His name is there and she won't see it.

The girl lifted her head and smiled brightly. 'Yes, he's here. He arrived yesterday. I'm afraid he left no address.'

Stella turned and walked out into the street.

A moment later Trevor Nyall came out of the office, smiling as he walked towards her. 'Well, my dear, and so you see ...'

'He's here!' She looked up at him, her face radiant.

The smile left his face. 'I told you to stay here, to mind the car. I have important papers in my briefcase. They might have been stolen ...' He glared up and down the street.

'I'm sorry, I didn't understand.' In her exultation she hardly noticed his displeasure. 'I was right. He's here, and he'll go to Eola. We must find him before he goes!'

Nyall seemed disturbed, at a loss. He looked vaguely around him. To Stella he seemed less impressive, less handsome than he had before, and she thought that his good looks were based purely on his confidence, his belief that he was always right.

'He came on my plane,' Stella said softly, 'and I don't remember him. I was with him for twelve hours. I don't remember a single face on that plane.' She turned to him. 'What does he look like? Describe him.'

'I don't remember him either,' said Nyall. He was staring down the street at a naked child squatting in the gutter and playing with a paper cap. 'Well, we must find him, I suppose.'

He fixed her with his most penetrating regard. 'Do you understand?' he said. 'If this gets out, it will reflect on me and my department. I could be thrown out.' He threw a wild glance to the skies as if imploring heavenly aid. 'You don't know what the word "gold" means in this country. You must be discreet.'

'I understand,' said Stella, cowering before his vehemence.

'You'd better leave it all to me,' he said. 'I'll find your Mr Jobe for you. You sit tight.'

She wanted to look for Jobe by herself, but she would not have dreamed of disobeying him. He was the inevitable extension of her father and husband.

'You'd better go back to the mess for lunch now,' he said. 'Come and have dinner and meet Janet tonight. No, not tonight, I'm going out. Tomorrow.'

She thanked him. 'Who went to Eola with David?' she said. 'Someone went with him.'

Nyall turned and looked at the child in the gutter, distracted. After a while he said, 'He went alone.'

'But he said he would take somebody with him – someone who knew a lot about the Papuans.'

'Only Sereva, who went everywhere with him. Good boy,' he mused. 'Oh, I believe he did intend taking someone, but he decided not to – the less people who knew about it, the better ...'

Work in Marapai stopped at 3.30. The sun was still strong, but past its fiercest hours, and the white administration employees scattered to the beaches, to the golf course, to the tennis courts, or to lie disconsolately in their stuffy ten by ten rooms and wonder why they had ever left Australia.

It was at 3.30 that Stella, leaving the Department of Survey, made her way along the path that crossed the parade ground. She passed a group of policemen who were saluting the Australian flag, and approached a low, stone wall and a row of ragged trees, behind which, she had been told, was the Department of Cultural Development.

Over to her right by the police barracks – a low green building with a thatched roof – half a dozen Papuans were kicking a ball around, yelling and shouting with laughter. They had tucked their ramis up between their legs like loin cloths and were kicking the ball with bare feet.

The surrounding offices, after a day in the hot sun with their louvres raised to suck up any passing winds, were closing for the night. Some offices were less punctual than others. Typewriters could still be heard and Papuans were sweeping the floors, standing in doorways urging little clouds of dust on to the ground outside.

The Department of Cultural Development was still open, its louvres raised, breathing in the afternoon winds, which blew dust and the scent of frangipani flowers from across the square. Casuarinas leaned over it, the shaggy fringes of their foliage hissing on the iron roof.

Stella stood in the doorway and looked around at the office where her husband had worked. It was little different from the Department of Survey. Seven foot walls partitioned it off like a milking shed. There was office paraphernalia – tables, desks, typewriters and filing cabinets. The strange, long, animal body of Papua and New Guinea and a map of the world with the British Empire marked in red were pinned on the wall. An oil painting of a native in a feather head-dress was propped up on top of the bookcase, and there was another drawing, which might have been done by a child, pinned on the opposite wall. Littered about the table among the files and wire baskets were half a dozen tins of bully beef, a round, yellow gourd with a boar's tusk stopper, three little wooden figures and a human skull. Down in one of the smaller offices somebody was using a typewriter.

She looked into the first office, but it was empty; the desk was tidy and the louvres behind had been closed. The second office was also empty. The third office looked and smelled like the basement of a museum. Bundles of spears and arrows were propped in corners; axes, masks and drums had been pushed under tables and on top of the bookcase; over the large, untidy desk, acting at times as paper weights for loose sheets of paper, were round, smooth stones.

At a small table in the corner sat a Papuan man. He had stopped typing and was studying a child's elementary reader.

He looked different from any Papuan Stella had seen up to date. He wore khaki shorts and shirt with an air of ease and familiarity. His hair was parted on one side and cut like a white man's, except that one heavy lock had been left rather long and stuck out like a cockade. His skin was light bronze and his face handsome. He had neither the flat features of the Mekeo, nor the beaked, semitic face of some of the darker men she had seen in town. He might have been southern European but for his thin wrists and long, shadowy hands. He wore sandals, and a watch, and smoked a cigarette. He stood up promptly when he saw Stella. 'Good afternoon.' he said. 'Did you want to see Mr Nyall?'

It seemed an extraordinary thing to say, when Trevor Nyall was playing golf. She blinked at him, puzzled.

'He's not here,' continued the man.'I am the only one.'

'I didn't come to see him.' She looked around her. 'Perhaps you could help me.'

'Would you like to sit down?' He drew up a chair, offering it and then stepping back.

She sat down. No one had told her that there was a particular way to behave in front of Papuans and she was not in the least nervous. She wondered why he did not sit down, but remained standing at attention in front of her. 'Have you been here long?'

'A long time. I work for the government ever since I was a small boy.'

She might be at ease, but he was not. He spoke like a courteous child talking to an adult.

'What's your name?'

'Hitolo, sinabada.'

It was a name she did not know. 'Perhaps ...' she began.

'I work for the government longer than anyone else in the village,' he said, and smiled broadly as if she must be glad to hear this.

'Perhaps you knew my husband, Mr Warwick.'

'Oh, yes.' Hitolo's grin split wide. 'I knew him well. I was his clerk, I used to go with him everywhere. He was a very great man. He came to my wedding – it was in a church and my wife wore a white frock and veil – and sat at the end of the table and made a speech.' He paused, and then said joyously, 'We had *sandwiches*!'

She felt a little of the difference in him then, and looked down at his hands, where this difference seemed most strongly to reside. 'I am Mr Warwick's wife,' she said. It was something that he seemed not to have grasped.

'How do you do. I am very pleased to meet you.' Smiling still, he held out his hand.

She pressed the strange, moist, unfamiliar fingers and drew her hand away. 'Perhaps you can tell me,' she said, 'where I can find a man named Sereva.'

He did not answer her but stood looking at her, smiling still. She waited, looking up into his face and noticed that, though his features had not relaxed, the smile had died. The life behind the eyes had gone; she might have been looking at a human skull. His lips drooped and his face became expressionless. He jerked his head around, still facing her, his cheek turned towards her but his eyes staring over his shoulder.

She had no idea what the gesture meant. Perhaps he had flicked back his head to avoid a blow, or had discovered something in her face that he could not bear to look at.

'Do you know him?' Something in his attitude – standing as if paralysed – disturbed her. Then a voice from the main office called out, 'Hitolo! Who are you talking to?'

Hitolo did not answer. It might have been death for him to move. Steps sounded in the passageway and around the partition of the office appeared the man whom Stella had hoped she might never see again, the man she had mistaken for Trevor Nyall the day before.

Hitolo had moved now. He had turned his head, blinked, and his face had become composed and expectant.

'What are you saying to this boy?'

Stella met the hostile glance defiantly. Now that she had met him she experienced a peculiar exhilaration. She felt for him some of the comforting hatred she felt for Jobe. She met his dark-ringed eyes, larger than life behind his glasses, and her pulses beat with the excitement of intense aversion. She was certain that he would attack. 'I was asking him where I could find Sereva,' she said.

For a moment he did not answer. Then he said, 'Sereva is dead.' His voice was flat and dry.

'Dead!' she whispered. To those who have lost someone

near to them, death, any death, even a stranger's, becomes personal, like a shadowy repetition of their own tragedy.

'Hitolo doesn't like to speak about it. He saw it happen and it was not, I believe, very pleasant. They were brothers.'

She glanced at Hitolo who looked quite composed. But she understood now that his peculiar attitude, neck drawn back and cheek averted, had been a gesture of grief. 'When did it happen?'

'What do you want to know for?'

She looked at him in surprise.

He shrugged his shoulders, picked up one of the stones on the desk and held it in the palm of his hand, looking into it as one might gaze into a crystal. 'I suppose you'll find out, and you'll make something enormous out of it. He died in the field with your husband.'

'In the field?'

'It's a term meaning outside. This last trip he made into the Bava valley. Sereva went with him as usual, and he died before they reached the station at Kairipi on the way back.'

Stella could scent her prey, and her eyes shone. 'What did he die of?'

'It's hard to tell. There was no doctor.' He put down the stone and looked up. 'He was taken suddenly with some sort of convulsion and died a few hours later in great pain. I never thought to see such pleasure taken in a man's death,' he said quietly.

Stella, who could not know that a fanatical light suffused her face, said angrily, 'Pleasure! How could I ...'

'I can see,' he said bitterly, 'that you welcome it. That you see it in some way explaining what you stupidly want to know – the reason for your husband's suicide. It enhances this mad wish you have.'

She forgot her promise to Trevor Nyall and answered coldly, 'David did not commit suicide.'

He lifted his hands, held them helplessly in the air and then flapped them down to his sides. 'Ah! So that's it!' He turned away, his shoulders drooped, and he trailed his hand over the desk like a blind man. Her eyes followed his hand. His fingers fumbled on the smooth, round stones, and closed around a small, black coconut, carved in a white design. He picked it up and looked at it, blinking his eyes as if waking from a fit of abstraction, then turned it over and examined it minutely.

Stella looked about her at the littered table, the thick, anthropological volumes in the bookcase, the bundles of spears, the masks, the mysterious round stones. 'You're David's assistant,' she said. Her discovery was extraordinarily gratifying, and her voice rang with triumph.

He smiled ironically. 'Is that what he called me?'

Stella attacked him furiously. 'Now I know all about you! You hated him, you were jealous of him! And you don't like me because I'm his wife. You don't like anything connected with him.'

She had wanted to make him angry, but he just stood looking at her with an air of helpless sadness. 'I forget,' he said at last, 'that you're so young.'

They were the most terrible words that anyone had ever spoken to her. She felt instinctively that they threatened the whole basis of her faith. She hated him more than Jobe for destroying her husband and breaking up her life. He had implied that she was too young to love. She could only repeat, 'You hated him because he was more successful than you!'

'I didn't hate him. I only said I wasn't a particular friend.'

She loathed the gentle quietness of his manner. His attitude towards her had changed. I forget you are so deluded. This is what people meant when they said, 'I forget you are so young.'

'*Everyone* loved him!' she replied.

'Some did,' he said, 'but you aren't among them.'

She floundered in the very heart of rage and pain. She could not speak. His face broke and blurred in the tears that started to well in her eyes.

His quiet, ruthless voice went on. 'You expect the best of

him. If you loved him you would accept the worst. You never knew him — how could you? He had no choice but to hide from you what he was.'

If I don't love him, she thought, what am I doing here? Where is the significance in what I'm doing? 'You're trying to get rid of me,' she said desperately. 'You don't want me to find out the truth. You know something that you don't want people to know. You have an agreement with Jobe. You've arranged for him to go back to Eola and get the gold and share it with you.'

'You don't believe that,' he said wearily.

'What else can I believe? You know something. Why were they killed? What did they find in Eola? David was killed, Sereva was killed. They went to Eola and then they were killed before they could tell anyone what they saw.' She stopped. 'Hitolo was there.' She looked around, but Hitolo had gone.

He shook his head.

'But you told me yourself. You *told* me he saw his brother die. You lie so badly even I can catch you out. You *said* he was there.'

'He didn't go into the village. Only Sereva and Warwick went. Just the two of them. *Nobody* else. Nobody else. They left the rest of the patrol outside.'

'I don't believe you. Hitolo said he went everywhere with David. Hitolo!'

'Hitolo's a liar. He was only trying to be important. He was frightened and stayed behind. He's afraid of sorcery.'

'Sorcery?'

'Purri purri. Eola's full of sorcerers – vada men. All the carriers were terrified and wouldn't go near the village. Hitolo was frightened too.'

'I don't believe you. He's educated, he wouldn't believe in sorcery.'

He laughed dryly, then looked back at the little black object in his hand and stroked it with the pad of his thumb.

'I don't believe you,' she said fiercely. 'You're only trying to mislead me. Where is Hitolo?' She brushed past him and ran out into the main office. Hitolo was squatting down on the floor by the bookcase. He looked round quickly and stood up. 'Hitolo, did you go to Eola?'

He smiled. 'Yes, sinabada. I went with Mr Warwick,'

'Right into the village?'

'No. I stayed behind to look after the carriers. They were frightened. They don't like the people of Eola. They are only village people, and they are frightened. Sereva went into Eola and when he came out he died.'

'What made him die?' she said. Hitolo's soft, quiet voice had a steadying effect, and she spoke more calmly.

'The people of Eola made him die,' said Hitolo. 'They're bad people. They made his food bad and killed him.'

'You see.' The white man had followed her into the outer office and leaned now on the wall, one leg crossed over the other. 'He thinks the vada men of Eola made purri purri on Sereva.'

'Mr Warwick thought so too,' said Hitolo quietly. 'He told the boys not to eat any more of the food they brought out of Eola. He said to the boys that the vada men had made all the food bad and that was what killed Sereva.'

Stella, looking over her shoulder, spoke sullenly. 'What happened?'

The man shrugged his shoulders. It was a gesture she was beginning to expect from him. It contributed to his air of listlessness. 'I'm not sure, probably just what Hitolo says. Warwick had to say something to the carriers. Sereva's death terrified them. He probably died of food poisoning; one of the tins was bad perhaps. It had nothing to do with the vada men. But the carriers thought it was purri purri, and Warwick had to tell them something they would believe and understand. They're only primitive people, right on the border of the patrolled area. He told them that the vada men had made magic on the food and as long as they didn't touch it they were safe. That's the only defence against sorcery, to know you are safe. Once they get it into their heads that they aren't, they're quite likely to lie down and die.' He stopped and his eyes fell on Hitolo. 'But you ought to know better,' he said. 'I thought you'd got over this idea about your brother. You're trained and educated. You're meant to lead these primitive people, not rush about like a bird or a wild pig at the very mention of a vada man.'

'I don't believe in purri purri, taubada,' said Hitolo. 'I work for the government. Purri purri isn't true.'

Stella turned to the door. She had nothing more to ask, had every reason to leave, but she was reluctant. Hitolo was again squatting on the floor, and the white man, still watching her, had lit a cigarette. Outside in the bright afternoon sunlight, she knew, were all the waiting demons – fear, loneliness, and the knowledge of being unloved and unwanted by any human being in the world. Here in this room she had at least been alive. She looked back. 'Thank you, Hitolo, for what you've told me.'

Hitolo stood up again and flashed her a dazzling smile. 'I am very glad to help you, sinabada. Mr Warwick was my boss. He gave me a cigarette case for my wedding.'

'I'm sorry about your brother, Hitolo. I didn't say it before, but I'm very sorry.'

'One day,' Hitolo said 'I shall go back to Eola and find those vada men who killed my brother. One day I shall make payback for my brother.'

She went out through the door into the sunlight. Her anger had gone, and she felt drained. Even the weight of grief had lifted. From that hour she would never again believe so confidently in her own despair. Her faith was shaken not only by the words still echoing in her ears, but also by Hitolo's averted cheek. She knew there was something here that she did not understand. She fanned the dying ashes with the desperation of one pursuing a lost cause. I shall find Jobe, I shall go to Eola myself and see what happened. With her eyes bent to the ground she did not see the tall, slim man who walked down the path towards her.

And Washington, his eyes on the open doorway of Cultural Development, did not notice Stella. He walked into the outer office where Hitolo was still kneeling before the bookcase. 'Hello, Hitolo. Anyone in?'

Hitolo grinned broadly. Washington was popular with the boys, or had been until lately. He had an easy, friendly manner that was only occasionally condescending, and he was rarely as rude to the Papuans as he was to white men. But he was inconsistent and this bewildered them.

'Mr Nyall. He's in the office, Mr Washington.'

Washington nodded and walked on down the passage. He found Anthony Nyall sitting on his desk, staring out of the window and tossing up and catching a small carved coconut.

'Hello, there,' said Washington, in a manner which had once won him the reputation of being charming. 'Busy or anything? Am I interrupting?'

This he saw immediately was an unfortunate remark and hoped it would not be taken as irony. It was common knowledge that Anthony Nyall was never busy, and that you could not possibly interrupt him. This was rather common in Marapai, but Nyall was inclined to be touchy about it. He did not smile, but put down the coconut, slid off the desk, walked around it and sat in his chair.

Washington, who wanted something, tried to restore any possible damage to his cause by comments on the weather, which had over the past few days been particularly pleasant, with a fesh, cool wind and no mosquitoes.

Anthony Nyall did not respond but stared at him over the top of his glasses. Washington found his intense, serious gaze oddly disturbing. He had never liked him much. Like all men who talk too much, Washington was suspicious of reticence, and Nyall was altogether too quiet.

Nyall interrupted Washington's chatter about the weather. 'Can I do anything?'

'Well, yes,' said Washington, trying to sound casual. 'I more or less did come begging. I want to borrow a book.'

'What book?' said Nyall, folding his hands. Washington did not meet his eye. He lit a cigarette, blew out the match, and said. 'Williams, *Drama of Orokola*.'

'Sorry, can't be done.'

'Why on earth not?' He was not surprised but put up a fine show of indignation.

'You know quite well,' said Nyall tersely, 'that this book,' and he nodded at the case behind him, 'is the only copy in the Territory.'

Washington did know it. Most of the anthropological library, supreme court records and district officers' reports had been destroyed during the war. Officers in charge of what remained guarded their few treasures jealously. The books in Nyall's bookcase were precious because they were irreplaceable.

'Good God, I won't eat it! I have got some sense of the value of the book.'

'I don't doubt it, but I'm afraid I can't let you have it.'

Washington was well aware that Nyall was not being unreasonable, but he chose to be angry. The books, he told himself, would be rotting away. They were probably half devoured by cockroaches, and Nyall would never touch them, that was certain. 'How typical!' he said, raising his eyes and appealing to the heavens. 'And we ask ourselves why nothing gets done in this country. You go to Transport for a jeep and you can't have one without filling in fifteen pink forms, by which time you don't want it any more. You go to Housing to get a door for your bathroom and you can't have it because Plan P hasn't any doors and Plan X hasn't any bathrooms. Everywhere you go you're up against some petty regulation made by a doddering old fool in Australia who has never been out of his home town and thinks that a yam is a kind of oyster. And, to crown it all, when you try to find out something about the poor innocent brown victims you're slowly killing off with tuberculosis and whooping cough ...' He stopped and mentally cursed himself. It had slipped out, he had not meant to say that.

Anthony Nyall's expression had not changed. There was perhaps the faintest flush in his cheeks but his gaze lost none of its steadiness.

'God knows why we stay here at all,' Washington said more softly. 'We should have packed up and cleared out years ago.'

'Why don't you take your leave, Washington? It's due, isn't it?'

The leave that he could not take always enraged him. He forgot to be discreet and said fretfully, 'Why should I take it?' Damn him for preaching at me! I'll show him, and his big sleek brother too. He'll be glad to lend me his books. But he kept his temper. 'Could I just glance at a reference, under your eye as it were?' he said, glancing at the bookcase.

There was no reason why Nyall should refuse this request, but he did not move and only said, 'Perhaps I can tell you what you want to know. I'm familiar with the book.'

'Well, yes, maybe you can. There's a chapter on ...'

'Vada men?' Nyall said, raising his disconcerting eyes. 'Yes, there is, I know. But then sorcery is such a loose subject that you're not to know whether the Orolola vada men function in the same way as those in the Bava valley. The two areas are some distance apart. But as we have no knowledge of the Bava valley, I suppose it's the best you would have to go on.'

Washington laughed to hide his consternation. 'Now

what would give you the idea that I'm interested in Bava valley sorcery?' he said, and then immediately wished that he had not spoken.

Nyall did not look at him. He opened a drawer and produced a tin of cigarettes. 'Since Warwick's trip ...' He shrugged his shoulders. 'I assume you want to know about the most extreme form of magic, magic to kill.' His eyes were fixed across the room, and his voice had the cool, impersonal tone of a lecturer. 'There are several methods used. There is pointing or stabbing from a distance. The sorcerer hides, or is invisible, stabs at his victim with some sharp instrument which produces a fatal illness and the victim dies. There are various local explanations. Some say that he manages to inject into the victim some foreign matter, others that he drags out the victim's soul. Then there is another specialised type of magic, performed in company. One man waylays the victim and shoots him, others come behind, cut him up and extract his soul. Then others come and put him together again. He is brought to life and sent back to his village. He remembers nothing of what has happened, but he has no soul and so he lies down and dies. The victims in these cases would not have actual evidence of sorcery. They would either be told about it, or fear that it might happen, or, if they should become ill, assume that it had.

'Then there's the personal leavings magic. You're probably familiar with that; it's common all over the Territory. A substitute for the victim is obtained, something that has been attached to him, something that has been impregnated with the sweat of his body – a discarded arm-band, for instance – or scraps of food he's been eating, or a lock of his hair. This undergoes various treatments and is usually placed in a piece of hollow bamboo in some sort of dirty mixture, often the victim's excrement. When the bamboo blows its stopper' – he displayed the palms of his hands in a gesture of finality – 'finish ... the end.'

'I see.' Washington threw his butt on the floor and

ground it with his heel. He knew all this and knew that Nyall knew that he knew it. He picked up one of the stones from the desk and inspected it. 'Who are the vada men?' he said.

'Just about anyone. There are, of course, notorious sorcerers, but anyone can practise sorcery, providing that he persuades himself that he knows some of the charms, spells, the right sort of mixtures to use and persuades others; and that's even more important.'

'And how do they protect themselves? The victims, I mean?'

'By counter-sorcery. It seems to be the only way. If you are afraid of sorcery, you buy a sorcerer of your own to make counter-magic.'

'And the dead?' said Washington, staring at the stone he held in his hand.

'The dead? You mean are they afraid of the dead?'

Washington spoke lightly and laughed. 'I mean would they fear, for instance, a dead sorcerer making payback?'

He need not have composed his features into an expression of nonchalance because Nyall did not glance at his face. Throughout the conversation they had studiously avoided each other's eyes.

'They might. They'll believe just about anything. The sorcery is elastic and constantly changing. But for the most part they seem to forget the dead. They revere and fear them a little, but not as strongly as we do. A live sorcerer would be much more fearful to them. The dead are more harmless. The notion of a spirit seeking revenge is more European. With Papuans the living make revenge, and death dilutes their power. They don't have, perhaps, such a complicated sense of guilt as we have.'

Washington did not smile. 'Guilt!' He put down the stone and picked up the black coconut with the carved face. 'But it would be possible; it is heard of?'

'A dead sorcerer making purri purri? Of course it's possible. Anything's possible providing you're sufficiently credulous.'

'I see you don't think much of it all.'

'Oh, admittedly strange things happen. But there isn't much that can't be put down to suggestion.'

'Don't you think it's rather childish,' Washington said crisply, 'to dismiss so scornfully those phenomena that we ourselves may be too insensitive to experience?'

Now Nyall turned his large eyes full upon him. 'Childish or not,' he said, 'it's wise. I only know that in this country you've got to keep your two feet on the ground. Men up here, as you know, do nothing by halves. They act and think grandly. People don't just drink here, they're dipsomaniacs; when they make money, they make fortunes; when they lose money, they go bankrupt. And when they grow fanciful, they end up by going mad,' he paused, 'or killing themselves.'

Washington threw back his head and roared with laughter. 'Like poor Warwick, you mean. Well, that won't happen to me, I assure you. I have far too much to live for. And as for keeping your feet on the ground, I don't agree with you. This country has been ruined by people with their feet on the ground. It needs men of imagination, and men of vision, not the stuffy, government clerks with their red tape and carbon copies, or brawny beef and muscle men from the bush. What we want are men who'll take the trouble to understand the people, who'll find out how they think, and think in the same way.'

'A few years ago I would have agreed with you, but not now. You'll never understand the Papuan, Washington, and you know it. We're here to guide and guard, not to understand. Only children can understand children, and we aren't children any longer. It may be unfortunate, but it's true. Sometimes we would so like to be, but we can't turn back. We've lost the eyes that see fairies. All our fairies are gone. There are only a few left for drunkards and madmen.'

'Oh! And which am I?' said Washington shrilly. A feeling of having been caught out enraged him. He lashed out at what he hoped might be the other man's Achilles' heel. 'Guide and guard! That's pretty good coming from you.'

He would like to have said more but dared not. The rest was understood between them. 'Everyone knows you haven't done a stroke of work for six months. You would have been kicked out months ago if you weren't Trevor's brother. Warwick would never have put up with you much longer.'

But Anthony Nyall's expression did not change and all he said was, 'You've been here too long and you need leave.'

Washington was thoroughly unnerved. He had a feeling of having said too much or not enough, and to rectify the latter error, talked on. He spoke in the sweet, sharp tone that had lost him most of his friends. 'I happen to be one of the few people in this country who considers it sufficiently interesting to be studied,' he said. 'I've never liked the average white man here, carrying up from Australia with him his pub, racecourse and golf links. When I sail I go in a canoe, not in a yacht. I like Papuans, and I'm interested in them. If there were a few more who made an attempt to understand them, instead of imposing on them half-baked canons of white conduct, we might get somewhere.'

'I believe that you've sacked all your boys,' Nyall said coolly.

'I won't have thieves!' Washington said passionately. 'I'd rather be without boys if I can't trust them.'

'Now that's very powerful magic,' said Nyall, pointing to the coconut in Washington's hand. 'Orokola magic. There are a lot of them used up in the hills, probably in the Bava valley too. They're mostly harmless, but if you know the right charms and stuff them with the right herbs, they can do just about anything. If you hang it up on your door, it'll keep the thieves away.'

'I'll thank you not to be funny,' Washington said frigidly.

Nyall stood up. 'Well then, don't ask for information under false pretences. This is a small town and practically every man's life is public property, particularly a man like you who's always lived unconventionally. The place is getting you down. You're a pack of nerves. You've quarrelled with every boy you've had in your house for the past two months. You've got the wind up and it's time you got out. You know as well as I do what happens to people who stay when they get into your condition. You can't fight this place. Get out and don't be a fool!'

It was all so true there was nothing Washington could say. He could no longer be angry. He felt exhausted and stripped of his defences. He thought of Sylvia and momentarily longed to be with her. He slunk from the room.

When Anthony Nyall looked back at his desk, the small black coconut had gone.

Next morning Trevor Nyall entered his office ten minutes after Stella. He stopped only five minutes to collect some papers from his desk and put them in a brief-case. He patted Stella on the shoulder, enquired kindly after her health, said he would be back before twelve, and left. He did not mention Jobe.

But he did not return at twelve, nor during the afternoon, and Stella worked alone all day. There was only one interruption. At about five to twelve, as she was collecting her hat and bag to return for lunch at the mess, the door of the office opened and a man came in. He stood, standing in the doorway, with a brief-case in his hand, and said, 'Mr Nyall not in?'

Stella smiled at him. There was something about him that instantly made her feel friendly. His bright eyes sparkled beneath thick, overhanging eyebrows. His face was florid and jovial. She could not remember having seen him before, but he reminded her vaguely of someone who had been kind to her.

'No, he's out,' she said. 'He's at a conference.'

'Conference? Ha! Ha!' He rubbed his hands together and his eyes sparkled. 'Always at a conference, these government fellows, eh? Wouldn't be happy without one. If they didn't talk they might have to work, eh?'

'I don't know,' said Stella. 'I've only just arrived.' It seemed to her that he was looking at her closely, though it was impossible to be sure, his eyes were so deeply set, like two small animals in ambush, behind his ragged, tobacco-coloured brows.

'Well, well. Just arrived, eh? How do you like it here? Not a bad sort of place. Except for the natives,' he added. 'Used to be all right. The beggars used to work in the old days. But the government's ruined them with this newfangled education. Place has gone to the pack. A pretty thing like you now ... all alone, you want to be careful. Funny things go on up here.'

'I'll be careful,' said Stella, smiling.

He walked across to Nyall's desk and put down his grey, felt hat, its black band soaked in sweat. Stella wondered why this hat, seen in thousands in Australian cities, should, in this country, give to its owner a disreputable air.

He looked quite worried. 'You want to look out for the boys. Can't trust them. And don't you go walking around alone at night.'

'I must go now,' said Stella, 'or I'll miss my lunch. Will you wait for Mr Nyall? He said he'd be back, though it's so late I doubt if he will. I expect he'll go straight from the conference to his lunch.'

'I reckon I'll stick around,' he said and settled himself into a chair. He held the tattered brief-case over his knees.

Stella was to have dinner that night with Trevor and Janet Nyall, and at 6.30 walked once more up the hill towards their house. The sunset was less brilliant that night than it had been two evenings before. The sky was overcast and the long, purple clouds were fired only on the edges. There was no wind and the air was heavy. The road turned ahead of her, and she saw, walking down the hill, a white man. He lifted his hand and waved. It was Trevor Nyall.

'I thought you might be lost,' he said, as she drew near. 'I suppose you don't know the way.'

They walked on together side by side. 'Have you found out anything about Mr Jobe?' she asked.

He had taken her arm and patted her hand. She felt comforted by these gestures. 'Well, not anything much, my dear. It takes time. He's not at the hotel, and he's not in the mess. Sometimes these strays sneak a bed there. My guess is he's left already. Now here's where we go up. It's quite a climb.'

They had left the road and faced the flight of steps that Stella had climbed two nights before. She looked up in surprise. The steps led straight ahead through the green, flat-topped trees.

'It's a nice spot, isn't it?' said Nyall, putting a hand under her elbow. 'In a few weeks, round about Christmas time, these flame trees will be a picture. There's nothing like a Marapai Christmas. You must spend it with us. The fun never stops. I believe someone came in to see me today when I was out. Who was it? What did he want?'

But he seemed more interested in the trees and before she had time to answer, he said, 'There, look at that one, isn't it a beauty?'

'It was a man. He didn't leave his name. He came at about five to twelve. Didn't you see him?'

'No, I didn't finish until 3.30. One of the girls told me he had been in. Did he leave his name?'

'No.'

'Didn't say what he wanted?' He had turned to look at her.

'No.'

'Beautiful trees.' He smiled around him. 'The Grafton people boast about their jacarandas, but there's nothing like the flame tree.'

They had nearly reached the top of the steps. 'Mr Nyall,' said Stella, 'I feel somehow that he isn't the whole answer any more – Jobe, I mean. There's more to it. I've found out that Sereva is dead.'

'Sereva?' he said vaguely. He took a long pace forward, and she had to spring up to keep level with him.

'David's assistant. They were the only two who went into Eola, and Sereva died before they got back to the station.

Something happened out there that we will never find out from Jobe, and I think that's where I must go. I will never find out what happened to David unless ...'

They had reached the top of the verandah steps. She had been talking so earnestly that she had hardly noticed that they were approaching the same house that she had been turned away from two nights before.

'We'll find Jobe,' he said, pushing her up the steps ahead of him. 'Don't worry.'

But Jobe had now become only a secondary goal. 'I know we will,' she said confidently. 'But I must go to Eola, Mr Nyall.'

The steps were narrow and she walked just ahead of him. She turned to look at him earnestly. His head was just below her shoulder. His eyes lifted, and looked for a moment fully into her own. Then she was forced to turn around again to watch where she was going. She had, now that the moment of contact was over, a peculiar impression of having looked into nothing, of having turned her gaze, not upon a man's face, not upon eyes and lips, but upon a kind of void.

'Eola,' he repeated, speaking behind her. 'Now you must go in and meet my wife.'

His hand between her shoulder blades pressed her forward, and she entered again the bright, golden room with its drifting draperies, bamboo furniture and enchanting air of not being a room but an extension of a garden. The same soft breeze fluttered the hangings in the doorways and stirred the green, shiny leaves that reached in from the shrubs outside.

Then she forgot the room and could only look at the woman who came to meet her. She hesitated, afraid of committing a social blunder. What was she doing here? She *could* not be Trevor Nyall's wife. But the woman was coming forward with a hand outstretched and Trevor was saying, 'Janet, this is Stella.'

She looked some ten years older than Trevor, in spite of her hair, which was cut into a mass of short, frothy golden curls. Beneath this fantastic aureole her small pinched face looked shrunken and wizened. She was small and painfully thin, with tiny, white arms that reached out from the sleeves of her dress like the arms of a starved child. Her dress was made of some fine, transparent beige material patterned in green, and fashioned in a wispy style reminiscent of the 1920s. It fluttered like rags against her bony limbs. Stella felt that she had not walked forward but had been picked up by the breeze and wafted across the room like a withered leaf.

Her eyes were large and wide-set. They must at one time have been beautiful, but beauty was now entirely submerged in nervous evasion. Her eyes disturbed Stella profoundly, though she did not know why. The woman did not speak, but pressed Stella's fingers and then drew her hand quickly away, stepping back with a look of uncertainty about whether she should ever have stepped forward. Then she threw a glance at her husband and waited like a servant expecting an order.

Stella was no more certain how to behave. Janet Nyall did not look actually deranged, but Stella sensed that she had a grip on life so limp that she might at any time drop her hold altogether. The woman moved back across the room, hovering uncertainly from chair to chair. She appeared to have a profound distrust of everything around her. For no apparent reason she put out a hand and touched a table, like a blind woman reassuring herself that she was on the right path. Then a man came forward from the back of the room, took her hand and led her to a chair. Stella, her gaze turned on Janet Nyall, had not seen him before.

'And this,' said Trevor, 'is my brother, Tony.'

He bowed slightly. '*You*!' said Stella. 'You are Mr Nyall's brother?'

She could see now how like he was to Trevor Nyall, and why Trevor when she met him had seemed familiar, like someone known years ago and met again, older and changed. Even though Anthony would be a younger brother, in many ways he did not look younger. Experience, suffering, frustration or disappointment had marked his face and left his brother's smooth and clean. Sickness, too, had possibly attacked him and passed his brother by. But there was more that made him seem a shadow of the older man. All that was strongest, richest and happiest in the parents who had produced these men had gone into the making of Trevor Nyall. The younger brother looked to be battling against the liability of being the last, of being born when the best of life's gifts, talents and powers had been bestowed elsewhere. And he wore these liabilities in his face with bitter resignation.

Stella did not acknowledge his nod but stared at him coldly, her body rigid with aversion. The words that she had tried to cleanse from her mind over the past forty-eight hours spoke again. 'You didn't love him ... you didn't know him ...'

'So you've met before?' said Trevor, looking at her with surprise.

'Yes. I met him in the Department of Cultural Development yesterday afternoon. I knew he worked with David, but I didn't know you were brothers.'

This discovery struck her as being enormously significant. She had come here for comfort and peace, to be helped by her husband's friend, to be looked after, to be guided and directed as she had always been, but the house was stirring uneasily with its own currents, and the origin of this strangeness was Anthony Nyall. She felt apprehensive and bewildered, as if she were on the brink of some sinister discovery. Remembering something that Sylvia had said, she looked around at the walls, the corners, the ceiling, and saw that in this beautiful room that had so charmed her, something of great importance was missing.

Trevor laughed and thumped a hand twice on his brother's shoulders. 'That was the only reason he would put up with you, eh? Lounging around all day getting under everyone's feet. We are a united family, aren't we Tony? We stick together at all costs.'

Anthony Nyall's reply was a faint smile. Stella had never seen him smile before. She preferred him serious.

'You won't find in the whole of Australia, Stella, a more loyal family group than this.' Trevor looked from his brother to his wife. The smile died from his face, and he turned away and went to a table set with glasses and drinks. Janet, who had been gazing up into his face, followed him with her eyes. She half rose to her feet and her wispy hand extended in a vague, unrealised gesture.

'I'm pouring you a pink gin, Stella, is that all right?' Trevor said from the table. He shook the bitters into the bottom of a glass. 'You must excuse Janet, she's been sick. Can't take the climate. You've got to be husky in this place. It all looks pretty harmless, but it can be deadly.'

He stood with his feet slightly apart, his broad shoulders thrown back; his firm, deep voice rang out loudly. His white teeth and brilliant eyes flashed in the dusky light. He dominated the room, and his bitter-faced brother and faded wife looked insignificant beside him. 'You wouldn't believe what the tropics can do to people. Take Janet here' – he pointed a hand at his wife, who sat with a fixed, bright smile – 'you wouldn't believe it, but six years ago she was a beauty, the loveliest woman in Marapai. She's only forty-two. Ten years younger than me. You wouldn't think it, would you?'

'You wouldn't think it, would you?' said Janet, looking up at Stella with the same fixed smile. 'It's just as Trevor says, the tropics don't agree with me at all.'

'So you see, you'll have to be careful,' said Trevor. 'You fair-skinned, delicate girls don't wear well in the tropics.' He threw back his shoulders, conscious of being one of those who had worn well.

'I think on the whole that women look exceedingly youthful here,' Anthony Nyall said quietly.

'No, Tony,' said Janet, 'you can lose your looks in a day. You heard what Trevor said.'

Tony looked down at Janet and smiled. It was, this time, a very different smile.

Stella had been waiting for the right, dramatic moment to bring out her accusation. Your brother tried to stop me from seeing you, he lied to me, he drove me away. She had been savouring this delicious moment of retaliation. But in the meantime Tony had smiled and she knew she could not speak. She did not know what to think of him. In the moment of pinning him down, he had eluded her. This glance, cast towards a sick woman, had thrown dust in her eyes. She saw that an enemy could be tender and she could not battle with tenderness.

'Where's that boy?' said Trevor suddenly. His voice rang with displeasure. '*Where*'s that boy? We want ice.' He moved to a door and shouted, 'Where the hell are you. *Bring some ice*!'

Janet immediately began to flutter her hands. Her eyes were turned to her husband's back. She half stood and sat down again. 'I don't know. I expect he's in the boyhouse.'

'Well, he ought to be *here*,' said Trevor crisply. 'Kora! Kora!' He raised his voice. 'He ought to be in the kitchen from *six o'clock*,' he said, addressing his wife.

Her eyes watched him frantically. Stella found her disturbing. She did not know why, but she suddenly wanted to leave, to go away and not see Janet Nyall again. Janet had touched a chord that revived a forgotten horror in her childhood.

Janet stood up and made a few uncertain steps about the room. 'He's a good boy,' she said vaguely. 'A nice, polite boy.'

'Where *are* you going?' said Trevor in a tone of undisguised exasperation, and then went out calling, '*Kora*! *Kora*!'

They waited. Janet was quiet now. She sat on the edge of her chair, her hands in her lap. Stella, feeling ill-at-ease, made an attempt at conversation, but was only answered with a vague yes or no. Anthony still held his stance behind the chair. He did not speak either, but Stella felt his eyes on her face. She stared out of the open louvres at the sky into which the stars were breaking, but once she glanced up and met his eyes. She looked quickly away. She was afraid, not just of Anthony, but of Janet too. They looked to her in that moment withered, twisted and pitiful. She felt that they were united in some devious partnership, and shared together a secret that cut them off from the normal world. If she looked at them long enough she might know what the secret was. She felt that Anthony Nyall, staring at her so fixedly, was attempting to communicate it, was actually trying to draw her into their mysterious intimacy. She kept her eyes turned away. She did not want to know what message he was sending her. She had forgotten that he had smiled so gently.

When Trevor came back with a bucket of ice, she turned to him a face radiant with relief. Sanity, kindness and normality had taken over from sickness and despair.

'You'll have to be firmer with those boys,' he said. 'God knows you ought to be able to manage boys, you've been here long enough.'

Janet visibly brightened. 'I can't manage boys,' she said to Stella. 'I should be able to. I've been here too long.'

Trevor dropped a cube of ice in a glass and handed it to Stella. 'You're all very quiet,' he said. 'Stella expects to be entertained.'

'Tony's having a new house built,' said Janet, drawing herself up. 'Aren't you Tony? He's staying with us till it's finished. It's going to be very nice.'

'Of course,' said Trevor, 'not as big as this.' He handed a glass to his wife. She clutched it and held it tightly in her small white hand. She looked at it, raised it to her lips, glanced at her husband and put it down on the table in front of her. She clasped her hands in her lap.

'But that's to be expected, isn't it?' said Anthony.

He's jealous of his brother, thought Stella. She fastened on this fresh reason for disliking him. No wonder he didn't like David, no wonder he didn't want David to be loved. No wonder he couldn't bear to see anyone loving David.

Trevor laughed heartily. Turning to Stella, he waved a loose arm at his brother. 'Tony suffers from the disease of all youngest sons,' he said. 'He thinks he always gets the short straw. He's the defender of the weak. In every successful man he sees his big brother who always had the fattest potato.' There was no irony in his words – he spoke charmingly, with the good nature and confidence of the invulnerable, and patted his brother on the shoulder.

Anthony smiled faintly. 'You misrepresent me,' he said. 'I have no quarrel with successful men, only with the world that's taken in by them.'

Stella forgot her pleasure in finding him out and her anger was rekindled. He's talking about David, she thought, and about me.

'You see, Trevor,' he went on, still smiling, 'I know so well what it is that goes to make a successful man. He's composed for the most part of little drops and shreds of the brains and hearts of other people.'

Trevor chuckled; his eyes still smiled and his tone was kindly. 'Well now, that doesn't only apply to successful men, does it? After all, we've all of us, haven't we, surely, had our meals off brains and hearts – some of us more immoderately than others.'

Stella did not see the expression on Anthony Nyall's face because she was looking at Janet who had stretched out a slow, apparently almost reluctant hand and picked up her glass. She lifted it to her lips, tipped it back and put it down on the table. It was nearly empty.

Stella stared at her, and a look of slow horror came over her face. She realised that Janet Nyall was drunk. She had seen women drunk before, though not often, but she knew instinctively that this woman was different. Janet drank all the time. There must be some dreadful reason.

She found she could hardly bear to sit near her. Mentally and physically, she shrank from this deranged spectacle. She left as early as she could without being rude, and as she walked down the hill with Trevor Nyall beside her, the cool, night air washed the pollution from her body, or so she felt. She reasoned with herself, feeling that there was some abnormality in the violence of her reaction. But it was useless. At the thought of Janet Nyall her mind and body shuddered. For Trevor she felt pity and admiration. How bravely he had been through it all! One would think he did not care. How lighthearted he was when his spirit must be in misery. In consideration of his troubles she did not speak again of her own.

When she reached the house it was only 10.30 and the light was still burning in Sylvia's room. She knocked on the door and entered. Sylvia was lying on her bed in her black dressing-gown, her hair in pins. She was writing a letter.

Stella sat down and stared before her. 'I've been to dinner with the Nyalls,' she said.

Sylvia threw a glance at her pale, strained face, and smiled faintly. 'You didn't know what to expect?'

Stella shook her head.

'Don't look so miserable. It's not so unusual up here. Marapai is full of drunks, temporary and permanent.'

'But why her?'

Sylvia shrugged her shoulders. 'Philip swears Trevor beats her, but you can't rely on him. He's got a bee in his bonnet about Trevor, thinks he was done out of a job. He doesn't realise that no one in their senses would give him anything to do. He's very clever, brilliant really, but not in that way.'

Stella was not listening. 'Do you know anything about the younger brother ' – she hesitated over his name and brought it out reluctantly – 'Anthony?'

'Not really. Only what everyone knows, the big scandal. I've always thought he seemed a decent sort of fellow.'

'What scandal?'

'There was a hullabulloo about a year ago. Anthony made some frightful blunder. He was terribly enthusiastic and full of bright ideas – thought everyone else very conservative – and rushed around doing things without considering the consequences. He used to say that everything was too slow, that if we didn't do something quickly it would be too late. He took some highland boys to a school in one of the coastal villages. I think there were about a dozen of them, and they all died in an influenza epidemic. Some Papuans are like orchids; they won't stand transplanting, haven't any resistance. Anthony, who didn't anticipate anything like that, was devastated. There were some Sydney reporters up here, and they got hold of the story and made headlines out of it. They said we were murdering the locals for our own foul ends. The administration was in a spot and I think would have kicked him out if it hadn't been for Trevor. I think he pulled some strings and fixed it so that Anthony was cleared of some of the blame. Anyway, he's still with us.'

'I see.'

She had hoped for something different, and this, like the smile bent to Janet Nyall, only further confused her. She rose to leave, then hesitated. 'Sylvia, I remembered what you said, and I looked around the room. It's beautiful, like a pavilion in a garden, but there were no geckoes.'

Sylvia regarded her silently, then said, 'It's only a saying. Stella, I think you are too sensitive and fanciful for this country. Soon you'll be seeing ghosts and believing in vada. Be careful, and if you want a confidante come to me. I don't believe in vada, and I'm tough. I have to be.'

A week passed and Stella found out no more about Jobe until one morning Trevor brought her the news that he had left Marapai and taken a job as skipper on a small coastal boat trading between New Ireland and the mainland. No one knew when or if he would return. It was obvious that he was not going to Eola and had been frightened off Eola gold and the possibility of deportation or another term in gaol.

For the first time Stella began to doubt her convictions. Those two words of her father's, had she heard them or imagined them? Had Sereva, after all, died of food poisoning? And had David committed suicide? They were all questions which she had never before asked herself and now they more and more insistently tormented her. She had been in Marapai for nearly a fortnight and was beginning to realise that suicide was not, after all, impossible. It was not that life here was unbearable, but it was different. People changed; they were no longer recognisable as Australians. Aberrations of behaviour seemed normal and did not startle you. Frustrations and misfortunes festered into wounds here, deranged the mind and poisoned the blood. No, suicide was not impossible.

Another question presented itself and her convictions almost entirely crumbled away. How could she be right and Trevor wrong? He had known David and the country, he had been involved in the affair with Jobe, and he was older and wiser by some thirty years. He was authority, he could not be wrong.

She woke up one morning to find that she had lost her faith. It was an experience almost as terrible as the loss of her husband, except that by now, being used to loss, she accepted it more calmly. There was no longer any reason for her to stay in Marapai. There was no reason for her being anywhere, but Marapai with its dazzling seas and brilliant flowers was the last place on earth where she wanted to be. She did not think where she would go or what she would do; just to leave was for the moment enough. Once she made up her mind, her heart lifted slightly. Her sense of urgency was now attached to her departure. It was desperately important to get away as soon as possible. Marapai had become unbearable, and she resisted its beauty with a feeling of horror.

She booked a seat on the plane for the following week. Then she met Philip Washington.

It was a Thursday evening. Washington left his house at about 5.30 and walked down the hill to the shacks where he kept his jeep. The sea was pink and green and calm as ice. Canoes on their way home to the village hung poised, their slack sails barely moving in the intermittent puffs of wind.

He turned the nose of the jeep to face the road and allowed it to run down the hill towards the sea-front. He was just swinging out to turn at the bottom of the road when a woman stepped out from the footpath and waved her arms above her head. It was Sylvia. She was dressed in a sleeveless black silk dress, with a cluster of frangipani flowers on top of her head and another cluster over one ear. This time of the year was particularly humid and her face shone under its make-up.

Washington drew up the jeep beside her. He was tremendously pleased to see her. Apart from the visit to Anthony Nyall and a trip into the village, he had not been out of his hut for nearly a fortnight. He had been in bed most of the time with a fever, partly genuine, partly induced, and preferred in times of sickness to be left alone. Sylvia had been instructed not to visit him. He knew he looked unattractive when he was sick and it wounded his vanity to be seen in such a condition. He hailed her gaily.

'You're better,' she said, and looked at him closely. 'Oh, but Philip, you look dreadful. You should be in bed.'

'I'm on the mend. Still can't sleep, that's all. And where have you been, my sweet, all dressed up to kill?'

His moments of sweetness were rare these days and she smiled gratefully. 'I've been drinking tea with the upper crust,' she said. 'Mrs Lane, believe it or not.'

Mrs Lane was the wife of the Controller of Civil Construction.

'Good God!' said Washington. 'Why on earth would she ask you?' He had never been to the Lane's house. They had only been in Marapai for a few months and had taken over a new block of flats on the harbour road.

'I met her on the beach and she seemed to like me.'

That Sylvia should go to houses where he himself was not entertained was ludicrous. Sylvia was a dear but she was hopeless socially. She did not know about clothes and, in spite of her beauty, always looked a mess. 'Well, she's new to the place,' he said sullenly. 'And I suppose she just doesn't know any better.'

'She's nicer than most,' said Sylvia mildly. 'She isn't a cat – not yet.'

'Not yet, she isn't,' said Washington. He had forgotten his pleasure in seeing Sylvia and looked at her with hostility. 'But *really*, an afternoon tea – I thought at least you were going for cocktails, rigged up in that thing with the blue stuff all over your eyes. Haven't you any idea of what's appropriate? She'll never ask you again. And even if it hadn't been afternoon tea, you don't seem to know that you should never wear black in this climate. You know what is said about the tropics? Never trust any man in braces or a woman in black.'

Sylvia only smiled and said placidly, 'I don't like pale colours. I know I haven't any taste, but I dress to please myself.'

'Obviously,' he said sharply. 'You couldn't dress for anyone else. Why don't you watch you boss's wife? She's one of the few women in this town who doesn't look like a trollop. God knows where half of these men find their wives.'

Sylvia rarely fought back, but this time he had hurt her.

'Why should I watch her? She's a vile woman; no one's safe from her. Not even you.'

'What do you mean?' he said immediately. 'What's she said about me?'

'She was talking about you this afternoon,' said Sylvia, relenting. 'It was nothing really.'

'What was it?' he said. 'Tell me. I want to know. Don't drop hints then crawl away like a cockroach.'

Again she was hurt. 'She said you couldn't keep boys, that you were too familiar with them. She said it was disgusting the way you went on, and how could you expect to keep boys when you let them wear flowers and play mouth-organs and talk to you like a friend. She said they were servants and ought to be treated as such, and that people like you were ruining the country for others; that it was people like you who had caused the rise in wages and made the locals insolent and demanding and that you ought to be put out of the country.' She stopped and was immediately ashamed. 'The usual nonsense. She's just a fool; nobody listens to her. They know they get just as much as soon as they go out of the room.'

'Oh God!' he cried passionately. 'These women! These fat sows who think they know all about Papuans!'

'It was Rei,' said Sylvia. 'He went up to her sister's house and wanted a job as cook boy.' She looked up at him and said gently, 'Why did you sack Rei, Philip? Heaven knows, I don't like natives much. I can't understand them and I'm sure my laundry boy steals my gin, but Rei was a sweet boy. You should have kept him.'

Washington stared gloomily ahead. 'He's disobedient. I went out for half an hour last week and left him in charge. And when I got back he was talking to someone in the boy house and three dogs were scratching around in the rubbish bin. I won't have dogs in my place! If he can't keep the dogs away he can go. And he prowls around at night. I told him not to.'

'You're imagining things again,' she said gently. 'Rei loved you. I'm sure he wouldn't take anything. You're all on edge.'

Was it Rei? he thought. It must have been Rei. And if it wasn't Rei who was it? What was he doing there? It must have been Rei – that man who wore no rami, who stank and who was too small by far to be Rei.

'I've got a better boy than Rei.' He was feeling a little mean for having been so rude about her dress, and said with a charming smile, 'Hop in. I'm going down to the village to pick him up, and then I'll drive you home if you like.'

The village was about two miles out of the town. Before the war it had been a typical sea village, a collection of grass and timber huts built on piles over the water, each house reached by a narrow, rickety jetty stretching out from the land. At low tides the houses on their stilts were left high and dry, like strange grey birds, crane-legged, standing in the mud. During high tides the water rose up just below the floors of the houses. But this village had been destroyed during the war, and when the re-building started the government decided that it was better for the people if they built on the shore. So the old sea village had gone and the houses were now huddled up on either side of the main road. The villagers had not re-built in the traditional manner with walls of woven sago palm and thatched roof, for the government hinted that it would build a model village with wooden houses, tin-roofed, in the white man's style. Unfortunately there had never been sufficient material for the few houses needed by the Europeans, and of the new model village only two houses had been constructed. The rest of the villagers had built themselves temporary dwellings from old army scrap, pieces of tin and the broken bonnets of trucks and covered the holes with odd pieces of sacking. This had all happened in the years immediately after the war and the word 'temporary' was now almost forgotten. There was an undeniable air of permanency about the rusty little town.

But the village still had charms. These were a fishing

people and their slender log canoes with outrigger and sail still floated at the water's edge. Their woven nets sewn with cowrie shells hung from the verandahs. Some of the women wore dirty calico and tied up their hair with Christmas paper, cheap plastic clips and diamante bows, but others squatted in the doorways, their grass skirts swelling up over their knees and their hair studded with flowers and leaves. They wandered in twos and threes down the village street, carrying wood or yams in long woven baskets, that were supported from their foreheads and dangled down over their backs. In the evenings round an open fire on the beach the young boys and girls still shuffled their feet and swayed while they sang their own songs and mission songs. And there were always the small, naked, pot-bellied children scampering after pigs and skinny dogs, or crouching in the firelight, their bodies shining and their huge, black goblin eyes ringed in china white.

There was a warmth and vitality about the village that was lacking in the European-inhabited town a mile or so away, where people were boisterous but not gay, and suffered always from a sense of incongruity.

Six months ago Washington had contemplated living here, but he had not dared. Such a step would have been to transgress unforgivably the laws of white conduct. But he always, even now, felt a sense of relief and peace here. It seemed to him that in the white town everyone was poised for departure, ill-at-ease, bewildered, longing for some other land and resentful of this one. The village people sprang from the primitive soil and were not entirely separated from it. Knowing no other life, they did not question what they had. Conflicts were only just beginning. Satisfaction was only just starting to wane and, to the onlooker, at least, they still appeared happy. Washington was not worried by the rattle of rusty tin and the flapping rags; he had long since ceased to notice them.

Sylvia, however, saw nothing else. She was passing

through the inevitable stage of mourning for the grass huts. 'I hate this place,' she said, as they drew into the centre of the village. 'It's so drab, filthy and miserable.'

'Nonsense,' said Washington. 'You don't know beauty when you see it. You've got a silly, magazine mind. You're wasted in this place; you ought to go to Honolulu with a lei round your neck. You only look at the sky when there's a red sunset. You wouldn't look up on a grey day. Papuans have to be under twenty-one for you, all done up in dog teeth and garnas with hibiscus in their hair – you wouldn't glance twice at a woman in calico. I'll show you someone beautiful. You wait till you see Koibari.'

He was waiting for them. Half way through the village was a large nut tree. Its leaves had turned to autumnal hues and fluttered in red and orange rosettes around the fresh, green plumes of the new foliage. Around its trunk had collected a group of Papuans with bundles and packages, apparently waiting for some transport; village boys in cotton ramis, and strangers from outlying villages wearing the necklaces, feathers and armbands of less sophisticated places. As Washington pulled up his jeep a man rose from the fringe of the group and came towards them. He walked with a stiff-jointed shuffle, slightly sideways, like a crab. His yellow face was seamed and withered; his lips had disappeared, but a few black betel-stained teeth gaped into a grin. He wore a tattered khaki rami hitched about his waist with a piece of string, and as he waddled forward a black bag that was fettered to his waist flapped against his thigh. His legs were stained with the purple scars of ulcers. His great bush of fuzzy hair started up from his forehead, and crowned his monstrous ugliness with a wreath of pink coral flowers. As he slowly moved towards them the others in the group crouched back or slid away, flashing the whites of their eyes.

'Oh, no!' cried Sylvia, lifting her hands in a childish gesture and pressing her fingers to her cheeks.

Washington's face was alert and eager. 'Isn't he wonderful! Isn't he superbly and diabolically evil! Look at his little mean red eyes, like a scheming pig.'

'Oh, what do you want him for?' said Sylvia shuddering. She did not know exactly what filled her with horror. It was not only the sight of the old man, who had stopped and stood, chewing and spitting, a little way off. She was more frightened by the look on Philip's face.

'All the people around here are scared of him,' he said. 'He's a very powerful sorcerer. People pay him to make sorcery against their enemies. See that little black bag he has – that's got all his stuff in it. Bits of old bones and shells and stones, and God knows what. It's illegal. He's been in gaol twice for sorcery. The district officer got hold of his bag last time and burnt it, but he soon made up another one.'

'What do you *want* him for?' she cried.

The excitement died out of his eyes. An expression of recognition and then reticence passed over his face. He might have been jerked back to earth wishing to disguise that he had ever been away. He smiled. 'I'm only amusing myself. I like these old characters, they interest me. There aren't many of them left, and they're the only ones who can tell you what the old life was like. These boys' – he waved a contemptuous arm around him – 'don't even know the songs their fathers knew; they've forgotten the old legends. I know more of their culture than they do. It's just as well there are a few men like me who are willing to talk to the old men and learn about the old days before it's too late.' He beckoned to the old man who lurched forward in his shuffling, crablike gait. The black bag flapped at his thigh, and his strong, musty odour travelled before him, like breath.

She did not look at Philip again but huddled down in the seat beside him. Koibari was heaving his bulk into the back with strange, animal grunts.

'Right? All fixed?' Philip said gaily, and started up the engine. The jeep moved off, back along the harbour road. They did not speak; Washington sang, Koibari sucked and grunted. As they passed through the main street of the town, Sylvia, who had been leaning out of the window with her head in the wind, straightened, turned and spoke. 'Philip! Take him back! I'm frightened!'

'Don't be silly,' said Philip, annoyed.

But she leaned across, gripped his knee, and spoke with an intensity quite unlike her. 'Philip, why don't you stop all this nonsense and get away. Get out of that house. Living up there on the hill by yourself, it's not healthy. It gives me the creeps with the fireflies and glow-worms and flying foxes and the damned Keremas beating their drums all night. *I'm frightened*!'

He took his eyes off the road for a moment to stare at her scornfully. 'And where would I go, may I ask?'

'Leave that house and go into a mess where there are other white men around you.'

A man living in a mess was to Philip the lowest of all creatures. To go to a mess was to lose utterly all distinction and claim to respect. That Sylvia should even think of him in a mess filled him with rage. He swung the car into the gutter, leaned across her and snapped open the door. At first he did not speak, but there was a pulse jumping in his cheek. When he did speak, it was with all the icy contempt of which he was capable. 'Go to a mess! Live in a ten by ten with a bunch of drunken morons. I'll thank you not to think up such notions for my well-being. If you can't mind your own bloody business, you can get out and walk home.'

Sylvia got out on to the road. Tears had started into her eyes, but she spoke calmly. 'You shouldn't have said that, Philip. I've taken a lot from you, but I've had enough. I don't want to see you again.'

Enraged with himself for having lost his only friend, but incapable of contrition, he threw back at her, 'Do you imagine that breaks my heart?'

The jeep swung round and spurted off down the street. Sylvia stood and watched it go with tears on her cheeks.

Five minutes later when Stella walked up from the beach on her way home, she remained standing there. Stella recognised her from some way off, and waved her hand, but Sylvia did not see her. She stood in a peculiarly ungainly attitude, as if she had forgotten her body. Her hands hung limply at her sides and her hair, half an hour ago so immaculately smoothed and piled on her head, hung in wisps about her shoulders. Stella, approaching nearer, saw her face. 'Sylvia, what's the matter?'

It shocked her profoundly to see Sylvia crying. She was so collected and debonair and moved with so much assurance, and it did not seem possible to Stella that a woman like her could cry. She divided her world into the vulnerable and the invulnerable, and Sylvia had obviously belonged to those who were strong and safe.

Sylvia turned slowly and faced her, blinking long lashes that were gummed together with tears and mascara. 'I hardly know,' she said. 'I don't know why I'm crying; he's not worth it, damn him.' She spoke with a touch of bravado, but Stella was not deceived.

'Philip?'

Sylvia could only nod.

'Come home and we'll have a drink,' said Stella. 'You'll feel better.' They turned and walked slowly up the hill.

'If he's unkind to you,' said Stella, 'why do you have anything to do with him?' Sylvia's emotional life puzzled her. Her own view of it was beautifully simple. People who were kind like David, her father and Trevor Nyall, you loved. People who were cruel, who went out of their way to wound, like Anthony Nyall and apparently like Philip Washington, you disliked or avoided. She had no notion of what it was like to love someone who was cruel or even unkind.

Sylvia, who had never loved anyone who had been kind to her, and had treated such people with the contempt that Washington now meted out to her, stared at Stella in astonishment. 'Good heavens! You don't love people for their characters.'

'I couldn't love someone I didn't respect,' said Stella.

The suggestion that Philip might not be worthy of love caused Sylvia to forget her tears. She rushed to his defence. 'But I *do* respect him. He's brilliant. That's the trouble with him, he's too brilliant for this place. It's no place' – she quoted Philip himself – 'for men of imagination. He knows more about the Territory than anyone else in Marapai and just because he lives unconventionally people won't have anything to do with him. The only thing that they have against him is that he treats the Papuans like human beings.'

'But why is he so mean to you?' said Stella.

'He doesn't mean to be,' said Sylvia. 'He doesn't know he's mean. He's so much more intelligent than I am. And he's nervy. He needs leave. He's as jumpy as a cat on hot bricks. He hasn't been the same since he came back from the Bava valley.'

'The Bava valley ...' Stella slowly turned her head and fixed on Sylvia her wide, empty eyes.

Sylvia was never quite sure why she told Stella this. She had promised Washington she would never speak of it, to anyone, particularly not to David Warwick's wife. 'I don't want weeping widows falling all over me,' he had said. Certainly she had not been careless, she had not forgotten her promise. But Washington had hurt her, and this was one of those small acts of spite by which people seek retaliation against those they love. She did not aim to injure him, merely to display her own hurt. But looking now at Stella's face she began to wonder if she might have gone further than she had intended. 'What's the matter?' she said sharply.

A strong emotion in Stella's face gathered. 'I didn't know he went to the Bava valley,' she said with stiff lips.

'He went with your husband,' said Sylvia. It was the first time that it had been admitted between them that David Warwick was Stella's husband. 'I wish he hadn't gone. I don't think he's strong enough to do these jungle treks. They must be exhausting. And then of course your husband's death ... it upset him terribly. He's far too sensitive, he's not like other men.'

Stella strode up the road to the top of the hill. She had forgotten Sylvia now, dejectedly sitting alone in her room. She burned with indignation.

They had lied to her: not only Anthony Nyall, who was jealous of her husband and from whom lies were to be expected, but Trevor, her friend and protector. She saw now that he had never helped her, that he had refused help also and had deliberately tried to impede her search for justice and truth. She was not only angry, but bewildered and dismayed, for she had never before distrusted a friend. That he was a friend there was no doubt, because David had loved and admired him. She felt the anguish of a child who hears it said for the first time that there is no God.

Half way up the hill she heard a jeep behind her and moved over on to the side of the road to let it pass. The jeep drew alongside and slowed down. The driver was Hitolo. He leaned out and smiled. 'Would you like a lift, Mrs Warwick?'

'Are you going to Mr Nyall's house?'

He nodded, and she got in beside him. 'I am going to pick up Mr Nyall's luggage and take him down to the airways,' he said. 'He is going to Rabaul tomorrow. Usually I go with him, but not this time. But I make all the arrangements for him. I help him get away.'

Stella was not listening. 'Hitolo, did Mr Washington go with you to the Bava valley?'

'Yes, Mrs Warwick,' he said. 'He is a good man, Mr Washington. He is a friend of mine. He came to my wedding and made a speech.'

'Why didn't you tell me?' cried Stella, wringing her hands. She had a sensation of fighting against time. For nearly a fortnight she had known nothing about Washington.

'You didn't ask me,' he said, taking his eyes from the road to glance at her. 'I think you know.'

'Did he go into Eola with Mr Warwick and Sereva?'

'Yes, Mrs Warwick.'

He fell silent then and she felt that he would not say anything more. She had, once again, an extraordinarily acute sense of his grief, though he turned to her as before only an expressionless copper cheek. Then his slim, shadowy hands twisted the wheel a half circle. They drove through the gate and pulled up under the mango tree at the back of the Nyall's house.

Stella did not hesitate. She did not ask herself what David would have done, by which door she should enter, or whether she should knock or ring. She walked deliberately up the front verandah steps and in the open door. Trevor, Janet and Anthony were sitting together with a tray and glasses on a table between them. Janet half rose and then fluttered back into her chair. Anthony and Trevor both stood up, and Trevor stepped forward and held out his hands.

'Well,' rang out his warm, hearty voice, 'how very nice!'

The wonder and excitement of the new discovery meant little at this moment. Stella burned with rage, and she turned savagely on Trevor.

'You lied to me!' She spoke softly but the words, let out in gusts of fury, had the quality of spark and smoke. 'You lied! I can see it all now. You don't want to know the truth. You don't want justice for David. You know something happened at Eola, but you'd rather not know what it is, and you're doing everything in your power to stop me from finding out.'

'Hey! Steady, steady now!' Trevor Nyall smiled at her.

He spoke with the soothing indulgence with which you might address a spirited pony.

'It's no good,' she said. 'You've never tried to help me. I can see that now. You just want me out of the way. And I nearly went. By next week I would have gone. Somebody murdered your greatest friend, but it doesn't matter to you. The truth is too much trouble for you. It might upset the administration. It might upset the Papuans. You sit back and let this discredit hang over David's head.' She was crying now, but she did not turn away or blink her eyes. They blazed with unabated anger behind the her tears.

Somebody repeated the word 'discredit'. It was Anthony. His eyes behind the magnifying circles of glass were staring at her, extraordinarily brilliant. She saw his lips move.

Janet was fluttering her hands. They waved about, vague and purposeless. 'Trevor wouldn't lie,' she said. 'Trevor's so kind. Listen to her, Trevor. I would never say that you lied. I wouldn't say that.'

'I can't believe anything you've said to me,' cried Stella. 'I'm going to this man Washington by myself. I'm going to find out what happened. And I'm going to Eola. I'll find some way. I'll go to the police. I'll go to the administration, and I don't care if it causes trouble. You haven't considered me; why should I consider you?'

'Stella!' Trevor put his two hands on her shoulders. She tried to shake him off but could not. He pulled her around to face him. It was hard to suspect a man who looked straight into your eyes. She was reminded of her father, of the nuns, of her husband, of the procession of adults who had all directed and guided her, who had put their hands on her shoulders and said, 'Now, listen to me, Stella, now tell me, Stella, now, Stella, it's not like that ...' and had died and left her alone. Her will slowly bent before his.

'I see now that you've found out about Philip Washington,' he said. 'You can't blame me for keeping it from you. It was because I have some sense of responsibility towards you that I did keep it from you. Of course I want to stop you in this mad enterprise. Because I *know* you're only doing yourself harm. And even if you *are* right, which you're not, I'd still try and stop you and do the investigations myself. I wouldn't let you put yourself in danger.'

'Don't you see that I don't *care*!' Stella said. She had whipped herself up into a fresh frenzy of faith. The light of fanaticism in her eyes burned brighter than ever.

Anthony Nyall turned abruptly away from them, strode across to the door, and then came back.

'And *you*,' she said, facing him. 'Why didn't *you* tell me?'

Trevor looked at his brother and said, 'Yes. Tony, why didn't you tell her?'

There was a faint, derisive smile on Anthony's face. He answered his brother, not Stella. 'Oddly enough,' he said, 'for exactly the reason you've just stated. It's strange isn't it, that we should have the same motives? We may end up by doing the same things, but no one would imagine us to have the same motives.'

Trevor laughed. 'Now, now, no jibes, little brother.'

'Don't be rude to Trevor, Tony,' said Janet. 'He's very good to you; he lets you stay in his house.'

'You have no cause to protect me,' said Stella stiffly. She had forgiven Trevor, but she did not believe Anthony would ever try to save her from pain. You didn't know him ... you didn't love him ... he had said. 'Why should you? she said. 'You didn't like David. You don't like anything connected with him.'

'It apparently pleases you to think so,' he said quietly. 'But you're wrong. We disagreed over matters of policy, that's all. We represented two opposed anthropological points of view. There was no bitterness on my part.'

Trevor turned petulantly to a boy who had been hovering in the doorway, trying to catch his eye. 'What *is* it?'

'Please, taubada, boy come long taubada's sometings.'

'Tell him to wait.'

The blood was draining out of Stella's face. Her moment had passed. She felt tired and numb. 'I'm going to see Washington,' she said mechanically. 'I'm going to Eola.'

'Well, yes,' said Trevor. 'You must certainly see Washington. You must hear from him what happened. *I* can only give you the briefest details. But if you really want to see him you shall, though I think you'd better wait a few days. He's been ill.'

The suggestion of a delay reignited her enthusiasm. 'I can't wait,' she cried. 'I've waited for days – for weeks! I can't wait any longer! Jobe may be at Eola now! He may be gone before we can find him.'

Trevor answered with a touch of sternness. 'The man's had a fever, he's not at all well. He hasn't been to work for a fortnight. And Jobe is in Rabaul.'

But doubt, once admitted, fingers every word and thought. 'How do I know he's been ill?' she said. 'How do I know you didn't send him away until I had left the country or until you had convinced me, as you nearly did.'

Trevor's brows drew together and Anthony smiled.

'I'm going to see him tonight ... now,' she said.

'I'll take you,' Anthony said.

She looked at him in surprise. 'I think you'd better let me take you,' said Trevor and smiled charmingly. 'Let me redeem myself in your eyes. I obviously need to.'

'I'll take her,' said Anthony, in a flat, decided voice. He took Stella's hand and drew it through his arm.

She found herself moving off with him towards the door. She did not know how it happened that she left with this bitter, wounding man, leaving behind his brother who was kind, her husband's friend, who had in his misguided way tried to look after her, and who would never have said, 'You did not love him.' She looked back over her shoulder and said, 'I'm sorry I was rude. I know you were trying to help me, but I don't want that sort of help.'

Trevor said nothing. He had swung his tall body around

to watch them go. Beside him sat his wife, her yellow hair burning like a candle, her white hands dabbing about after a mosquito that had long since decided against her emaciated arms and had settled on the bronze dome of Trevor's forehead. The light was behind him and his features were only a dark blur, but there was no doubt of his friendliness for her, for he lifted his hand and waved.

She was glad. She could not have borne to quarrel with David's friend.

Still with his arm linked to hers, Anthony led her around to the back of the house. The Nyall's cook boy was sitting on the back steps talking to Hitolo. Anthony paused. 'My luggage isn't ready, Hitolo, but you can drive us to Mr Washington's house.' He helped Stella into the front seat and climbed into the back. Nobody spoke. Stella tried to think of Washington and the meeting ahead. She tried to assemble the questions she wanted to ask him, but her thoughts kept sliding away and she found herself wondering instead about the man sitting next to her. She turned to speak to him. He had been leaning forward in his seat and her head almost knocked against his. She felt his breath on her cheek and caught the faint scent of his body. For an instant his eyes blazed into her own.

You rarely look for long into the very heart of another's eyes. And Stella felt she had done more than look, had seemed to plunge, to drown. She had no idea what she had encountered, but her nerves sprang from contact with the unknown, and she turned away. 'Why are you taking me?' she said.

He drew away from her. 'You'd go anyway.'

'That's not consistent. I would have met your brother anyway, but you wouldn't help me then.' She had wanted to quarrel with him, but found herself speaking quietly.

'I've changed my mind,' he said, 'about you, since ...'

'Since the night I came to dinner,' she supplied, though she had no idea what she had done then or why he should change his mind. Her words rose from a conviction that after that night many things had changed.

He did not confirm her statement but only said, 'You will go on.' He spoke without emotion, as if he recognised her course as inexorable.

The road they drove on turned in towards the hills past low buildings that hummed with cheap music and a tangled pile of army scrap that rusted beneath tendrils of encroaching creepers. It was darker here and rather cheerless. Even the Papuans looked different. Along the sea-shore they walked with long, swinging steps, talking, laughing, sometimes singing. The yellow skirts of the girls swished gaily around their shining calves. But in this valley that the sun had left some of them had already lit their fires and sat huddled around them. They did not laugh, but beat their drums, and here and there broke out a monotonous, quavering chant, 'Ba ba ba aa a aa ba aa.'

The road came to an end by some empty tin sheds and a clump of coconut palms. Hitolo swung the wheel around and pointed the jeep back the way they had come. The government offices were on the left. There were no houses anywhere. The palm leaves rustled overhead and every now and again creaking, scratching sounds came from the derelict sheds. Anthony Nyall pointed without speaking up the hill and began to climb. Stella and Hitolo followed.

Then she saw the little thatched hut perched above them in a bright garden of frangipani and variegated shrubs. A light was burning in the window. A flight of wooden steps led up between the trees to the overhanging verandah. It was almost overgrown with tall, red shrubs, and Anthony, half way up the steps, paused and held back the branches for Stella to follow. The verandah was covered by a creeper with shiny leaves, and there were speckled orchids in hanging pots, their small twisted flowers dipping in the light breeze. 'Are you there, Washington? May we come in?' called Anthony.

There was a murmur of voices within, a grunting sound

and a subdued scuffling. Then came a man's voice, clearly but softly speaking words that Stella could not understand.

They waited. Through the open doorway they could see a dim yellow shape and the outlines of a table and chairs. Stella, so not to appear to pry, turned and looked back the way they had come. The red shrubs, their leaves against the sun, were now pale transparent pink. A mosquito whined towards her.

'Just a moment,' called the voice. 'Who is it?'

'Nyall,' said Anthony.

'Oh, you, Trevor ...'

'Anthony.'

'Oh!' The voice fell away.

Stella looked back at the doorway. The shining green laurel leaves drooped around the open frame. Her eye was caught by a small object fixed to the outside of the door by a piece of string tied round a nail. It was oval in shape, but pointed at both ends. It was black, highly polished and carved in a design of fine, feathered lines slanting in from the sides and joining at the centre around two eyes and a mouth. It suggested both a human face and the head of a fish. She had seen it before, or one like it, on the desk of Anthony's office. Anthony was looking at it too.

Washington said, 'Come in, sorry to keep you waiting.'

The room was dimly lit by a single lamp fixed into a large glass bottle that was almost quarter full of the dead bodies and fallen wings of flying ants. The lamp threw a soft, golden light on the thatch above. Small pink geckoes lay waiting on the rafters to pounce on the insects that scratched and scuttled there. The walls were festooned with various weapons: masks and ornaments, axes, spears, arrows, drums, bamboo pipes and long strips of coarse cloth decorated in bold brown and red designs. Against this decor Philip Washington presented an incongruously elegant figure.

He was sitting in a large cane chair with his feet on a wooden stool. He wore a yellow silk dressing-gown with a deep black collar and borders to the sleeves, and fanned his dripping face with a Chinese sandalwood fan. On the table beside him was a wooden Balinese head, a glass of rum and an untouched plate of bully beef and hot boiled potatoes. The tin that had contained the bully beef was on the floor at his feet.

She had accused Trevor Nyall of deliberately hiding him but decided now that she had been unjust. Washington did look ill. It was not exceptionally hot, though the climb up the garden steps had made her skin prickly and moist, but Washington's face ran with sweat. His eyes were pouched from lack of sleep and there were sharp, haggard folds around his lips that did not appear to belong to a face otherwise young.

As soon as she entered the room she knew he was hiding something. He lay, making no attempt to move, languid as a Yellow Book poet, but she felt that the body under the silk gown was tense and defensive. She felt that he knew who she was and why she had come, and was prepared for her.

'You will excuse me for not getting up.' He spoke in rather high-pitched, drawling tones and waved a long, elegant hand at two cane chairs. 'This damn fever leaves me weak as a chicken. Oh, hello there, Hitolo. Nice to see you again. Sit down over there.' He pointed to the corner and Hitolo came quietly in and squatted down on his haunches.

Stella, who had no idea that in Marapai it was a breach of etiquette to invite a Papuan to sit down in the same room as a white woman, took no notice of this. She sat down too, but Anthony remained standing. 'I've brought Mrs Warwick to see you, Washington,' he said. 'She's only recently learned that you went into the Bava valley with her husband.' He spoke quickly, almost casually, as if to get this visit over as soon as possible. His words subtly deprived the meeting of emphasis. Stella did not know whether to be angry or grateful.

Washington had turned his extraordinarily light eyes towards her, and in a manner as elegant as his dressing gown said, 'Believe me, Mrs Warwick, you have my deepest sympathy. I knew you were here, of course, and I was going to get in touch with you. You probably think it unpardonable of me for not having done so. I should have written, but I am one of those poor wretches who go completely *under* in an attack of fever. It just prostrates me. I am useless. You will excuse my not getting up, won't you? Perhaps you'd like something to drink. Hitolo, fish around behind that curtain and you'll find a bottle of gin.' His eyes returned to Stella. 'I have no ice, I'm afraid. The boys used to carry it up from the freezer for me, but, alas, I now have no boys. So you must excuse the mess.'

Stella said nothing. She was shocked to find him so charming. There was something light and brittle about the way he spoke that – against her inclinations – amused her, an inflection to his voice that made everything he said sound witty. She did not like being charmed, and she profoundly distrusted him.

'What about Rei?' said Anthony.

He shrugged his shoulders. 'Rei ... That's right, Hitolo, and there are glasses there too and water in that jug. Put back the cover or the ants will fall into it.' His voice faded. His eyes had wandered and were fixed now on the darkening doorway. He leaned forward suddenly in his chair and peered outside. Both Stella and Anthony turned to follow the direction of his gaze. The leaves of the creeper formed a sharp, serrated edge around the doorway. Night had fallen quickly, and behind the frangipani trees, the sky was pricked with stars.

Washington's unblinking eyes probed the dark shapes of the bushes. His face was tense and a small pulse throbbed in his cheek. 'Hitolo, be a good boy and have a look outside, won't you. I think somebody's waiting out there.'

Hitolo left the drinks and walked obediently outside. He stood for a moment on the verandah and came back in again. 'Nobody there,' he said.

Washington leaned back in his chair. His face relaxed.

'We're keeping you from your dinner,' Stella said, and struck at a mosquito on her leg.

'Oh, that's nothing. It's inedible anyway. Are the mosquitoes troubling you? Hitolo, pass over that switch to Mrs Warwick.'

Hitolo unhooked a long, horsehair switch from the wall and Washington picked up his plate and prodded a potato with a fork. Stella switched impatiently at her legs. She opened her lips to speak, but Hitolo forestalled her. 'Taubada!' He had moved forward into the centre of the room. He was staring at the empty meat tin by Washington's feet. 'Mr Washington, don't eat that food. You die!'

Washington lifted his eyes and stared at Hitolo. His lips were half parted to receive the food. Then he glanced down at his feet. When he looked up again his eyes were bright and angry. 'Don't talk such nonsense!' he said. 'Go back and sit down this instant!' Digging his fork into the bully beef, he scooped up a large piece and thrust it into his mouth.

'No eat 'im, taubada,' chanted Hitolo. He appeared not to have heard Washington's rebuke. He stood with his arms hanging at his sides, his eyes wide and glazed. There was a strange, whitish flush around his lips.

Stella looked down at the can. Its lid was rolled back round a key. It had a scarlet label with yellow lettering. Washington spoke again. His voice rose, a note of hysteria in it now. 'Do as I tell you! Sit down and be quiet or you can get out!' He ate a little more and pushed his plate away, grimacing. 'There!' he said defiantly to Hitolo, who had slunk back into the corner again. 'Do I look as if I'm going to die? My God, you're a spoiled crowd. There used to be a time when a piece of smoked magami was good enough for you. Now you scream for tinned meat and fish. And if you strike an off tin that gives you a belly-ache you wail about that and want fresh beef from the freezer at five shillings a pound. That's where we've gone wrong with these people,' he said to Anthony. 'All we've done is to create unnecessary needs without developing a sense of discrimination.'

'Mr Washington!' said Stella desperately.

'Yes, Mrs Warwick, you were wanting to ask me some questions. I'm sorry I was not more prepared for you. Oh, dear, that doesn't seem to be agreeing with me.' He ran his hand over his stomach. 'I shouldn't eat with fever. I never feel I can touch a thing.'

As he spoke Stella became conscious that the room was becoming filled with more and more tiny flying insects. The circle fluttering about the lamp was slowly thickening. They seemed frenzied and pelted about like snow. The table all around the glass bottle was littered with fine, shining wings. They had settled on the ceiling, too, and scratched and whispered in the thatch. Two or three large cockroaches joined them and flopped about the room. In the confined space they looked as large as birds. The geckoes waiting on the rafters were darting to and fro, and a lean black cat that Stella had not noticed before was sitting on a rafter directly above her head cracking something between its jaws.

Desperation seized her. Somewhere here, she believed, hidden in this house, in the body and mind of this man, was the truth, the justice she sought, but the hut was equipped to distract and bewilder her. The masks, the string of dogs' teeth and the curved half moons of the boars' tusks caught and mesmerised her eyes; the amusing elegant manners of Washington trapped her; Hitolo with his talk of deadly meat had momentarily banished David Warwick from her mind, and now nature itself, the sky with its hordes of winged insects, had rallied to attack her. She felt that her sight, her senses, her passionate purpose was blurred in the flutter of myriad wings.

'Mr Washington,' she said again, leaning tensely forward. 'When you went to Eola ...'

'Just a moment, Mrs Warwick. I'm afraid we'll have to turn off the light or we'll have these things in hordes. They'll pass over in a moment.'

She lashed at her legs with the horse-hair switch in a sudden revulsion against the tiny pricking, tickling creatures. Along the arm of her chair they had settled in a thick, wriggling, greasy patch. She looked up and her eyes met Anthony Nyall's. He was staring a her with an expression of grave sadness. Washington put out a hand and snapped off the light.

There was a moment of silence, at least of human voices. In fact the little hut was filled with sound. The flying ants flopped and battered their wings against the lamp; through the open louvres they could be seen, a twirling, spinning multitude against the night sky. The thatch was alive with scraping, cracking, creeping insect life, and from the ceiling above Stella's head swayed a cluster of strange, bamboo objects – some sort of musical instruments, she guessed – that tinkled in the breeze like wind bells.

'Who's that?' said Washington sharply, and they heard him move forward in his chair.

'There's no one there,' said Anthony in a flat, tired voice. 'It's only the flying foxes. There's nothing to be afraid of. Nothing can come in. You're well protected. You have magic hanging on your door'

Washington laughed. It was a strange high, dry sound. 'Oh, so you noticed it. Now don't expect me to be ashamed of myself. I can't help it, you know. All the nicest things I have are pinched. My fingers itch and there's absolutely nothing I can do about it. You're not going to take it away, are you?'

'Not if it gives you any comfort,' said Anthony. His voice was low, and it was difficult to tell whether it was menacing or gentle.

Stella struck a desperate blow at the mosquitoes that were attacking her legs. She was beginning to feel hysterical. The whole evening – this strange, elegant, unstable man, his fantastic house, Hitolo, the flying ants – seemed unreal, dreamlike.

'There *is* someone there,' said Washington tensely.

Now Stella had heard the sound. It was a low, scuffling

noise that seemed to come from under the house. Then there was a subdued yelp.

Washington leapt to his feet. She saw his tall body dart across the room to fill the doorway that looked out towards the boy house. 'Koibari! Koibari! Where are you? You there! There's a dog under this house. Get it away, I tell you! *Get it out here*. I won't have dogs scratching around in this place!'

Her first thought was, There's somebody there. And he said there was no one. He's a liar too.

Washington's voice rose almost to a scream. 'Get him out of here! Kick him! Stone him! Get him away! I won't have those damn Kerema dogs in this place!' The yelping and scuffling increased and Washington's voice screamed on. 'Get him out of here! I won't have those damned dogs!'

He's mad! she thought. The scene had changed abruptly from dream to nightmare. The walls of experience shot back and she found herself glimpsing into regions of the human heart that she had never dreamed existed. The flying ants were still thick in the air, brushing her face as they passed. They had poured down the hillside in a united stream, using the house as a tunnel, sucked in through the louvres on one side and out through those on the other. Stella sat motionless in her chair, her hands clenched at her sides and her heart beating violently.

A voice spoke quietly in her ear. 'Look at the glow-worms,' said Anthony Nyall. 'Aren't they beautiful?'

She looked up. In the thatch above her head pale, soft lights were breathing on and off. They were not sparkling, hard, metallic like the firefly, but bright, soft and tender. She felt an immediate sense of relief. She smiled and moved instinctively to hold out her hand, then collected herself and drew it back.

'You must excuse me, Mrs Warwick,' said Washington in a more normal voice. He was feeling his way back to his chair. He flopped into it and fanned himself. She could smell the faint sour odour of sandalwood. He was breathing deeply, and though she could only see the outline of his head and one rapidly moving hand beating the fan, there came from him a suggestion of almost desperate exhaustion. 'I'm not at all well,' he said. 'Fever always puts my nerves on edge and those damn Kerema dogs come over and root up all my vegetables.'

'Mr Washington, when you went to Eola ...'

'Yes, Mrs Warwick. What were you wanting to ask me? I'm sorry about the interruptions.'

'Please can you tell me what happened?'

Anthony Nyall spoke now. 'Mrs Warwick believes that the trip to Eola might have had some sort of bearing on her husband's suicide.'

Stella's lips tightened at the word 'suicide', but she said nothing.

'Nothing,' said Washington quickly. 'Nothing at all.'

'What happened?' said Stella patiently. Nothing would come from this man, she knew. He was not attending to what he said. She had a strong impression of his thoughts flitting about the room like the flying ants, and only returning now and again to give the briefest check over the words he was speaking, which sounded forced and mechanical, perhaps rehearsed. But she was not discouraged. She felt she might learn what she wanted to know, not from what he said, but from what he did not say.

'Well, we went by flying boat to the station at Kairipi. It's on the coast, at the mouth of the Bava River. The district officer took us up the river in the station boat to Maiola, which is the end of his patrol. Here we picked up a couple of guides and we had eight carriers with us from the station and Hitolo, and ...'

'... Sereva,' said Stella.

'Yes, and Sereva. It was rather a crowd to take, but we were carrying some trade goods for the Eolan people, who haven't got much of a reputation for friendliness. Nobody knew anything much about them, but we were considered rather foolhardy going in – by the natives that is. So we took cowries and pearl shells from the coast. We had trouble getting the natives to go with us. But two of them ran away as soon as we got near the village and the others wouldn't go any further.'

'Why were they frightened?' asked Stella.

'Vada, Mrs Warwick. Vada. Eola has a reputation for vada men.' He had lowered his voice and spoke with an inflection of awe, almost of reverence. 'It's a type of sorcery. A very powerful type of sorcery. You've probably heard a little about sorcery but ...' his voice was slow and eager, and Stella, fearing another digression, interrupted.

'What happened then?'

'Well, we were at this village Maiola, which is the end of the patrol. The river narrows there and you can't take a canoe up it, so we struck out on foot, following along its bank.'

Stella listened and stared outside through the open doorway; the sky was now clear of flying ants and showed a deep, washed blue between the frangipani trees.

Anthony had sat down and lit his pipe and the white smoke moved slowly out through the door.

'I think that the flying ants have gone,' Stella said.

'So they have.' Washington stretched out his hand and switched on the light. They blinked at each other, their faces for the first few moments white and strained, their eyes pinched and drowsy. The cat above Stella's head had disappeared, the geckoes had crept into the corners of the rafters. The flying ants had dropped their wings on the table and just a single cockroach still banged against the lamp.

Washington had looked first at Stella, but now his eyes surveyed the room. Then his body grew rigid, his hand clutched the fan, and he sucked his breath in sharply. Stella glanced quickly into the corner, but she could only see Hitolo squatting on the floor, his long exquisite hands hanging limply down between his knees. There were two white spots of light on his burnished cheeks and his eyes glimmered like jewels.

Washington fluttered his fan. 'You startled me, Hitolo,' he said with a nervous laugh that broke into a giggle. 'I thought you had white paint on your face. I couldn't imagine what you would be doing with a painted face. Let me see, we went on till we were half a day's march from Eola, and then the two guides decided to run for home. We weren't yet really in Eola country but fairly near it, and they weren't taking any chances. But the carriers, who were mission boys and just one degree less idiotic than the two guides, agreed to go further. After a while they got the wind up too, so we went on alone. They made camp and waited for us outside the village. We were right in Eola country, and when we came back they were huddled together over a fire, nearly ill with fear, though they hadn't seen a soul. Everyone was in the village at a dance festival.' He paused and mopped his face with a handkerchief. 'My God, it's hot, isn't it? Hitolo, pass Mrs Warwick a fan.'

'I don't find the weather any different from Australia,' said Stella.

Washington laughed. 'You don't at first. This is a place, Mrs Warwick, that doesn't give itself away in the first five minutes. If it did it would be uninhabited, at least by white men. You stick around till it gets its claws into you and then starts spitting in your face. But it's too late then, you're no good for anywhere else.'

Stella, fearing from the tense eagerness of his tone that he had arrived on another of his favourite subjects, said, 'You went on. Who went with you?'

'Your husband, Sereva, myself.'

'And was there any gold?'

He did not seem surprised that she should know about the gold. 'Very little that we could see. Just a few neck ornaments, probably traded from some other part of the country.

He's hiding something, thought Stella. She was certain that Washington was lying, but just when he had started lying she could not tell. She felt that the questions she asked now were vitally important. She had a sensation of stalking – a bird, or an animal – creeping up slowly, sliding her questions through grasses and bushes noiselessly so as not to disturb the elusive truth within. One wrong step, one cracking twig or fluttering leaf and it would be off and gone. She felt that Washington knew he was being stalked. She could sense his nerves fingering the air around him.

'Like the ones that Jobe brought back,' she said. She clasped her hands to stop them trembling. She had lost consciousness of the strange hut where they sat, and of the dark, melancholy eyes of Anthony Nyall. She had a feeling of power that she had never known in her life. She saw the situation as important and dangerous, and she was dealing with it herself. No one was telling her what to do. She was actually pitting her wits against an older, and more experienced, man. She moved in her chair, her eyes shining.

A sharp, flicking glance, like the dart of a snake's tongue, flashed across at her from Washington's pale eyes.

'Yes, like those.'

'And was there more gold in the long house?'

'Well, just a little, I believe. It was hard to see, we could only sneak a look. These people are very cagey about their long houses, particularly with strangers. They use them for initiation ceremonies. A lot of harmless nonsense goes on, but they put great store by it, and with primitive peoples it's sometimes dangerous to nose around too obviously. Warwick fished about a bit, and then we came back to find Hitolo and the carriers huddled over the fire waiting for the vada men.'

'I see. And that was all?'

He waved his fan. 'That was all.'

'Except that Sereva died.'

The fan faltered. He laughed. 'Of course, one forgets. How easy it is to fall into the accepted attitude that such things don't matter. He was a good boy, a wonderful boy. Your husband was very distressed about it. I've never seen him so cast down.'

'Had you any idea what caused it?'

He waved a hand vaguely. 'It might have been anything. Fever, bad food ...'

'But to die so quickly.'

'It's not quick for this country. Or for a Papuan. It doesn't take them long to die. It might have been vada ...' His voice dropped.

Stella threw a glance at Hitolo. He sat as before with his hands hanging down over his knees, the light flashing on his blue fingernails. 'But you don't believe in vada.'

'It doesn't matter whether I believe in it or not,' said Washington quickly. 'The point is that Sereva would, and that would make it effective.' Then with a clipped note to his voice, he said, 'It's obvious that you've only just arrived in this country, Mrs Warwick. Don't forget that these people have lived here for thousands of years – or so we assume. Isn't it smug of us to laugh at the beliefs that they have built up through centuries? We're always looking for ways of living in the tropics without going off our heads, but it never occurs to us that *they* might have the answer. The fact is we've lost all but the last decaying stumps of our senses, and there's nothing for us to do but sneer.'

They fell into silence. 'Is there anything else you want to ask?' said Anthony.

'Yes,' said Stella. 'How long did the trip take? – from Maiola, that is, when you left the district officer and the boat.'

'Four days in all – you could do it in three. That's one way of course. It isn't far outside the patrolled area.'

'Is it hard going?'

'All jungle travel is hard going,' said Washington. 'But it's easier than most. You don't have to check your direction. The river leads you, and the paths are clear. But personally I loathe these treks. Hot, filthy clothes, unspeakable tinned food. Though I do like the local food. Yams are excellent if properly prepared. But mosquitoes, leeches ... No, I find it horrible.'

Then the direction of her questions was recognised by both men. 'Why?' said Anthony Nyall. The word fell into the stillness with a sharp, explosive sound.

'Because I am going there,' said Stella. She waited. Anthony did not move. He was looking at Washington. Behind him in the corner Hitolo stirred. Washington beat the air with his fan. 'What for?' he said in a high, aggressive voice.

She only replied, 'For many personal reasons.'

He appeared not to hear her. 'Aren't you satisfied? Don't you believe what I've told you?' His fan beat the air like an angry wing. 'Ask me anything you like. I'll tell you anything you want to know.'

'Mrs Warwick hasn't said that she doesn't believe you,' said Anthony Nyall. 'She wants to make the journey for sentimental reasons.'

Stella threw him a look of indignation. 'Will you take me?' she said to Washington.

'I?' The fan was still. He stared at her. His eyes looked blank and colourless. She might have been gazing into glass. 'No,' he said. 'No. No! No! No!'

Between each word there was a pause and into each pause washed a torrent of ... what? Anger? Fear? Each word was burdened by a whole fresh load of terror. The last 'No' was almost a scream. He sprang to his feet.

He backed away as though defending himself from something he saw in her face. She had never seen a man so terrified. Words babbled from his lips. Stella, almost as frightened as he was, felt that he did not know what he was saying, or even that he had spoken at all. His reason seemed to have flashed away and left a delirious body behind.

'Back to that filthy jungle, not on your life ... the mosquitoes and the mud and the damn mangroves and those filthy little beasts with their white faces and rotten tinned food and yams, yams, yams ... slimy leeches hanging out of your shoes, blood suckers, slimy beasts sliding along like lizards and *eyes*, eyes in the leaves and not a sound, only eyes in the leaves and foxes in the trees. Foxes hanging like filthy rags, while we crawl around with our bellies in the mud, sleeping and not listening' – his voice trailed away, became slower and clearer – 'go back to that rotten little corner of hell, not on your life!'

His face was white and dripping with sweat. He passed the back of his hand over his lips. Into his eyes – fixed at Stella but not seeing her – consciousness drained back like water into the dry bed of a pool. For a moment his face was violently expressive, and then closed up with caution. He waved his fan languidly and sat down again, arranging the yellow robe over his knees.

'I'm sorry,' he said and his voice was now under control, 'I couldn't possibly go back there. I'm working, you know. They'd never let me go.'

'If they would ...' said Stella.

'Well, I don't much relish these jungle treks. They're so damned uncomfortable. And when you've been in the tropics as long as I have you rather shy off that *Boy's Own Annual* stuff. And I'm not fit,' he added, and raised a hand wearily to his forehead, remembering his sickness with the air of one producing a forgotten asset.

'I think we'll leave,' said Anthony, standing up. 'You don't look well.'

Stella rose reluctantly. The man was useless, there was nothing to be learned from him, but she felt herself obscurely bound to him. She felt that there existed between them some sort of close, passionate relationship. It was not love, hate or friendship, it was different, and beyond them. She knew that Washington felt it too. Awareness of what they were to each other had only a moment before shone in his eyes.

He did not wish them to leave either. 'Go?' he said, starting up. 'Oh, don't go. Have another drink.' The asset appeared now as a liability, and he discarded it. 'I feel better. Really it was good of you to come. Fever is so depressing, particularly when it's getting better. One craves for company. I wish you'd stay, really I do. You mustn't take any notice of my jitters, they don't mean anything.'

'I'm afraid we must go,' said Anthony, but as he turned to say goodbye he added, 'Hitolo will stay with you for a while. He'll get you anything you want. You shouldn't be up here on your own when you're ill.' There was instant relief in Washington's face. 'You needn't worry about my luggage, Hitolo. Stay here with Mr Washington for a while.' He nodded briefly.

It was now dark outside. Anthony went first down the little flight of wooden steps, and turned to help Stella. They slithered down the rough path to the bottom of the garden.

Here the light from the hut did not penetrate, and they had to feel their way between the frangipani trees. It was quiet, except for the flapping of the flying foxes in the pawpaw trees, and somewhere nearby a tap was running. Anthony stopped. 'Who's there?' There was a low grunting sound and then a figure appeared, brushing aside the leaves, and crouched in the path before them. It was a squat, misshapen body, with a huge bushy mop of hair. It paused and then waddled off into the shrubs on the other side of the road.

Stella felt an eerie prickling in her skin. She shuddered, and the tremor passed down her fingers into those that held them. Anthony looked quickly over his shoulder. 'It's only a native,' he said. 'Don't be nervous.'

'Is he sick?' she said, looking back at the house. 'Is he mad?' They had reached more even ground now. He still held her fingers to guide her, but his hand was limp and unresponsive. 'He too,' he said, 'has his obsessions.'

'He too! Like me? Is that how I seem to you?'

She could not see his face but felt he was smiling. 'Well, it's how I seem to you, isn't it?'

She thought for a moment. 'You mean,' she said, 'in not liking David or your brother.' She found herself able to say this without animosity.'

His head turned sharply, as if she had shocked him. 'My brother? Don't I like him?'

'No,' said Stella. 'Perhaps it's an obsession. Why do you hate people with houses larger than your own?'

He did not correct her cruel simplification. 'Because I know too much of the material that builds them. The average man doesn't make a pretty victim.'

'What do you mean?'

'You've seen one tonight,' he said. 'They aren't humble or submissive, they're savage and dangerous, spiteful and treacherous. But they aren't responsible for themselves. They're man-made monsters.'

'How was he victimised?' said Stella curiously, wondering

if this explained why, in spite of everything, she had found it impossible to dislike Washington.

Either he did not hear her or chose not to answer. 'You can't force mediocrity on a man who isn't mediocre.' he said. 'He'll always find some way of being exceptional. That's what the levellers don't take into consideration, that if they lock the front door they force the spirit into back passages.'

'What do you mean? Back passages! Do you think this man killed David?'

'I've told you before ...' he began.

'You told me before!' she cried. She tried to be angry. Anger was their customary form of communication,and she was used to it. But now she could not feel anger. Her emotions were no longer direct but wayward, diffused. 'You lied to me,' she said. 'Everyone lies to me.' She stumbled on the road, her foot slipping into a deep rut. He gripped her fingers and then let them go.

'I won't lie to you again,' he said surprisingly. 'You're right. Everyone lies to you. Look how they've placed you now, chasing another lie, and God knows where it'll lead you.' He spoke with a ring of indignation.

Stella, recognising the direction of his accusation, threw back at him, 'You know what happened. You know everything.'

'I know enough.'

'And you won't tell me?'

'No.'

'But you aren't stopping me from finding out any more,' she said quietly.

'No. I can see now that you'll find out anyway. I couldn't stop you if I tried. I don't want to now. I now believe that I want you to go through with it. As you say, enough people have lied to you.'

'*Why* won't you tell me?' He entirely puzzled her. She felt more curious now about his motives than about the secrets he withheld.

They had reached the jeep. He paused with his hand on

the door and turned to face her. 'For one thing,' he said, 'I haven't any proof, and you would want proof, otherwise you'd never believe what I told you. You'd only hate me for it and find excellent reasons for my having said it.' He looked away and spoke more quickly. 'You can find out for yourself. I won't help you. You can make your own victims, I've got enough of my own. You've probably heard about them.'

The twelve men who died. She saw that he was not against her any longer or he would never have said this.

'I don't understand you.'

'You will when it's over, if you survive it.' He turned his head again and looked at her. He spoke quickly and intensely. 'Don't you see. *I* can't make victims. I'm not strong enough, or single-minded enough. I don't think you could ever understand it. Ever since I've been in this country my ability for any dynamic action has grown less and less. I feel that every step we make towards the so-called progress of these people is a step towards their destruction. There is only one thing to do, one reasonable course of action and that is to do nothing. Leave them alone and they will slowly imbibe our culture; force them and they will take only our greed and corruption.'

'But we can't leave them as they are. It just wouldn't do.' Stella searched for words. 'You just *can't*. They must take their place in the world.'

'No,' he said flatly, 'we can't. There's nothing else to do but what we're doing. Yet I feel more and more that *I* can't do it. *I* can't contribute. I can't even bring myself to attack what seem obvious evils – sorcery, head-hunting. I can't help to remove the fear from native life, because I know what goes with it. Good and evil, beauty and ugliness, if they exist, aren't separate and distinct in these people's lives. If you drag out one thread, you tear down the whole house. What incredible arrogance! Any fool can see that there's more dignity and integrity in a Papuan than in the average white man who comes up here from the south because anyone can get a living here without earning it.' He paused, and in his next words there was a note of pleading. 'That's why I'm so helpless and incapable of doing anything about it. Ten years in this country have paralysed my will. I'm convinced that it's invariably better not to act.'

She looked up at him, trying to read his face in the dim light. She felt disturbed and excited. No one had spoken to her like this. No one had ever exposed their weaknesses before her. 'But this is different,' she said. 'I only want to know the truth.'

He shrugged his shoulders. 'Exactly. You're looking for victims. And you'll find them, some of them innocent.'

'How could that be? Who?'

'Well, one for certain – yourself!' Startled, she drew back. He continued. 'But that's what you want. You're bent on self-destruction. Well, I won't help you. I've got enough murder on my hands. We'll make this another suicide.' He shook his head. 'It's no good, you don't understand me. And anyway you're right. It's better to know the truth. But I will be here for you to turn to, afterwards.' She did not speak, and he went on. 'When this is over, if you survive it, what then? I don't think you've thought about it. I have.'

What then? The words had a hollow ring. He was right, though she only now realised it. She had counted on not surviving. All that there had been to survive for would have finished. 'I don't think beyond it,' she said.

'And you have been counting on there being no need to think, on not coming through,' he added gently. 'But you'll want to, when it's too late. You'll see it then as an obsession that wasn't worth your trouble.'

It was only then that she caught the meaning of what he had been saying. 'You ...' she stopped.

'I think I could love you,' he said quietly. 'Perhaps I already do. I know I love what you're doing, and I don't think it's only that. It gives you a strange, possessed quality that I can't get out of my mind. I have a picture of your face, when you say these terrible, misguided things, that hangs there in front of me and never goes. I know you can't talk about this now because it would be against everything you're after – to think of me, I mean, as anything but an enemy.' Stella said nothing. She was astonished and confused.

'I've never loved anyone before,' he said in a rather puzzled tone. 'I can see that quite clearly now. I thought I loved Janet once, but that was only pity and something to do with Trevor. I think I need you,' he said, almost grudgingly. 'I think what I admired most in you was your courage, your tenacity. That was why you made me so angry, because you were doing what I couldn't do, and what I felt I should do. I wanted to stop it, I still do now, because it's so misguided and destructive, but I admire it because it's dynamic. Perhaps you would be able to teach me to act again. Action is your strong point.'

'You need me?' Stella murmured.

'Yes. I didn't realise how much I was in need of help. I didn't want help. I was proud of being the only one who knew that it was better to do nothing. Now I'm ashamed. You might teach me to be single-minded again. You might break up this paralysis I have. I haven't done any work for months, would have been thrown out months ago if it hadn't been for Trevor. I don't mind one way or another – or rather I didn't mind, I would have enjoyed being sacrificed, but he wouldn't tolerate it. I literally haven't done a thing. I'm afraid to. I'm afraid of the consequences of working. I'm afraid to pay my boy for fear of what he will do with the money. I'm afraid to open a book for fear that I might read something that will tempt me to act. It must be like the sloth of old age when all actions are futile. I feel older than anyone in the world.'

'How terrible!'

He stood silently in front of her. She did not speak. Words of protest, even of outrage flashed into her mind, but she dismissed them knowing that they would in no way express her real feelings. These feelings were too strong to remain entirely unacknowledged. She was tremendously shaken and very proud.

He opened the front door of the jeep and she got in. They did not speak again for some moments. They drove down past the men's mess and the jangle of voices and wireless sets grew fainter behind them. The road turned along the sea-shore. Stella leaned out through the window to catch the breeze in her hair. She felt suddenly tired. Anthony's declaration of love became like a burden on her spirit. She had never had responsibilities. She had always been the responsibility of someone else. She realised vaguely that whatever she said or felt towards him, here was a person she must do something about. She could not just shrug him away, she owed it to him. She had never felt this before, even about David. Their relationship had been so simple. She loved him, she admired him, she obeyed him. That was all. She had been able to transfer to him quite naturally the attitude and behaviour that had belonged to her father. There had never been any problems, at least, not any that she knew about.

But Anthony's wife would not be cherished and looked after. She would not follow a prescribed course of conduct, for none would be plotted out for her. Everything would be left to her, and there would always be problems. Questions that arose would be as much the property of one as of the other. She shifted uneasily, conscious of a strange disquietude. It seemed to her that an unrestful, emotionally turbulent and unstable existence was promised for Anthony's wife.

They had reached the town. Cars were drawn up under the palms outside the hotel and women in long dresses could be seen in the foyer.

'What will you do now?' Anthony said, as they turned up the hill. 'Go to Eola?'

'I shall try.'

'I must go to Rabaul. Will you wait till I come back?'

'I don't know.' She spoke stiffly, and did not look at him. She was not surprised by his demand, had expected it, really, and accepted it as the first of many demands that he would make on her. It annoyed her, but she felt no sense of injustice.

But she was afraid. He will ask me not to go because he loves me. He will corrupt me. I shall be like him, unable to act. 'I shall do what seems best,' she said quickly.

'I shan't be long,' he said. 'I'll be back on Friday of next week.' They had stopped in front of her house. She shrank away from him.

'I don't know, I may not be able to go.'

He leaned back as if to spare her from the necessity of shrinking. The movement so touched her, and this emotion was so new that she said, without thinking, 'I'll try.'

She asked Trevor next morning if he would help her to get to Eola. He instantly refused. 'I wouldn't take the responsibility for one thing,' he said, 'And it wouldn't be in my power, for another.' He did not look at her but opened and shut the drawers in his desk, looking for papers and files. He was going out again and had not even taken off his hat.

'It would be in your power,' said Stella calmly. She had come to realise that people lied to her more often than they did not, and examined all Trevor's statements in the light of this. 'You're the head of this department. People are always going out in the field. If you wanted to arrange it you could send a surveyor at least as far as Kairipi and from then on nobody needs to know where they went, or why I went too.'

He did not refute this but merely said, scowling into an open drawer, and then closing it with a sharp slap, 'You don't know what you're saying.'

It was true. She spoke with her old intense determination; her eyes, fastened even more rigidly in one direction, looked neither to right nor left, but Eola might have been a village in a fairytale. She made her plans as one spends money in a lottery. 'If you don't help me,' she said. 'I shall go to the administrator and ask his help. Or to the police. Or to the district officer at Kairipi. Perhaps he will go with me.'

This statement was not, as it might have been two days

ago, innocent and uncalculated. She knew exactly what she was doing and looked him steadily in the eye as she spoke.

He gave her a faint, tight-lipped smile. 'Blackmail, is it? You're trading on my wish to keep this quiet. Either I help you or you shout, "Bava valley gold", all over the Territory. Not very fair tactics when it was through David's indiscretion that you learned about it. The responsibility will fall on me and my department, and he isn't here to protect us.'

'No,' said Stella, 'he isn't here. He's been murdered.'

He brushed his aside and went on. 'And the natives ...' he began.

'I am beginning to realise,' she said, 'that people up here only worry about the Papuans when it suits them.'

He was stuffing papers into his brief-case but paused and threw her an outraged glance. She felt his antagonism like a physical blow. She lowered her eyes and thought of his wife. You would always have to seek to please him, she thought. When she looked up his face had cleared and he was smiling. 'You mustn't assume that is true of us all,' he said. It isn't true of me, he had implied, but Stella saw that once again he was lying and that it was exactly of him and his kind that it was true. They could not by any other means remain as clear-browed and bright-eyed as this. Here, in this country, confidence and serenity were sins.

He came over and touched her shoulder. 'Wait for a day or so. I'll have to think about it.' The hand he reached out might have been her father's or her husband's hand. Her resolution weakened, and the startling glimpse she had seen of a new and different Trevor Nyall retreated. She thought only, He is my friend and I must not offend him.

'I'm sorry,' she said. 'But I must go. You don't understand. I *must*. But I'll wait.'

'Why do you want to go?' he said. 'What on earth do you expect to find out?'

She was silent, unable to answer what she dared not admit

to herself. His hand flapped absently on her shoulder and a moment later he was gone.

But Stella was not dismayed. She felt convinced that she would set off for Eola some time soon. Indeed it seemed now not only inevitable but inescapable. And when that same day Hitolo came to her and asked if he might go too, she listened to him without surprise. He was waiting for her outside the office, squatting in the thin shade of a clump of casuarinas. She did not see him until he rose and walked hesitantly forward.

'Mrs Warwick. Excuse me.'

'Hitolo.' She stopped and waited.

'You go to Eola, Mrs Warwick.'

'How do you know?'

He stared at her blankly. He could not know that his knowledge was a prediction, and blinked with an air of vagueness customary to his people when asked to account for knowledge that they held instinctively.

Stella understood. 'Perhaps, some time soon,' she said.

He smiled at her. His eyes were bright, his voice soft. 'Mrs Warwick, when you go you take me.'

'Aren't you afraid of the vada men?'

He smiled again and shook his head. 'I am not afraid. Purri purri not true, sinabada.' He waited, watching her. Then he made a vague movement with his hand. 'You take me, Mrs Warwick, I'll show the way.'

That was all the bargaining he put forward. She nodded. 'I'll try, Hitolo.'

At six o'clock next morning Washington rolled out of bed. He had hardly closed his eyes all night and felt around for his gown and slippers, weak and dazed with weariness. The room lurched and tottered, and he gripped the doorpost to steady himself. The sky was not yet golden, and masks and tapa cloth, dog teeth and lime gourds glowed in an eerie, greenish light. The sweet, cool morning breeze stirred the thatch outside the window. For once he was not afraid. His heart was filled with hatred and there was no room for fear. 'Well it couldn't be worse than this,' he muttered. 'Koibari! Koibari!' There was no answer. He went out to the back door and called again, but no sound came from the boy house. Washington lit the primus himself and filled a kettle. His hands trembled.

'Filthy, stinking savage,' he said aloud. Then he attacked himself. It was his own fault. What an insane impulse, getting rid of Rei and hiring that old wizard with his bag of tricks. Was the house any less haunted? He had hung coconut magic on the door, tufts of copra tapped in the wind on the trees in the garden, and Koibari sat on the steps and murmured slogans. But it was useless, there was nothing to be done.

He filled the teapot and carried it back into the house. He hardly knew where he was, his mind was dazed with rage and despair. But the tea revived him. After his second cup he was thinking more clearly. He lit a cigarette. Well, it would be good to get away from here, he thought, looking around him. The hut had turned against him. It was no longer friendly. It had gone over to the enemy, and no manner of coaxing would win it back. He would not have been able to stay here much longer. His health was breaking; his nerves were in pieces. But if he survived what was ahead, this place would capitulate, he would have won. He could move on then to all that the future had once promised – a home for his sister, a house on the hill, position, wealth, power, a garden full of flowering trees, a view over the sea, and a shoulder shrugged at Trevor Nyall.

He swallowed a third cup of tea and started to dress. His hands had steadied. The longed-for future seemed closer, more possible. It's only a few days, he told himself. It's only a matter of keeping your head, maybe for an hour or more. There was a three-day walk, but he tried not to think of it and fixed his mind on the salvaged future. The trip ahead was a hurdle, but it was a risk worth taking.

At eight o'clock he made his way down the hill towards the Department of Survey. He had been shut up in his hut for a fortnight now and it was with a sense of immense relief that he turned his back on it.

Most of the survey staff were already seated at their desks when he entered the building.

'Well, hello!' said a red-haired typist who had set her heart on him in spite of his consistent rudeness. 'Quite a stranger here.'

'Oh, God. The little ray of sunshine.' He felt better than ever after that. Rudeness was invigorating. It was proof of how little he cared for anyone.

The girl laughed heartily as if he had said something extraordinarily witty. 'You look sick, Philip. You shouldn't have come in.'

He ignored her and said to the man behind her, 'Nyall in?'

'Not yet.'

He went on down the passage and pushed open the door of Trevor's office. Stella was sitting at her desk, her hands in her lap, staring at the map on the wall. For a moment he forgot that it was better to be leaving Marapai than to be staying behind. He saw her as an agent of his enemies and looked at her with hatred. He noted coldly the unscathed freshness of her face, like a moth just out of a cocoon, its colours brilliant and untarnished. Oh brave new world, he said to himself, his mind filled with visions of calculated cruelty, You'll learn, Miranda, you'll grow up.

When he smiled his lips were tight and there was a sparkling brightness in his eyes. But Stella, turning her head and seeing only the dark smudges of sleeplessness on the bridge of his cheeks, did not read in his face that he hated her.

'Good morning,' he said, cheerfully. Anyone who knew him, Sylvia for instance, would have detected the irony, but Stella accepted it at face value.

'Good morning, I hope you're better.'

'Oh, much better, thank you, much better. The world looks like a different place.'

'I'm afraid that Mr Nyall isn't here yet.'

'Well, I'm not here to see Mr Nyall.' He sat down on the edge of the desk and nonchalantly swung one leg. 'I came to see you.'

She said nothing, but waited, her large, expectant eyes raised to his face.

He looked away, his hatred of her abating a little. It lost, in the face of this look, its sharp edge. He could not help pitying her. 'I've been thinking over what we were talking about the other night.'

'Yes.'

'I've decided that if it can be arranged, I'll take you to Eola.'

'You'll take me *back* to Eola,' she said. There was not, as there had been the other night, a glow of feverish enthusiasm in her face. She accepted his changed attitude. She looked at the map as if in imagination she were already half way there.

It struck him that she was not surprised. 'Thank you,' she said. That was all. She did not question what must have surely seemed extraordinarily inconsistent behaviour. Perhaps she understood, even more than he did himself, the inevitability of what was happening. He wanted to justify his actions in more rational terms. 'I was tremendously upset when you came up on Tuesday night,' he said. 'I always get a bit silly with fever. I must have sounded terribly abrupt and rude. I do hope you'll forgive me.'

'Of course,' said Stella gently. 'I don't think we shall be allowed to go. Mr Nyall is against it.'

He felt suddenly released. Going to Eola had now become desirable. 'It won't be easy,' he declared. 'It's not a picnic and you don't exactly look husky.'

'I shall stand up to it all right.' said Stella. There was the faintest emphasis on the 'I' and she looked at him as if she fully understood that he might not. He could not meet her eye and prattled on about leeches, mosquitoes and tinned food.

'I don't think that Mr Nyall will let us go,' she interrupted him again.

'You'll see,' said Washington confidently. But she shook her head. She was convinced that Trevor would do everything in his power to stop them. She did not examine this conviction. She was oddly reluctant to do so. But she was wrong. The next day he gave his permission without protest.

The three of them discussed the journey in his office. Now that it was agreed upon, Washington was anxious to start straight away. Stella on the other hand hung back. The strong, slow current that had borne her along steadily and in safety had gathered speed and swept her on with new ferocity and determination. She had a sense of events flashing past before she could detect their significance.

'I can't go till next week,' she said. 'Till Friday.' The reluctant promise made to Anthony was a life-line to cling to.

Both men turned and stared at her. They had found out

that the coastal boat was leaving for Kairipi in two days and wanted the party to leave on this. 'Why not?'

She made no reply.

'Friday?' repeated Trevor. 'I'm afraid we can't wait till then. It will have to be Thursday of this week or not at all. Washington has other work to do, Stella.' He spoke sharply. He did not pretend that he gave in with good grace, and it was plain that they were no longer friends.

'I want to take Hitolo with me.'

'He belongs to another department,' said Washington quickly. He had forgotten that he had once almost pitied her. 'What do you want to take him for?'

'He's been there before.'

'So have I,' said Washington gaily. 'I'll look after you, and don't imagine that Hitolo would be any use in an emergency. They're all the same – they panic and run like rabbits. Look what happened the time before. As soon as the carriers started talking about purri purri he wouldn't budge another step.'

'It would be different this time,' said Stella.

'I'll see what can be done,' said Trevor. But whatever he did was not effective. Hitolo was not granted permission to leave his work.

They made preparations for departure. Washington worked late with three village boys during the two remaining nights, fencing his hut.

It was Thursday morning, the day of their departure. Stella had collected her equipment from the front verandah ready for it to be taken down to the wharf.

She stood alone in her room looking around her to see if there was anything she had forgotten. She had not yet fully realised what had happened. Arrangements had been made, clothing had been collected, mostly under Washington's direction and with little thought or meditation on her part. She had followed instructions mechanically, ticking off the items on his neat, pencilled list with no thought of the uses to which they would be put. She might have been ordering groceries.

Her gaze moved around the walls and came to rest in the flame trees outside the window. Morning sunlight bathed the floor and the faded cover of the bed. The trees were breaking daily into more and more scarlet blossom. She had ceased to think them overdone and had come to regard them as miraculously beautiful. She found herself thinking now, as she had on the first night of her arrival, I like this place, I should like to live here.

But over the past few days, her mind had been subjected to internal censorship. It might have been composed of a series of forbidden doors. Her thoughts fluttered but would not penetrate. Hundreds of questions – Why am I going? Why is Washington taking me? Why has Hitolo not been allowed to go? What will happen to me? Shall we ever return? How could I break my promise to Anthony? – faintly stirred in the depths of her consciousness. But to ask them was dangerous. There was also danger in thinking, I like this town, I should like to live here. And the spirit that guarded her plan for self-destruction snuffed out the wish like a candle flame. There was still something further to be done, that she had left till the last moment. She picked up a pad and pencil from the dressing table. 'Dear Anthony ...'

She looked helplessly at the blank page extending beneath. What can I say? She had broken her promise and to Anthony it would seem that she did not care. She found that she did care, deeply. Being unable to probe the censored regions of her heart she explained to herself that he was her responsibility and she must act with integrity towards him. She would not tell lies and make dishonest promises as others had to her. '... I am sorry I broke my promise. I had to go. I shall explain when I come back.' She signed her name. She put the letter in an envelope, sealed it and addressed it to 'Mr Anthony Nyall, Department of Cultural Development, Marapai.' She paused and read what she had written. Then, obeying an unexamined impulse, she underlined the word 'Anthony'.

She left her room and knocked on Sylvia's door. Sylvia had finished breakfast and was standing in front of the mirror powdering her face. Her black hair had not yet torn loose from the knob at the back of her neck. She glanced around as Stella entered, but did not speak or smile. 'I was wondering if you would do something for me while I'm away,' said Stella.

Sylvia picked up her lipstick, dragged her lower lip tight across her bottom teeth and swept the lipstick from corner to corner of her mouth.

'I was wondering,' said Stella more hesitantly, for there was something stern in the movement of Sylvia's hand, 'if you would give this letter to Anthony Nyall. He won't be back till next Friday. Perhaps you could walk over to Cultural Development on Friday and give it to him.'

'Why don't you post it?' Sylvia said, clamping her lips over a red handkerchief.

'I'd rather he received it by hand.'

Sylvia slid her tongue around her lips and surveyed them intently. Then she turned and faced Stella. Her lids were narrowed, her eyes bright and hard. 'Why should I? Why should I help you?' Her voice, normally soft and drawling, was high and strident. Stella, shocked, caught a glimpse of a child in slum streets, of women shouting at their drunken husbands and starving dogs picking about in gutters. She did not speak, but her eyes grew wide and frightened.

'Why should I help you? Do you help me? Do you care about anyone but yourself and your crazy notions?'

'Crazy notions!'

'You think I don't know where you're going and why,' Sylvia said passionately. 'Do you think you'll ever come back? You don't care, but *I* do. I want Philip alive, and he'll never come back.' The diamond brightness of her eyes shimmered into tears. 'They all die,' she sobbed. 'Warwick died,

Sereva died, and now Philip. Now Philip! And all because of your bloody justice!'

'I have to find out,' said Stella, in a voice that she did not recognise as her own. 'I have to find out the truth.' She was powerless in the grip of an old dream that was almost meaningless now. Her mind, strength and will plodded forward doggedly in the old direction, but it seemed that she had left her heart long behind, perhaps when Anthony Nyall had said, 'You did not love him.'

'Philip's more important than the truth,' Sylvia said scornfully. 'Why do you want the truth?' Her body sagged, her lips fell open and she stretched out both her hands in a gesture of appeal. She could not have pleaded more abjectly if she had sunk to her knees. 'Don't go. *Please*, Stella!'

For the second time in her life Stella recognised love in another. She knew, as she had known when Hitolo had turned his cheek, that this was a world she had never entered. 'Oh, Sylvia, he's not nearly good enough for you!' was all she could muster.

'Good God!' cried Sylvia. 'Do you suppose people love goodness!' Stella was silent, for this was what she believed.

Sylvia's hands fell to her sides, and she turned away. 'He wasn't always like this,' she said. She picked up the letter that was lying on the table, glanced at the address and put it in her drawer. 'I'll give it to him.'

'He'll be all right,' said Stella. 'We'll be back. You'll see.'

A faint smile touched the corners of Sylvia's lips. It died, but the corners of her lips were still raised. Her face, with its tear-stained cheeks, looked ghastly. Stella turned to the door, feeling her way with an outstretched hand. She believed, then, that they would not come back. She closed the door and looked down the steps to the road. For a moment she hesitated, understanding what Anthony had meant when he said it was better not to act. Then a transport truck drew up at the gate. A driver flung open the front door. They had come for her luggage – it was too late.

The skipper started up the engines at 10.30. The crew was unfastening the ropes that held the ship to the wharf. Washington had gone into his cabin and closed the door.

Stella stood alone, looking down into the water lapping under the jetty piles. No light fell here, and she could see scarlet and white sponges bursting out from the wooden stalks of the jetty. Fish as thin as leaves, wearing brilliant, improbable colours, flashed about like hummingbirds. Her mind was dazed and empty. Sylvia had been thrust away behind the locked doors; broken promises had sunk like dregs to the bottom of her heart. There was nothing but the water slapping on the sides of the boat. Patches of coloured oil spread out in changing shapes, a swollen, burst cigarette butt dropped on the pier floated by. Someone had spat out a gob of betel juice that broke and spread like an opening flower. Beneath the intermittent surface scum, the water was pellucid. Transparent and blue at depths where it should have been black, it offered to the eye an ocean bed which, in temperate lands, would have been decently obscured. Huge, hyacinth-blue starfish clung to rocks, sliver cans winked and flashed, and seaweed waved like bleeding fingers over the obese, spotted bodies of the beche-de-mer.

Stella leaned on the rail, fascinated and horrified. The churning of the engines went on unheeded. She hardly realised that they were leaving until the marine world quivered and broke with the movement of the ship. The jetty drew slowly away and the water fanned out from the sides of the ship in long corrugated ribbons. She looked back at the town, its bleached tin roofs scattered about like white stones among the flame trees.

They were leaving this ordered outpost. Soon Marapai would be a spot on the map, a tiny ink blot on a page of virgin ferocity. They were striking out into the wilderness, where they would be competing for existence with mud, leeches, sea-snakes, slugs and crocodiles. Here, all the defences they had drawn on in Marapai would be useless. In this environment they must discard all they knew and adopt a different attitude. In the jungle, the rules of the golf club and the private school would no longer apply. They would fall back upon less refined defences, instinctively adapt their behaviour to that of the hungry bird and the sea-slug. Nothing that her father or David had taught her was now of any use. She was on her own.

Behind them the wharf grew smaller with extraordinary rapidity. With each moment Marapai was more infinitesimal. An hour ago it had been the whole island, now it was almost swallowed up. As they moved towards the long coastline stretching ahead, the land they were seeking reached out to them, hungry and waiting for victims.

Stella turned her back on the sea and faced the human bustle of the little ship. She felt dismayed and lonely. Not loneliness from being without a husband, a father, a counselling voice or supporting hand, but the loneliness of an insect in a forest or a bird in a desert sky. She dived back into the hustle of the ship, clinging to human beings.

On the top deck they were carrying twenty or thirty passengers: women with grass skirts bunched up around their knees, babies at their breasts; small, owl-eyed children who sat and stared with placid acceptance; and old men whose skin hung in purple folds from their shrivelled shoulders. Stella stood looking at them. One of the women shyly smiled, but no one else seemed interested in her. Then she noticed one who stood leaning on the rail of the ship, occasionally throwing her a serious, expectant glance. He wore a pair of khaki shorts, a wrist watch and a slim string of coloured beads round his throat. It was some moments before she recognised him.

'Hitolo!'

Instantly he smiled and came towards her.

She was conscious of a profound relief. 'What are you doing here?'

He planted himself, smiling and triumphant, in front of her. 'I came,' he said.

Had Trevor obtained permission for his release, or had Washington arranged it? she asked herself optimistically. These questions with their implications of well-being and goodwill the censor permitted.

'I tried to get permission for you, Hitolo, but they wouldn't allow it. They said you belonged to another department and could not leave your work.'

'They tell me that too,' he said and his grin split wider. 'I came here five o'clock this morning and sat with the women. They are only natives; so no one noticed me.'

Her hopes sank away. But he had come – it was something. 'I'm glad you came,' she said. 'You will stay close to me, Hitolo, won't you?' She cast a glance at the dense, forested coastline dipping on their right. 'I'm frightened' – his eyes seemed to widen and darken, though he still smiled – 'of the jungle,' she said. 'I've never been in the jungle. I shall need help. Don't leave me alone, Hitolo.' He smiled and nodded. But she felt he had barely understood. Perhaps he had not even heard her. His mind was turned inwards, to a purpose no less urgent than hers. She knew what it was and understood that helping her, if he should undertake to do so, would be incidental.

They drew in to the wharf at Kairipi at four on Friday afternoon. Stella, standing on deck, looked across the diminishing strip of water at a small, wiry man with a lean face, a beaked nose and a ginger moustache, who stood waiting for them on the wharf. Three Papuan policemen stood rigidly behind him. He made no movement and gave no smile of welcome. When he lifted his hand and touched the brim of his topee, the salute was so obviously not for her that she turned her head to see who he was greeting. Washington was standing just behind her.

She had hardly spoken to him since they left Marapai. He had retired to his cabin and his meals had been taken to him there. The skipper had said at dinner that he was a bad sailor, but Stella doubted this and felt that he was avoiding her. She saw him later in the evening leaning over the prow of the ship eating a mango and dropping the rinds into the water. They exchanged only a few polite words.

The district officer boarded the ship. Thomas Seaton was an abrupt, methodical man who had been in the Territory for twenty-five years. He was tough and inarticulate and admired these qualities in others above all else. He distrusted comfort and learning and held in contempt the university-trained patrol officers who came up from south. They had been scientifically prepared for the jungle, rather than cast forth in innocence to learn the hard way. He drank a glass of beer with the captain and then left the ship to take his two guests on an inspection of the station.

Kairipi was built on an island. It was safer in the old days, Seaton explained to Stella. Now it was rather inconvenient, as they only had two boats and something was always wrong with them. The fools in Marapai had no idea about engines. He could manage better himself, and he was no mechanic. Just two hands and commonsense was all he had.

The island was quite small, not more than a mile all round. It was flat-topped and its steep sides were covered with coconut palms that leaned out over the sea. The top of the island was like a large garden. An avenue of palms had been planted from end to end, and small paths, which led to the police barracks, the court, Seaton's house and the patrol officer's house, crossed it at right angles every hundred yards or so. Flowering shrubs and trees had been planted along every path and under the coconut palms – frangipani, crotons, caliphers and hibiscus. Everything that grew in this place looked larger and more luxuriant than in Marapai, and Stella, who felt that she had seen nature at her most vivid and opulent, looked around her with fresh astonishment. She saw now that Marapai was tamed. Perhaps the white culture, that had cooled the native blood, had in some way reduced the flowers too. Here were the limits of extravagance. Here anything might happen.

They walked slowly. Stella hardly spoke. Occasionally Washington asked a question. Seaton talked in short, clipped sentences and pointed out landmarks with his cane. At 5.30 they had exhausted everything that he considered interesting. They had visited the courthouse, a new building, constructed from sago palm, that prisoners were thatching. One of the police boys had been sent up a palm tree to pick a spray of orchids for Stella. Seaton and Washington had taken off their hats and stood with bowed heads by a scrupulously kept grave where a former illustrious district officer had been buried. They walked now on the landward side of the island. The district officer waved his cane through gaps in the palms, pointing to the mouths of rivers. Below them the land dropped to the water. The bay was sheltered and the water still, bearing on its surface perfect, undisturbed images of the land behind. All around stretched undulating, forested hills. There were mountains behind, but the clouds clung low above the forest and flattened the horizon. The land was grey and soft behind a mist that seemed to breathe from the forest. 'And that,' said Seaton, waving his stick, 'is your river. The Bava River.' The point of the stick quivered, their eyes swung round. Neither spoke. 'There,' the point of the stick jabbed at the sky, 'round that point the river turns. That is the Bava River.'

Stella stared at the break in the grey shore line, eyes fixed like a sleep-walker's. She was afraid.

Washington cast a glance at Seaton's profile. Had he guessed what it was all about? Did he know more than he appeared to? Beneath the ginger moustache, Seaton's lips were closed like the mouth of a trap. Washington had a profound distrust of silence.

Seaton glanced at his watch. 'Six. Time for a drink.' He swung around abruptly and marched down the path. Washington fell into step beside him and Stella walked behind.

'Can you take us up the river?' Washington asked.

Seaton fixed his eyes on the path ahead. 'Could be done. Though it's time the administration realised that district officers aren't tourist bureaus. We don't sit on our tails all day like these book-fed boys they send up from the south.'

'I'm sorry,' said Washington, trying to be charming. 'I don't like it much either. It's orders, you know, and, by the way, confidential. The director doesn't want it to get around.'

'I don't gossip,' Seaton snapped. Just as Washington distrusted silence, Seaton distrusted loquaciousness, and any sign of such a vice in himself was repressed. He had lived in the Territory long enough to know something of the results of indiscretion. As he saw it, there was no greater evil than a gossiping tongue. He never talked of personalities and never made a statement unless certain of his facts.

They were now walking down the main avenue. The tall trunks of the coconuts formed a deep shaft down which the sunlight drained to the path at their feet. 'Of course not,' said Washington. 'I was instructed to tell you, that's all.'

Seaton grunted and his stride lengthened. 'You won't find it easy to get anyone to go with you,' he said abruptly.

'Why not?'

'Boys seem even less keen about the place than they were before.'

Washington was silent. He wanted to question Seaton further but dared not, for fear of what he might learn. Yet it was best to know, it was best to set off armed with all the information he could gather.

'Do you know why?' he said at last.

Seaton shrugged his shoulders. 'Same old thing – vada. The boy dying upset them. Hard to get out of them what it's all about. Funny stories.'

'What stories?' said Washington.

'Nonsense, all nonsense,' said Seaton, twirling his cane and turning up the path that led to his house. 'Bigger and better vada. Say they've learnt to fly. They say they can walk without leaving footprints. You know, I don't care much for anthropologists, but they are the only people who can take fear out of a Papuan's life.'

'Without footprints!' Washington laughed inanely.

'Everything gets put down to them. Anyone dies. Pigs stolen at Maiola. River floods. The people are scared to death. I was in Maiola three weeks ago taking the census. If you'd been earlier you could have come with me then. Confounded nuisance going up the river again so soon. Doubt if you'll get those Maiola boys to go nearer than a day's march, you know.'

'It won't matter,' said Washington, 'as long as they can put us on the way.' The news cheered him in a way. The sooner the boys dropped out the better. It was all to the good if they refused to go far. He was, in a way, as dazed as Stella and realised no more than she what was ahead. He dared not even think of Eola. His mind shrank from it. He had laid his plans but had not yet realised that they must be executed.

Seaton had stopped abruptly, slapping his heels together as if about to salute, and waited for Stella to catch them up. They faced the house, a large, low building. On a patch of lawn in front of the verandah a flag fluttered from a white pole. Seaton led the way up the steps, calling for his boy.

The house was so austerely furnished as to appear uninhabited. There were no curtains on the windows, no cushions on the cane chairs, not even grass mats on the floor. Washington looked around him with contempt for the barren soul that was content to live like this. Half a dozen dusty books, their covers gnawed by cockroaches and blotched with mould, sloped in a home-made shelf. A detailed map of the district was pinned on the wall. On a low wooden table were three hibiscus flowers in a jam tin – a concession to visitors.

'Sit down,' said Seaton, pointing to the chairs.

Stella appeared not to hear and wandered over to the louvres. She stood looking out to sea, the spray of orchids still in her hand. Every time Washington looked at her she appeared younger and more helpless, carrying a mute air of acceptance. She seemed merely to wait.

Seaton was pouring out gin. He half filled a tumbler, slopped a dash of water into it and handed it to Washington, who sipped it with distaste. It was lukewarm. It angered him that a man who could have lived like a king on this flowery island should put up with warm gin. He saw no virtue in schooling the body to accept anything.

'Anyway,' said Seaton, swallowing and wiping his moustache, 'you won't be wanting as many boys as you had last time. Regular battalion.'

'No, this time three would be enough. An interpreter and two carriers.'

'Should take a police boy,' said Seaton.

'It wouldn't be necessary, I have a gun.'

'You shouldn't have a gun,' said Seaton sharply. 'You should take a police boy.'

'But that only means another carrier,' said Washington. He did not want a police boy. A good one might be reliable and he did not want reliable boys. 'If you say carriers are going to be hard to come by ...'

'True,' said Seaton, chewing the end of his moustache.

Stella turned around and faced them. She blinked her eyes into focus. 'Hitolo is here,' she said.

'What!' Washington put down his glass with a snap on the

table. His voice rose slightly. 'He wasn't allowed to come. I made the arrangements myself. He was refused permission.'

'He's here,' said Stella. 'It's too late.'

'How?' He struggled to hold his features impassive and looked at her through narrowed lids. 'Why is he so keen to come?'

She answered without thinking. 'It was my fault. I wanted a boy I knew and could talk to. I can't speak motu, I can't talk to the carriers and guides. I wanted him to come, and I think' – she looked away – 'I think he must have misunderstood.' The lie was not premeditated, it had come out quite simply. How easy it is to lie, she thought, and sometimes how necessary.

'Misunderstood!' Washington said sharply. 'They understand and misunderstand just what's convenient. He should be sent back immediately.'

'Don't send him back,' Stella said.

'He might as well go with you now that he's here,' said Seaton briskly. 'And it disposes of one of the carriers.'

'He's a clerk,' said Stella. 'Not a carrier.'

'If he's here without leave,' said Seaton, 'he loses his status. He can carry. We ought to be able to find you two more somewhere.'

Washington tipped back his glass and swallowed the rest of the gin. He saw it would be unwise to protest further. The gin made him optimistic. Hitolo's cowardice was well proven. He had caught the fever of terror as quickly as any of the primitive Maiola boys.

Washington looked at Stella over the rim of his glass. She had won. But how had she managed it? She must have paid him well. He would not relish the Bava valley. And if she had tried to protect herself did she know what was ahead?

Stella came and sat between them. She put down the spray of orchids on the table and picked up her glass. Her eyes met his, and she smiled, sweetly, vacantly, as if she had no idea on earth who he was.

It was barely light. A thick mist hung over the river and bound the trees on either bank. The water was black, and mist steamed off it like smoke rising from boiling oil. It was deathly still. The long, animal shape of a log rocking slightly just off-shore seemed to move through some sluggish pressure of life within itself.

But in the stillness there was a curious tension. Stella felt that the jungle was sleeping and would move, when it wished, beyond the accepted limits of plant life. The huge spreading roots of the trees would stretch and claw in the mud, sucking up some rich, black substance to swell the succulent trunks and the gigantic blades of leaves. Branches would reach out, feeling their way in the air, following scents and sounds, to clutch at the life that moved there.

Stella felt that the jungle was more animal than vegetable, that there would be danger in touching a leaf or breaking a twig, that the plant thus assailed would retaliate in a hungry, primordial fashion of its own. As she climbed from the boat on to land, she felt she had stepped on to putrid human flesh. Her foot sank into mud – not soft, boggy mud that slid up around her instep but strange black rubber matter that the foot sank into but did not break.

Washington took her hand and helped her up on to firmer land. They stood side by side, looking back at the boat while the boys heaved across the stores. The district officer had given them two – one a police boy – who came from a lower Bava River village, and they had picked up one other boy from Maiola when they arrived the night before.

They did not speak but kept silence as if in fear of waking someone. And even the district officer – not a fanciful man – gave his orders in a low voice. Some presence brooded in the trees. To have spoken out loud, laughed or whistled would have been like blasphemy and aroused vengeance. They were all on shore now. Hitolo came last, his dark body moving like a shadow out of the water. He stood a little way off and the mist folded around him, shrouding his ankles and wrapping about his shoulders. Stella, looking across at his dim shape thought, This is how we all look to one another. This is how I look to them. The process of annihilation had begun.

This meditation brought in its train no fear or regret. Never in her life had she held such a loose grip on reality. The hour itself was dreamlike, but Stella's senses were already befogged. She had lost the power to make all but one decision, like a swallow beating its wings south by instinct, undismayed by weather, preferring death to retreat, held doggedly to its course by the knowledge that there is no other choice. The past, which had endangered this journey, existed in her mind as a void out of which disturbing sensations she could not afford to examine sometimes emerged. She had even forgotten David. She was no longer lonely. She did not remember having loved or having lost love – even these memories were dangerous. She just stood at Washington's side, waiting for the carriers to collect their equipment and the first step forward to be made.

The village, a little ahead and hardly visible under its umbrella of palms, was showing signs of life. There were hushed sounds of movement and here and there a figure appeared in the doorways of the thatched houses. Half a dozen children stood staring at a distance – small, shadowy creatures with enormous, gnome-like heads, appearing at this grey, sunless hour more like jungle goblins than humans.

Maiola was the most northerly point of the Kairipi district and they did not see white men often, nor even uniformed native policemen.

Seaton was coming ashore, assisted by two police boys who stood ankle deep in the mud.

'Well, you're all set, I think,' he said. 'If you get going straight away you'll have the best part of your day's march over before it gets too hot. You don't want to walk in the afternoon, Mrs Warwick, if you can help it.'

Stella nodded, but his words floated far over her head. As she saw it they would never stop walking. They would go on and on like pilgrims in legends until they reached their destination. It did not seem to her that they would grow hot or tired or that they would need food and rest. Their bodies only existed to get them to Eola, and would make no demands on them.

'Might rain – might not,' said Seaton. 'After noon. Won't rain before. Uncertain time of year. Should be all right. Too early for rain. And if you get lost, Mrs Warwick, you've only got to remember, follow the river. Fact is, you can't get lost. Follow the river, it's well tracked on this side, your husband told me. Can't see that anything can happen to you.'

Only Eola, she thought. Only Eola can happen to me.

Seaton was holding out his hand. 'I'll be back for you in a fortnight. If you're not here, then you'll have to get hold of canoes and come down on your own. Unless you'd like to wait for a couple of months when the patrol officer will be back.'

'We'll be here by then,' said Washington. He spoke loudly, but his voice dropped away towards the end of the sentence. He cast a quick, nervous glance at the smoking wall of trees. 'How long does this mist hang around?' he asked in a whisper.

'Only a couple of hours. Don't ask for the sun. You won't like it when you get it.'

It was hot now, but there was steamy moisture in the air. Stella's hands were moulded together by an emanation from her skin. She thought of the beche-de-mer that crawled on the sea floor at Marapai.

Seaton was saying goodbye to Washington. She did not hear what they said. Their voices rang out like whispers in empty rooms. There was nowhere for the sounds to drift to, no emptiness. The air was thick like a sponge, sucking up their words and the breath they exhaled. As they stood, breathing and speaking, the air around them grew closer and thicker.

'Well, goodbye again,' said Seaton, lifting his hand in a sharp salute. The engines of the little boat started up. Seaton, sitting now in the stern, was a white shape with a grey, featureless face.

Neither Stella nor Washington moved. They waited while the last link that bound them to the law of Marapai and the western world broke loose. Two long, oily ribbons broke out from the stern of the boat as it moved slowly down stream. The water swirled, as if to reveal monstrous, muddy, submerged life boiling beneath the mist. The boat disappeared round the bend of the river. Only the sound of its engines outraged the silence.

Washington turned to face the village. 'Well, we might as well be off.' He had tried to be jovial, but there was a hollow ring in his voice. Faces in this gloom were bloodless and pale and Stella, glancing up at him, wondered if she also wore a moon pallor.

They walked side by side. 'I must say,' he said in the same jovial whisper, 'I'm all for starting a bit later than this.'

'We might as well go on,' she said, 'since we're awake and ready.' She did not know her own voice.

The village was built in a semi-circular form, leaving a broad half moon of mud between the water and the houses. They could see them more clearly now – squat grey shapes that looked alive on their stiff wooden legs, the ragged thatched roofs like the drenched plumage of birds. In the centre of the village was the large, downy shape of the men's long house, with its curved back swooping up into the sky like the prow of a canoe and its tall, conical face shuttered down upon its secrets. No dogs barked, but here and there they crept out from under the houses and slunk back and forth, mangy hides rippling over their bones. A few of the older men had come out to look at the departing whites. One of the women belonging to the guide followed a little way and then dropped behind. Stella glanced over her shoulder and saw her standing in front of her house, her frayed leaf skirt bunching out from below her hips, one hand dangling at her side, the other held across her swollen belly.

Notions of civilisation are only relative, and now that the district officer with his motor boat and his western law had gone, Stella saw that these people, who had seen white men, who lined up for the census, who had a village policeman with a badge on his tunic and whose people had been tried in a court of law, represented order, security, peace. She watched the young woman drop behind with a sense of loss. Three children were still following them and two young boys, one armed with a bow and arrows, had crept out of a house and joined them noiselessly as they passed. Then the mist closed up behind and the village was gone. The path led on into the wall of trees ahead. The mist wept down from their leaves like white slime. Moving forward, they pressed against damp, heavy air.

The children left them first. Stella did not see them go. But glancing behind a quarter of an hour later she could make out a single file of the two boys from the lower river village, the guide from Maiola and last of all Hitolo with the two village boys. She felt a pang of regret for the little brown children who had gone home to sleep.

They walked for another hour. The jungle was still shrouded in mist. It still seemed that there was a demand for silence. They walked single file for, though the path was well trodden, it was narrow and the undergrowth sprang up on either side, grey, rank and forbidding. Then the path widened into a clearing under large trees. Here the undergrowth had been cut away; the villagers apparently used this part of the river bank as a landing-stage. Three long canoes made from hollowed logs were drawn up at the water's edge. The ground around them writhed with huge, twining roots. They could see through a gap in the branches the river, flowing more swiftly here. The steaming emanation of mist had almost gone and hung thinly among the trees on either bank.

Washington paused and looked back. The boys, who had not straggled much, closed up and stopped. 'Who are those two?' It was the first time he had spoken since they left the village. With the mist gone, speech was possible.

The two youths stood back shyly from the rest of the group. Side by side, their naked brown bodies and woolly heads almost identical, they looked on, serious and uncomprehending. 'Village boys, taubada,' said the police boy in police motu. He was a tall man with a thin, beaked face and distended earlobes that dangled in split strips.

'Tell them to go home.'

Stella did not understand the language that Washington was speaking, but as the police boy called out there was no doubt about his meaning. The two boys turned away, hesitated, looked back, looked at each other, and walked off down the path. She watched them, the outlines of their bodies growing more and more spectral. They were gone. She turned and looked at Washington. For no more than an instant they stared at each other and read each other's hearts.

Jobe did not kill my husband, she thought. This man Washington killed him, and now he will kill me.

It was then – as Anthony Nyall had said, too late – that she realised that she did not want to die. 'Are we stopping here?' she asked.

He looked away from her and nodded. 'It will give the carriers a rest.'

She felt the crystalising of their relationship shock him as it had shocked her. But her thoughts were clear and arranged. She knew that what she was thinking and feeling had been arrived at days ago and set aside for the moment of danger – the glimpse into Washington's heart.

Washington had sat down on the root of a tree and was lighting a cigarette. The carriers had dropped their loads. She sat down in front of him. 'Why did you send those two boys away?' she said.

He threw her a darting glace. 'We have enough. They might hang on for hours and then we'd have to feed them. And they might panic and upset the carriers.'

'Because of the vada men?'

He did not reply.

I must protect myself, she thought. She looked around her and her thoughts were quick and alert. She sensed that there was something to guard against in the fear of vada men. On the last trip the carriers had panicked and the white men had gone on alone. Even Hitolo had lost his head. It must not happen this time. Possible dangers, possible defences against them, passed through her mind. She did not feel afraid – not now – a new vitality had risen in her that gave her an extraordinary sense of power. It did not occur to her to turn back, though now she saw different reasons for going on. She was a match for Washington. She felt that. He looked pale and ill, his hands trembled. It's not only fever, she thought. He's afraid. And he doesn't want to kill me, he'll only do it because he must, because I threaten his safety, or because some other fear compels him. He'd do anything to get out of it.

Washington behaved as if he were the hunted one. His eyes searched the trees around them. Every now and again he would sit still for a moment and stare at the ground, then in the next moment his head would be raised, staring at the path ahead, the path behind.

She stood up and walked past the carriers to Hitolo. He too was squatting on a tree root, smoking a cigarette. He looked up at her, but did not stand. She felt he looked strange and suspected that for a moment he did not recognise her.

'Hitolo,' she said softly. 'Do you think these men will stay with us? Will they be frightened?'

'They stay, Mrs Warwick. Two days maybe.' He was using short, simplified sentences and unconsciously she addressed him in the same way. 'You find out what they say. You tell me, Hitolo. You do that?' He nodded, but there was no look of understanding in his face.

'And you stay near me, Hitolo. Don't you hang back at the end. You walk close behind, and you watch all the time and see I don't get hurt.'

'Yes, sinabada.'

She left him and went back to Washington. He had finished his cigarette and was grinding it into the mud with his heel. She stood looking down at him. She felt for him none of the passionate loathing that had been an offshoot of despair and that she had felt for Jobe. She believed she knew him and understood him. And you cannot hate someone you know, she thought, any more than you can love somebody you don't. And there again Anthony Nyall had been right. She had never known David – this was becoming more obvious – and looking back over the past few weeks she saw her actions as an hysterical protest against never having loved him. Her presence here was a final protest. She did not regret the loss of love. The return to Marapai was not now something to dread but something to work for with all her strength. 'Shall we go now?'

Washington started and looked up. Slowly he rose to his feet and they went on.

Washington looked at his watch. The luminous dial showed the time to be twelve. He could hear no sound outside and, within the hut, only Stella's soft breathing. They had stopped for the night in the first of the river villages where the carrier from Maiola was known. The people had been friendly and had given them the use of an empty hut on the outskirts of the village.

Within the hut it was hot and airless. He had discarded his shirt and lay only in shorts. The sweat on his body pricked and crawled like the feet of insects. He lifted the mosquito net, slid out from beneath it and fixed it in place before the insects could swarm in. He stood up and looked across to the corner of the hut where Stella was sleeping. The mosquitoes descended upon his naked skin. He flicked them away from his lips and eyes and felt among his clothes for a shirt to throw over his shoulders. There was no movement from Stella. He could not see her clearly, only the faint outline of her body beneath its dim tent of netting. Outside there was no moon, but the sky was light. The doorway faced into a wide patch of cleared ground, around which the village huts were collected. He could see the tops of trees and a few pale stars.

He moved quietly to the doorway, sat down on the steps that led to the ground and put on his socks. It was unwise wandering round in these places without shoes, but he did not want to wake the boys. Lastly he put his hand in his shirt pocket and drew out a midget torch and the small carved coconut that he had taken from Anthony Nyall's desk. He waited, listening.

He was not afraid. At least, not as afraid as he had been in his own hut at Marapai. Stella gave him confidence. She slept so deeply and peacefully in the hut behind him. They had walked nearly eighteen miles that day, and she had lain down at nine o'clock and slept almost immediately, like an exhausted child. Her attitude gave him courage; she was not intimidated by the jungle, nor by the people in the village. She accepted the bizarre situation they found themselves in as ordinary. Throughout the day she had been eager, practical, interested. They had not spoken much, but every now and then, glancing back over his shoulder, he had caught her looking about alert and wide-eyed. She seemed intensely curious about everything around her, and utterly unafraid. The uneasiness of the three local carriers had failed to impress her. The irony of this – that Stella should inspire him with confidence – did not pass him by, and he smiled in the darkness. Then he stood up and, flashing the torch on the ladder, climbed carefully down to the ground.

Hitolo and the three local boys were sleeping under the hut. Ahead, the path faded into darkness. Washington threw only a brief glance in this direction. Here the jungle closed in over the sky, and he could see in the foreground only a few dim shapes of the larger trees. Behind this the darkness might have been solid. He knew that if he looked long enough he would see receding planes reaching back into the trees, darkness moving, coiling like smoke, clotting into thick shadows that blinked with the orbs of eyes. He knew all the tricks of darkness. Its slow, heaving shapes and darting tongues had displaced sleep now for many weeks, its tiny lights stabbed his eyeballs as he lay in his bed in Marapai. He knew all the dangers of staring too long at a fluttering leaf or a firefly.

But darkness was there and he could not forget it. His feet touched the spongy ground at the base of the ladder. The spot of light from his torch bobbed just ahead like a white moth. He kept his eyes fixed there, and his mind on the snakes or scorpions that might endanger unshod feet. But it seemed that this Philip Washington, this cool concentrating man following the bobbing light of his torch and treading cautiously so not to break a leaf or twig under foot, sheltered another creature, hardly a man, who crouched in a huddled animal state of apprehension, ears pricked and hair raised on its spine, its nerves like the hundred hands of a sea anemone reaching out and fingering the night ahead.

The darkness behind did not worry him. That was the way they had come, it was the path to Kairipi and to Marapai. The village was wrapped in a warm, inhabited dark, cleansed of evil by the sweat of human bodies, the breath exhaled from sleeping men and women and the trust of children. The darkness ahead was different. Anything might reside here, and they were only two days' march from Eola.

The path led around the side of the hut to where the boys had built their fire. Down the front, back and one side had been built a ragged brush fence, possibly to form some sort of enclosure for pigs. The dying fire gleamed on the outstretched legs of one of the carriers, who lay with his head under the hut, his legs and thighs stretched out into the footpath. Hitolo and the other boys were well under the hut. Washington could hear them breathing.

He paused and looked down at them. The little coconut charm was warm and damp in his hand. The village was behind him now and out of sight, hidden by the corner of the hut. He was alone with the four sleeping men and the darkness that closed around them. There was no comfort in them as there had been in Stella. They were not restless, but he knew they had not surrendered consciousness with the confidence that she had. Their sleep was as uneasy as his own, haunted by vague shapes and flickering tongues of fear. He knew so well the sleep of terror, the anguish of almost breaking surface, of lying, limbs paralysed, mind half submerged, with the anaesthetic of sleep still fuming in the brain, while the voice of the outside world whispered, 'Danger!' There was no more terror than to hear this voice, to carry in the mind an awareness of the location and cause of dread, and yet to lie, physically still in sleep, tied and helpless, while fear plucked at the roots of the hair.

These thoughts unsteadied him, and he bent down quickly beside the fire and ran his fingers over the ground. The soil was damp and slimy, but there was no vegetation. He raised the torch and the beam of light lengthened. The pool of its termination settled a little further ahead. The long, shining trunk of a tree beamed out from the edge of the jungle. He quickly dipped the light. Something had flashed in the shadows beyond the tree.

He stepped a little further away from the fire and felt again on the ground. He only wanted grass or a few leaves. He hesitated – only a few steps were needed to carry him to the fringe of vegetation, but it needed enormous daring to make them. His gaze was fixed on the ground, but the grey form of the tree was still there, visible to those other watching eyes within that took no heed of these devices against fear but were always on the lookout, always infusing life into a shadow and movement into a log or a stone. These eyes were fixed now on the light that had shone out in the jungle ahead. It no longer flashed like a luminous insect but had settled on the ground at the foot of the trees and just behind, and beamed palely like a round, bright eye.

Would it be enough without the grass and leaves? he wondered, fingering the damp polished sides of the coconut in his hand. Would the intention be sufficiently clear? They could be regarded, Anthony Nyall had said, as fairly harmless without the appropriate trappings. There were plenty of them in the villages hanging about more or less disregarded and forgotten. So he reasoned, stroking the coconut with wet, shaking fingers. And all the time the animal within stared at the soft, bright jungle eye that beamed ahead.

The point of the torch moved on across the ground, showing only the slime of river mud. Not until that tree was reached would the ground yield vegetation. One more step forward and he could resist the drag of his lids no longer. He raised his eyes and suffered one fierce, almost annihilating instant of terror. The jungle eye glowed out from the ground at his feet. It was not gold, but a green, white light, ice-light, moonlight. It breathed. It was palpitatingly alive. It pierced the very core of his heart.

A nerve flicked in his wrist, the torch jerked up and the eyes died away in the circle of torch light. He was looking at a cluster of fungi that sprang up from the roots of the tree.

Luminous jungle fungi! He was almost sick with relief. His sweating body jerked with spasms of silent laughter. For an instant the world was safe and sweet. But the animal within was not confident of safety. Instinctively he knew that what was to be done must be done quickly. He clawed at the ground with his fingers. His hand closed over a piece of dead wood. He lowered the torch and the fungi burned out again just ahead. The next thing his fingers touched was a piece of dead pandanus leaf. He picked it and went quickly back to the hut and the sleeping men.

He squatted down by the fire, broke off the tip of the pandanus leaf and shredded it with his fingernails. His eyes did not move from the shredded leaf but a voice from the jungle ahead spoke incessantly, Look up, look up. All his will was bent on not looking up, and the shredding of the leaf was an act that he was hardly conscious of.

He tried to stuff the little sheaf of leaf fibre into the mouth of the coconut. But the opening was too small and the sheaf would not stay in position. He felt about desperately on the ground for a small piece of stick to prod the plug into place. But he knew there was nothing, and that he must return to the edge of the jungle. He squatted, quivering with rage. He knew he could not go back and that he was defeated by a coconut and a plug of leaves. He forgot that this was only a small, incidental obstacle in the journey ahead. It was the goal itself, the end of all doubt and fear.

Then he remembered the hut. He stood up and went across to the sleeping men, stepping over the legs of the boy who lay stretched out with his feet turned to the fire. He broke off a splinter of hard leaf from the side of the hut and rammed it into the mouth of the coconut. It held the plug firmly in place. Gusts of hysterical laughter broke out inside him. He need not have left the fire.

Biting back his laughter, he twisted the string that was attached to the coconut around a loose splinter jutting out from one of the beams of the hut. The little charm dangled now just over the heads of the sleeping boys. They would open their eyes to see it hanging there – the threat of a slow mysterious sickness, perhaps the visit of the vada men who cut out life from the body and left the shell to rot away, the fear of the unknown striking with weapons of magic.

The little black charm with its sprouting mouth of dead leaf and stick swayed in the faintly stirring air. The thought flashed through Washington's mind that one of the boys might die as a result of what he had done. It might need only the knowledge of guilt in one of these susceptible hearts, fear sufficiently intense, despair completely surrendered, and life might be handed over willingly to the sorcerer.

This possibility gave him little distress. He genuinely loved the Papuan people, but it did not seem to him that the death of a few of them, or even of a whole community, mattered. As he saw it, death for them was more natural, more likely, followed more closely and inevitably on the heels of life. Death for a white man was something to shudder at, to resist and fight against. To kill a white man or a white woman was the very last of all human acts to be contemplated, and then only when any other action was impossible. But a Papuan was different. He did not regard them as inferior, but as nearer to natural law, one with rock, river and tree, bird and fish, and destined for the same struggle and violent extermination. They were hunters, and like all hunters must accept the likelihood of being hunted.

He steadied the coconut charm gently over the three men's heads, and stepped back. It turned slowly on the frayed string and was at last still. The white, incised eyes stared into his own. It looked now, with the equipment of sorcery bristling from its mouth and its victims marked down, subtly animated and malevolent.

He turned away quickly, walked back to the front of the hut and flashed the torch on the steps. The doorway loomed above him; he went up the first three steps. He could not hear Stella's breathing. No light penetrated the black interior of the hut. He paused, and an unaccountable feeling of dread held him motionless, waiting. He listened for some sound, but there was silence. He was afraid to move, to look back at the deserted village, to stay where he was, to flash his torch inside the hut. The last feeble tongues of reason whispered, Do something, do something, you can't stand this. Something will crack and it will be too late. He stepped up on to the rickety verandah at the top of the steps and flashed his torch over the frame of the door. Hanging from the centre of the doorway, directly in front of his eyes, was a small, black coconut with two vivid white eyes that stared into his own and a plug of leaves bristling from its mouth.

He did not scream, he had passed beyond screaming. He stood in a sweat of terror and the magic poured out and pierced his veins. He was doomed, his blood was poisoned. He did not wonder how the coconut came to be hanging there. He believed it was his own coconut that, with gifts of thought and flight, had found its way to its true destination.

He knew that he had been discovered. The forces of evil had discovered him and would track him down till they destroyed him. With a sobbing cry, he flung out a hand and plucked at the coconut on the door. His fingers closed on emptiness. The vision faded. There was nothing there.

He clawed the wood with his nails. The palms of his hands burned with pain.

'What's that? Who is it?' It was Stella speaking from inside the hut. 'Is that you, Philip?'

'Yes.'

He saw her vague white form drift near and turned towards her, clenching his teeth to strangle the sobs that bubbled in his throat. He forgot for a moment who she was. Was she his sister, Doris, who had come to help him and comfort him? He wanted to run into the hut and clutch her in his arms. But he held out his throbbing palm and said querulously, 'My hand.'

She came nearer. 'Your hand? What's the matter with it?' She took it in her own. 'You're burning!' she said. 'Is it fever? You've cut your hand. It's bleeding. Give me the torch.'

She flashed the light on his hand. It was bleeding freely from a long scratch on the palm. He stared down at it and a deep shudder that he was too weak to control passed through his body.

'What's the matter?' said Stella. 'Why are you up?'

It struck him that she had changed; that she was no longer silly, deluded and helpless, that the jungle that had robbed him of reason and strength had given these very qualities to her. He had been rejected and she had been chosen.

'I heard something,' he said. 'Was there anything?'

'No. You must put something on that cut or it may fester.'

He followed her meekly into the hut. It will not be me who kills her, he thought. She will kill me.

They made a later start the next day. Stella slept soundly and was awakened only by the sounds of the village stirring. Washington was already up and folding his net. 'Why didn't you wake me?' she said.

He looked around. 'There's plenty of time.' His face shocked her. It was white and strained, and he looked like an old man. The skin folded loosely round his throat and chin. His heavy, bloodshot eyes told that he had had no sleep.

He had forgotten the anguished emotions of the night and turned on her a glance of cold hostility.

'Two of the boys are staying here,' he said.

'Why?'

He would not meet her eye. 'They are afraid,' he said, and went on folding the net.

'Which two?'

'Hitolo and the police boy are going on with us. We'll leave some of the food here for when we return.'

Stella went to the entrance of the hut and called, 'Hitolo! Hitolo!'

The boys were nowhere to be seen. A few silent figures moved about in the village, their legs shrouded in the morning mist that still hung over the ground. She climbed down the steps. 'Hitolo!'

Washington followed her out on to the verandah and stood looking down at her. 'What's the matter? What do you want?' he said. There was a nervous edge to his voice. 'You won't be able to persuade them. It's no use. They're terrified. They saw something last night.'

'What?'

'It doesn't matter what it was,' he said. 'They were prepared to be afraid and something frightened them. You can't bring reason to bear. It might have been a bird or a bat.'

Hitolo had appeared round the side of the hut. He stood looking up at them. Stella thought that his eyes looked wild. They were set in his head in a peculiarly unfixed way, as if at any moment they might roll round in their sockets like the broken eyes of a doll.

'What's all this about the boys not coming?'

'They come now, Mrs Warwick,' he said.

'You mean they've changed their minds?'

'Yes, Mrs Warwick. They come now. I tell them and they come.' A momentary smile of self-congratulation passed over his face, but his eyes still looked wild.

She glanced at Washington. He was leaning against the door frame, and she could not tell whether the expression on his face was anger or relief.

'All right, Hitolo, make breakfast.'

He shook his head. 'Boys no stop, sinabada. Kai-kai breakfast in bush. No stop here.' She looked at Washington again for explanation.

'They're afraid,' he said. 'They say that a sorcerer was here last night. He might come back and pick up their leavings. We'll have to walk for an hour and then have breakfast.'

A quarter of an hour later they started. The boys still looked frightened. They huddled together, walking almost on each other's heels, for the path was only wide enough to allow them to walk in single file. They whispered and grunted among themselves and kept throwing apprehensive glances about them. Washington kept near to the rest of the party and did not stride off in front as he had done the day before. He walked so close to Stella that he fell in alongside her whenever the path widened. Yesterday he had been silent, today he talked.

At seven they stopped for breakfast. The boys sat apart and ate like dogs, bolting their food, eyes on the surrounding trees. When they had finished they scraped a hole on the side of the path and buried the scraps, stamping the earth hard and flat with their feet. They hid the empty tin in the undergrowth and pulled the foliage of the bushes up around it so that it could not be seen from the path. Washington had finished his breakfast and sat watching them.

'Why do they do that?' said Stella.

'It's dangerous to leave scraps around. If a sorcerer finds a piece of food you have been eating, it can be used just as potently against you as leavings from the body.'

He spoke quietly, but there was an undercurrent of eagerness in his voice. She had noticed it once before, the first time she met him, when he spoke of the Eola vada men. He believes it all, she thought, watching him curiously, and he welcomes it. There is something here that he dreads but wants.

The jungle was lighter now, and she could see more clearly his worn, haggard face. A nerve fluttered in his cheek. His eyes did not dart about searching the trees like the eyes of the native men. His eyes were wide, and haunted. Terror lived within him now, not in the jungle outside.

She felt she should not pity him, but pity was there, struggling against judgment. Even the wicked, in the moment of executing their most monstrous plans, are pitiful. She was not astonished or shocked by this discovery – discovery now was an hourly event – but waited to find the new paradox in it.

Free from the illusion of having loved David, she was free from those opinions and attitudes of his she had worn as her own. She thought of Marapai, and of Anthony and Trevor Nyall. What were they really like? About Anthony she felt she knew, about Trevor she had no idea. People had always come to her second hand, stamped with the insignia of someone else's approval. Why had David liked one and disliked the other? His choice now seemed to her incongruous, and she could not understand it. She could not understand David for she had never known him, only his opinions. Perhaps he had never liked Trevor, but preferred it to be thought that he did.

She felt that everyone she had known had hidden from her, had protected her from the dangers of discovery because they had enjoyed in her a condition of innocence. All except one person, who alone had respected her enough to disclose what he believed to be the worst in himself.

The boys had huddled together on the path and were watching her expectantly. She glanced over her shoulder at Washington to see if he was ready to move. He was squatting down on the path with his back towards her. For a moment she could not see what he was doing. One knee was bent, his head was lowered, and his elbows jerked backwards and forwards. He was scraping the pieces of charred yam from his plate into a hole he had dug in the ground.

She felt her stomach lurch. She was frightened and revolted as if she had looked on something obscene. 'Don't !' she cried. 'Don't!'

He looked around. He crouched still, his head lowered. His muddied hands dabbled like paws on the ground. His eyes were turned in their sockets showing a rim of smoky, bloodshot white. He looked like a cornered dog. She could hear the sharp hiss of his breath.

'That's not for you!' she said. 'It's for *them*. It's all right for them. They manage. They know all the ways out and the loopholes and evasions. But you're a westerner! Don't be a fool!'

He rose slowly to his feet and turned to her, his muddy hands hanging at his sides.

'A fool!' he said. His teeth clenched and he was very white. He lashed back at her as if she had insulted him. 'A fool! You don't know what you're saying. Only fools are safe! Westerner! What place has the west here! Good God, this is the tropics! We are standing virtually on the equator! Don't you know that's where all living things – slugs, pigs, fishes, trees, flowers, mosquitoes, humans – are the same and survive on equal terms! Do you suppose it'll snow for us because we've got Nordic blood in our veins? *We* must give in.'

He stopped abruptly and stamped on the earth he had been digging. She glanced around her. Hitolo and the three carriers were still waiting, and watching. They won't stay, she thought, they'll leave us tonight.

Washington did not speak to her for some time. She realised he was angry at being caught and rebuked for his furtive digging. But after they had walked about half a mile the track widened into mud flats on the edge of the river and he dropped back and walked alongside her.

'You don't understand,' he said. 'You've just come here, you haven't been here long enough to realise these things. You can't know them intellectually, they don't bear examination, you've got to feel them. For hundred of years now the white men have been trying to live in the tropics and the only ones who have survived are those who have obeyed its commands and worshipped its gods.'

He seemed unaware of the half hour of silence that had passed between them and spoke as if in direct continuation of their earlier conversation. 'Isn't it possible,' he said, 'that this belt that circles the world demands some other sort of equipment for living?' He spoke almost in a whisper and kept looking into the trees on either side. 'In every tropical country, there are native peoples who have survived and built up cultures of their own. And always, always, with the people who survive you find witchcraft, magic, sorcery and a conglomeration of methods for harnessing and counteracting the forces of evil. They recognise evil. They *recognise* it and survive. But *we* don't survive. Not the whites, the westerners, as you call them, because they won't acknowledge what they can't explain as a scientific formula. They think it's childish; they won't climb down and admit their helplessness.'

'There could be other reasons for their not surviving,' Stella said.

'What other reasons?' His voice was again eager. His own theory seemed to fascinate him. 'Why is it that after a year or so up here or in any other tropical country, they lose touch with their own natures? Why do their personalities rot and crumble? Why is their work futile and profitless? Why do they end up in suicide and madness, drink, sex and sickness?'

He paused and spoke more loudly now, more passionately. 'Because they refuse to understand that all the phenomena that they have been brought up to be enlightened about, to be sceptical about, are still here. Oh, God! What fools! They think a jungle is an English wood. They've never spent a night alone in the jungle as I have. They refuse to live – with their goddamned superiority – as a native has learned is the only way to live – cunningly, instinctively and acknowledging their own insignificance!'

Stella did not reply, and he rambled on about instincts, feelings, the false trails that the intellect followed; the inner eye that the western world had lost. Every now and again he would stop and glance back over his shoulder and then the boys behind them would stop too.

They arrived at a village in the mid-afternoon and decided to stop there for the night. They were now a day's march from Eola.

While the other boys were preparing food in the evening Stella tried to talk to Hitolo, but she felt that he had ceased to be frank with her. He was wary and on the defensive.

'Will the boys come on tomorrow?' she asked. But he only shook his head enigmatically and would not meet her eye. 'If they don't, we shall leave food here and take presents and just a little food for the people at Eola.'

'We take no presents,' he replied indifferently.

'Why not?'

'Last time, Eola people send all presents back again.'

'Surely not. Mr Washington said they took a lot of presents. Pearl shells and cowries. And Mr Seaton said it too.'

He nodded. 'Plenty presents. Mr Washington and Mr Warwick and my brother bring them all back. The people of Eola bad people.' He looked away. '*Bad* people,' he said again.

'What do they say about them here?' asked Stella, pointing a hand to indicate the village.

'Bad people,' Hitolo said vaguely. He had become inarticulate, as if the jungle silence had made him feel the futility of words.

'Do they ever see them?'

He threw a quick glance around him. 'Vada men,' he said.

'They must trade with them,' she insisted. 'They're not more than fifteen or twenty miles away.'

'Vada men kill plenty people.'

They were no longer able to talk together. Whatever knowledge Hitolo had acquired of European language and customs was now muddled. The fear that was his birthright had claimed him. She wondered if he had forgotten his dead brother, or if this memory, too, was lost with all that he had started with. He no longer set himself apart from the other boys, seeing himself as an administration clerk, more white than brown. He walked away from her to the other boys busy around the fire with, she felt, an air of relief.

The boys did not, as she had half expected, stay behind in the village. She woke early at about four o'clock and lay for a few moments looking out through her net at the grey light outside.

'Are you awake?' she said.

'Yes,' Washington said. The relief in his tone suggested that he had been lying awake for hours.

This is the day, she thought. 'We should leave as soon as possible. Will you wake the boys?'

He said nothing but got up and left the hut. It was understood between them now that she should make the decisions. A moment later he returned. Stella was up and folding her bed.

'Are they coming?'

'Yes.' There was no telling what this meant to him.

They had breakfast and left as it was growing light. The day before they had walked through open country but now they were in forest once more. The path was narrow and only visible for a few yards ahead. The light was not daylight but a thin dark.

Washington tried to make the boys lead. 'They might sneak off behind,' he explained. But they refused, so he and Stella went first, walking abreast and continually knocking against each other on the narrow path. She felt that he sought this constant collision of hand, shoulder and knee as an antidote to his loneliness. More than once she noticed his fingers feel towards hers in the unconscious act of clasping her hand. But this statement of bewilderment and fear was never completed; consciousness intervened just in time and his hand was drawn back.

The boys walked close behind. They did not speak now and moved so silently there was no way of telling they were there. Every now and again Washington stopped and glanced over his shoulder, then the boys would stop too. His constant checking agitated them and they picked up his anxiety as a horse senses fear in its rider's hands.

They spoke only once, when a chuckling cry broke out of the jungle ahead. The party stopped as one; even Stella froze to a halt. 'It's only a bird,' she murmured.

Washington, stiff as a terrified dog beside her, said without moving, 'I've never heard a bird like that.' His eyeballs turned a violent half circle while his head remained stiff. He dared not turn to either side and expose himself from the other.

The cry sounded again, a little further off, and sounded less eerie and more birdlike. The boys shuffled and muttered; they moved on.

But the cry must have decided them. When Washington turned round again, not more than five minutes later, they had gone.

'They've gone!'

Stella turned sharply. The path was empty. It led back about twenty yards and then disappeared round a smooth-barked tree. She started to run. 'Hitolo! Hitolo!'

She could hear Washington running close behind her. Another fifty yards past the tree they came on the stores dumped down on the path. She stopped. 'It's no good,' she said. 'They would be running too.'

She looked down at the stores. They looked to have been thrown down in panic. 'Hitolo!' – she cupped her hands to her mouth and called – 'Hitolo!' But her voice was soaked up in the heavy trees.

Washington had stopped beside her. She felt him standing there, sensed his stillness but did not look at him. Now she was afraid.

'Hitolo!' She called again. There was some relief in calling. It postponed the fear, though she knew there was no hope of an answer.

To Washington her voice was an outrage, a flouting of the law of jungle silence. For a moment he did not move or speak, then he broke out hoarsely, 'Don't! Don't!'

Only then could she look at him. By speaking he had proclaimed the remnant of some sort of humanity. She turned, and they looked into each other's eyes.

They stood staring at each other. Stella's face was composed, but her eyes were filled with intelligence of what this moment might mean to her. It had not been sprung on her. It had been, all the time, a looming possibility, and she had not shut her mind to it, but had passed from village to village, point of safety to point of safety, knowing that each rejected fortress brought it nearer. It must be accepted if Eola was ever to be reached.

Washington was less clearly aware of their arrival than she. There was a dazed, vacant expression in his bloodshot eyes. The sudden terrible fact of finding themselves alone was all that he could grasp. They have gone, they have gone, they have gone, a voice whispered. Then the voice stopped and he became aware of the silence.

Stella had heard it too, for her eyes had moved away from his face and were fixed on the path ahead, searching for whatever it was that could make such silence. It was not merely an absence of sound – a hush in which no leaf stirred and birds were quiet – but a stillness that precedes violent action, as of a storm about to break or a beast about to strike. The jungle crouched with breath indrawn. For a moment they actually forgot each other and knew what it was to be alone.

Then Stella turned her head and looked at him again. His angry, helpless eyes stared into hers. He was trapped, it was no good, it was too late. The boys had left too late. He could never destroy the one creature that stood between him and the jungle and bring about by his own act the most appalling horror of all – to be alone on Eola land.

She understood and said quietly, 'Shall we go on?'

Her words steadied him a little. Suddenly everything was easier and less terrifying. She was not to die. He could not for the moment look ahead and face up to the consequences of her living. He felt only an immense relief. It was unthinkable – he had never even got around to thinking about it. He could never have killed her, not even if the boys had left the day before, before they reached Eola land. She was a white woman. He was not capable of destroying her. He had fooled himself all along into thinking that this simple, easy way out was possible. Something else must be done.

His thoughts were quick. They were the last vigorous gusts of life and drenched his spirit in radiance and optimism. 'We can't go on without the boys,' he said definitely.

'Why not?' She had already moved down the path, and paused to look back at him. He read resolution behind the contours of her youthful face, and his elation died.

'We might need help. It's dangerous.'

'You have a gun,' she said, pointing to the pistol in his holster.

'You don't use guns with boys,' he said sharply. It made him feel better to put her in her place. 'Having a bunch of them puts you in a position in which it isn't necessary to think of defence.'

'They didn't come before,' she said mildly. Her eyes were gentle but pitiless. He saw that she read exactly the reasons behind his excuses.

'That was different. We upset them before. We must go carefully. Besides, David was experienced with them. We aren't – not with primitive ones, that is. And besides ... the stores ...'

'We should get there by three,' she said. 'We can take a few tins and our nets and spend the night there. There'll be plenty of food. They'll give us yams.'

'Spend the night there!' It was all he could do to repress a shudder. 'You don't know what you're saying.'

'We can't go back now,' she said. 'It would be unthinkable.' She walked back and faced him. 'What is it about these people?'

It was the first time that anyone had asked him such a question. Not even Sylvia had dared. Now he saw they were to speak plainly. They had admitted between them that he was to have killed her and could not. There can be no closer relationship than between hunter and prey, and now she could ask him anything.

'They aren't like other people,' he muttered, looking away.

Stella did not answer him. She was bending down among the stores. 'We'll pick these up on the way back,' she said. 'Maybe the people from the village will come out for them. We can't actually be on Eola land yet. You carry your net, I'll carry mine. We'll take the water bottles and a few tins.' She was unpacking and re-packing one of the small haversacks.

He stood, helplessly watching her. Her large eyes, once so wild and fanatic, were clear and determined. Yet he felt that she hardly knew what she was doing, and obeyed, like himself – bending down and helping her – some irresistible compulsion. They moved the remainder of the stores into the undergrowth on the edge of the path and slashed the trees to mark the spot. Then Stella hoisted her haversack on to her back and started off down the path. She did not look behind to see if he followed. He stood for a moment dazedly watching her. The sun was up by now, but the light in the jungle was still dim, and the outline of her body grew hazy as she drew away from him.

Still he stood; his mind would not direct him. The silence drew nearer. A ring of watchers hidden in the trees had taken a step forward. A living band had drawn tighter. With a stifled gasp that was almost a scream, he raced after her.

'Wait!'

She paused and looked around. 'You've forgotten your haversack,' she said.

He looked at her helplessly and then back along the path to where the haversack lay. He felt he could not bear to leave her. To place even this small distance between them filled him with terror. He felt that if he turned his back on her and once lost sight of her she would be gone forever, swallowed in the jungle. He would be alone. She sensed his agony and said quietly, 'I'll wait while you get it.'

Only her command made the act possible, and he turned and walked obediently back to the haversack. She did not move on but waited for him to return.

They went on. The path bent away from the river and turned a little inland. It was hot now, and the air was thick and sticky. But they did not feel as hot and tired as they had during the noon hours of the previous days. They had forgotten their bodies and movement was mechanical to both of them.

Every now and again questions would rise to the surface of his mind. What am I going to do? What am I going to say? What explanation shall I give? But they would sink back once more like swamp creatures sucked down into mud. Most of the time he was hardly conscious of the past or the future. His body was not his own; his will had gone. He followed because Stella led and he could not live without her. He was not afraid, because he was beyond feeling. The jungle slid past like the backcloth of a revolving stage, each stretch of trees and undergrowth repeating what had passed before. Only now and again there would fall, like a shadow on his heels, the consciousness of that crouching, waiting, avenging silence that he only kept at bay by being with Stella.

Then Stella stopped. He did not know how long they had been walking. It might have been moments or hours. They were in a wide, open glade, entirely roofed in by trees. It appeared to have been at one time cleared right back to the trunks of the trees, but now the undergrowth was reaching forward on all sides and only a patch in the centre was bare.

All around them were straight-trunked fig trees with long up-sweeping branches that gave the effect of cathedral aisles. Down from the tops of the trees hung the tendrils of creepers, each bearing on its extreme end a single bright round fruit like an orange, so that the whole jungle was festooned with Christmas hangings. The undergrowth was thinner, and shining out among the roots of the trees in sinister purity were tall, white lilies.

'What a beautiful place.'

But Washington stared wildly around him. He felt like a sleepwalker who wakes in the mouth of a tomb.

'What's the matter?' she said.

'I know this place!'

'One would remember it.'

'We're only about six miles from the village!'

'That would be right. It's one o'clock. We should be there by three, though the paths are very overgrown; they look as if they haven't been used for ages.'

He did not hear her. He could not believe that their dazed marching had carried them so far. A shadow at night by his bed, a coconut face on the door – these were nothing. Even jungle silence was nothing. They were six miles from Eola. This turf had been pressed daily by Eola feet, the leaves touched by Eola hands, the orange fruit, the dazzling lilies were specific for Eola medicine. The trees and shrubs were bound over to Eola allegiance, the air thick with Eola curses and fanned by the spirits of Eola dead.

'I've been thinking how strange it is that we haven't met anyone,' Stella said.

He looked at her wildly. 'Met anyone?'

'I said before that the paths look unused.'

'They hunt on the other side of the village. They don't like this side.'

'The forest seems so utterly empty.' She stood listening. Then her eyes returned to his face. 'Why are you so frightened of this place?' she said softly.

He did not answer her and suddenly she understood. 'It was *here* that Sereva died.'

He nodded.

'Is he buried here?'

'Yes.' He looked wildly around. He could not see the grave and had no idea now where it was. That night he had been almost as dazed and frightened as he was now.

'I see.' Her face had grown sombre.

He had hoped that if he told her enough she would not want to go further. 'We camped the night here,' he said, 'after we left Eola. And it was here he died. Poor Warwick, he was heartbroken ...' Stella started to move on. He ran after her and caught hold of her arm. 'What's the good of going on?' he blurted out. 'There's nothing to see. It's just a village, just like any other.'

Her eyes regarded him, but she said nothing. She shook his fingers from her arm and moved on. When we get back, he thought, I will kill her for this. But another part of him yearned for her understanding. There was nothing for him to do but follow her. They walked on down the overgrown path into a more watchful silence.

The path was too narrow for them to walk abreast, so Stella led the way. Washington was almost treading on her heels. Only the front of his body, covered by hers, was in any way sheltered. He had a sense of something drawing in closer and closer behind him. He did not visualise it as a man but as a collection of images. Sometimes he saw it as a slimy substance crawling along the path at his heels. Sometimes the substance was grey, amorphous, writhing; sometimes it had only a hole for a mouth; sometimes a pair of round, lidless eyes. There was never a whole man, only parts: a disembodied arm that clutched forward, or a branch that clawed like a hand, a leafy spray infused with malignant humanity. Sometimes there was nothing, only a sense of collected, clotted wind that breathed on the back of his neck. He thought he could smell a faint pungent odour in his nostrils that hung in the air from no source. This was the most dreadful of all.

He could no longer resist the impulse to look back. There was nothing there, but he had a sense of having turned round just too late, at the end of movement. Something seemed to have flashed out of sight. Leaves, now almost still, vibrated with the agitation of something just gone.

'Do you know where we are?' said Stella.

She had stopped again. He put a hand on her shoulder. Now that they had stopped, walking was preferable. He looked around him. They might be anywhere. There were the same tall fig trees and tangled undergrowth struggling forwards to devour the path. Then he heard the river.

He thought at first that it was only the silence, a little nearer, rushing a little louder, or the hungry growth of the jungle, the roots clutching the mud and the sap swelling the flat broad leaves. But it was the river, over on the right through the trees. He could see the glimmer of water. They were no more than a quarter of a mile from the village.

'Stop!' he cried.

She was moving on and he reached out and clawed her back towards him. His hands, brutal with frenzy, clamped on her shoulders. 'You can't go!'

With strength equal to his own, she shook herself free and backed away from him. Her eyes, hard, cautious and pitiless, did not move from his face.

His arms were extended now in helpless yearning. 'Don't go. Don't leave me here alone!'

'You'll not come,' she said tonelessly.

He could not go on, he could not kill her, he could not remain here alone. He could do nothing. He could only repeat. 'Don't go!'

'Why?'

'You're nearly there.'

'Well?'

'I've got the gold,' he babbled, 'I've got it. You can have

half of it! You can have it all if you want it! You can have it! It's yours anyway. You have a right to it ... I should have given it to you before ...'

'You and David came to Eola and robbed these people of their gold. Is that it?' she said quietly.

'That's it,' he said. 'That's it.'

'You came here with that deliberate intention.' She had turned her back on the path ahead and faced him directly. It seemed to Washington that she had rejected the village and a faint hope rekindled in his heart.

'Yes, we planned it all. Nobody knew about it, you see. We only had to refuse Jobe his claim and nobody would come out here for years. We needed the money – I needed it. I didn't get my promotion. I should have had it ... I was the only one, but Trevor was scared to give it to me. He promised me something better. But I wasn't going to take it, I was going to walk out and start something of my own. I had to get out, I had to get away from him. He blocked everything I did. He prefers fools he can shove around, people he can bully and frighten like his poor idiot wife. And David needed it too. He owed Trevor money, a lot of money, and suddenly Trevor started pressing for payment. So we all put our heads together. Decided to come out here and have a look, then take what we could and put in an official report that there wasn't any.'

'And was there?'

Mistaking the glow in her face for greed, he nodded. 'More than we could carry back. We put it in the boxes we had brought the presents in. That's why we took so much and so many carriers. Warwick, Sereva and me. We only had to bring it here where the carriers were waiting. It's buried underneath my hut. We can't get it out of the country. That's the snag, getting it out and converting it. But we'll find a way.'

There was a long silence. Her eyes searched his face. He met her glance eagerly.

'Who killed David?' she said.

The hope died away. He started to cry. 'He killed himself,' he sobbed.

'Why?' But Washington, sobbing into outspread hands, could not answer her, and she went on, 'Because it was beyond him? Because he was too good for it and saw this – afterwards? Yes, I can see now. He would have to kill himself.'

He nodded over his hands. 'It's not so much,' he said in a stifled voice. He had forgotten her now and spoke to a presence within him that had waited these long weeks, patient but insistent, for his defence. 'It's no worse than the things we do every day. It's not so bad as giving them money they can't spend, or stopping their festivals, or telling them they can't dance. It's not as bad as giving them shirts that get wet and give them pneumonia or teaching them to value valueless things. We do it all day, not only here but all over the world. We teach them to gamble and drink. We give them tools and spoil their craftsmanship. We take away their capacity for happiness. We give them our diseases ...' He paused and dropped his hands. 'We're shocked by their head hunting and blow them up in our wars. Whenever you have an advanced culture in contact with primitive peoples the same thing happens. They perish. Look at Anthony Nyall. He tried to help them and he killed them. We wipe out whole villages with tuberculosis and whooping cough!' His eyes glittered and his face was knotted with excitement.

'That's half the picture,' said Stella. 'Good comes out of it ... or it will, one day.'

'One day!' he said.

She was still watching him intently, but he would not meet her eye. 'How did you get the gold?' she said. 'It's difficult, isn't it, to get into a village long house?'

'We frightened them,' he muttered.

'How?'

'With magic. We pretended we knew powerful magic.

We told them the gold was bad magic, that it would hurt them if they didn't give it away.'

She turned and looked on down the path in the direction of the village.

'You can't go!' He broke out again, 'You can't go. It didn't turn out right. They'll kill you. They'll kill us both! We must go back quickly now, before they find us.'

Not looking at him, she shook her head. 'That's not what you're afraid of,' she said.

He saw it was hopeless.

'Wait for me here,' she said. Her voice was flat. He felt that she had surrendered her will, that she was as powerless to stay as he was powerless to go. She could not look at him, and without turning her head went on down the path.

Washington held out his hands. 'Come back! Don't leave me alone!'

But the path ahead had turned, and Stella had gone. His voice died away and silence began.

‘Don’t go! Don’t go! Come back!’

The high, quavering voice, pitched almost to a scream, raved on and on, growing fainter and fainter, and then abruptly stopped.

Stella, walking on deliberately, held sensation away from her, pressing it back as you press on a door that threatens to burst open and let in a battalion of enemies.

The path turned slowly left towards the river and grew wider as she advanced. But it had not been cleared as much as the entrances to the other villages they had passed through. On both sides of the path the undergrowth pressed forward, and the creepers interlacing the trees trailed down ahead, so that she had to step around them or hold them aside and stoop beneath them. It was steamy and hot, for the sun was finding its way through the thinning trees. Mosquitoes and flies with long, fine legs steamed up from the undergrowth and settled on her face and hands. The path turned again and widened still further. On either side were huge, scarlet crotons and clumps of palms with spiky grey leaves. Ahead was the village.

Stella halted. At first glance it did not look remarkable. It was built on a flat, cleared space facing the river – a collection of raised huts made from timber, cane, woven leaves and grasses. In the centre was the men’s long house, its huge slanting roof thatched in soft grey leaf like the plumage of a gigantic bird. It faced the river, its swooping prow lifting up high above the roofs of the other houses.

Sunlight bathed the scene. There was a steamy thickness in the air that hung over the far bank of trees. There was so much about the place that was like other Bava River villages that a few moments passed before she realised that there was no sign of any living creature. When this understanding came on her she shrank back into the trees, and panic seemed to strain and shift the organs of her body.

She felt that the whole village had known of her coming for hours, perhaps for days and weeks, and had slunk away into their houses leaving the jungle and the village empty, and waited now in the dark doorways, turning upon her their watchful, revenging eyes. They would be capable of anything. Two white men had stolen their treasures.

There was nothing here, Washington had said. Was he right? What good would it do to step out from the trees, a target for Eola spears? The days of such deeds were not long past, and this was unpatrolled country. The arguments of fear were lucid and reasonable, but Stella could not obey them. To turn back now was unthinkable. She could not stop in the very act of completion. Anthony Nyall had seen in her ability to act some sort of salvation, and she felt vaguely that his future well-being in some way depended on her concluding what she had begun, that her own well-being depended on it too. It was bad enough to be as he was, incapable of the beginnings of action. Not to finish was unthinkable. The tears of Sylvia, the wild, mad hands of Philip clutching out for mercy would freeze into unforgettable memories if she could not raise above them the compensation of having arrived at her destination.

She took a quiet, halting step forward, but started back into cover once more. The red crotons beside her had sprung to life. They shuddered into a wild convulsed rustling. She stared in terror at the shaking, shivering shrubs. Something slid out on to the path ahead. It paused, looked sharply around and scuttled out into the sunlight. It was a fat, grey jungle rat.

She stood watching it. It was gross, obese like the sea slug and ran with a disgusting waddle. It was the only living thing visible, and she could not take her eyes off it; her skin was damp with loathing. It had reached the open clearing and the village houses. Here it paused again and looked around. It was confident, leisurely, unafraid.

Suddenly she thought, Not only are there no human beings, there are no pigs or dogs either. You could hide a man or a woman, or even a child, but it would be difficult to hide a dog unless you killed it.

The rat waddled on. It had reached the long house. Beyond were three large huts built in a row. Their doorways, with short wooden steps leading off the ground, faced directly across to where Stella stood. They were built close up against the trees behind and a long blanket of creeper with yellow flowers had fallen over the roof of one of the huts and trailed down across the open doorway. The house looked deserted, the thatch was damp, ragged and mouldy, and the creeper draping its door did not fall with the flowery lightness of garden decoration but like a shroud of cobweb fastened round an empty house that no one enters and no one leaves. In the very moment that this thought entered her mind the jungle rat scuttled up the steps and disappeared through the front door.

It was then that she knew what had happened at Eola; why Philip Washington dreaded to return and what had killed her husband. She stepped out into the jungle and followed in the tracks of the jungle rat. She was calm. She knew now that there was nothing to fear, and walked confidently. The only danger was in allowing the horror that was in Eola, that draped the village and inhabited the huts, that crawled and rotted on the ground, to invade her own body and mind. But some protective force that guards human beings at such times paralysed her senses and held her mind at a dumb, frozen level of consciousness.

She did not shirk her inspection. She made sure. She

walked across in front of the men's house, looking up at the tall peak of the roof, and then on to the group of houses on the other side. She mounted the wooden ladder on to the verandah and, parting the creepers with her hands, looked into the dark room within.

Three people had died there. Their white bones shone in the gloom. She could not see the grey rat but could hear its feet rustling on the floor and the scratch and crackle of insects feeding in the thatch.

The owner of the next house had died outside. He lay under the house on his back with his arms outstretched. A tight, moving patch of ants formed a black smear on the side of his skull. She thought how white and delicate were the bones of his hands. But his feet had gone.

She looked into the next house. It was empty, did not even house a pile of bones. But under the house she found a tin. It was the type that opens by the lid peeling back round a key. It was rusty and the label had gone. She turned it over with her foot. It was empty.

She left the houses and turned back into the centre of the village. Here in front of the long house were gruesome offerings of skulls and bones, sometimes complete, sometimes robbed by jungle scavengers, and some way from it was a rough open shelter and stone ovens that showed the scorch marks of flames. Scattered about among them were more tins, one still circled by the ragged remains of the red label of a tin of bully beef.

She walked on among the empty fireplaces. Some still contained bowls of ash that had not yet blown away and clung in the crevices of the stones. She found the bones of a child and a dog, and then a tin that had not been opened. She picked it up and turned it over in her hand. She noticed two small black holes – puncture marks – in the bottom.

Still holding the tin, she looked around her. There was no movement. The leaves of the trees hung limp in the stagnant air. A piece of thatch dropped from the roof of the shelter to her feet. There was no sound, but she fancied she could hear the village rotting around her – ants boring their tunnels in dry wood, the drip of thatch from the decaying ceilings and the crumble of ash in the stone ovens. The process of decay had been so swift the village almost appeared in a state of visible movement and change. She half expected it to crumble into dust before her eyes. Only the human beings, who had been the first to rot, were at peace.

She stood there, the tin in her hand. She did not move. This was her husband's murderer. Yet it was strange that at this moment she did not think of his death, but of her father's, and her eyes filled with tears.

He killed my father too, she thought. He thought me too young and innocent to face up to what he did, and so he killed my father. She dropped the tin on the ground and her heart was filled with bitterness towards him.

The force that had urged her on to this spot had abandoned her. She must move now of her own will or not at all. She felt the horror around her slide slowly nearer. She still did not move but her body was clutched and shaken with dread. A circle of insubstantial hands, from which the flesh dripped away, had reached out and touched her.

Then came a scream.

At first she thought the cry was her own, till it came again, sounding from the jungle behind her. It was a terrified sound, only just recognisable as human.

She turned and ran. She had reached the long house when the silence split and cracked. When she reached the jungle there was a second shot.

Caution did not occur to her. She knew the second shot was final. But she wasn't surprised. She understood now that when she left Washington she had not expected to see him alive again.

I killed him, she thought as she ran. I killed Washington. So many murderers. Washington, David, Anthony and I are all murderers. Trevor is the worst of all, because he never saw his victims.

Then she stopped. The path had swerved away from the river and opened into the small glade where she had left her companion. He lay sprawled across the path. But he was not alone. A boy was crouched over him.

In Marapai she had seen boys from outlying villages who had come in on their canoes, wandered painted and ornamented about the streets, dog-teeth necklaces round their throats, beads in their ears and flowers and leaves stuffed into the bands round their arms and calves. But she had never seen anyone so strangely and gorgeously daubed and festooned as this.

He was a brown man, slim, lithe and not very tall, naked except for a thin strip of bark wound round his waist and drawn between his legs. His body was streaked with brown and white and his face painted in a dramatic design. There was a splash of yellow down the bridge of his nose, white lines sprayed out from the corners of his mouth and curled down to converge in a beak on his chin. His arms and hair were decked with green and yellow croton leaves. He carried bow and arrows and looked more like a bird than a man.

He stood quite still, staring at her. He did not appear to threaten her, though there was threat undeniably evident on his face. Though he was brilliant and gay and strangely beautiful she knew he was dressed for death.

Then she saw the watch on his wrist. It was Hitolo.

They spoke simultaneously.

He looked back at the man at his feet. The birdlike painting of his face rendered it expressionless, but she saw his eyes flash in their whitened sockets and knew he was terrified. She ran forward and knelt down over Washington. His head was shattered. The pistol had dropped to the ground beside him. She could do no more than glance at him, but there was no need. She turned away. 'What happened, Hitolo?'

Hitolo shook his head. Speech seemed to have deserted him.

'What happened? Tell me!'

'He tried to kill me,' he said. 'Mrs Warwick, he shot himself. I did not shoot him. He shot at me, he shot himself.'

'Of course you didn't kill him. I can see that. You have no gun.'

'Why did he shoot at me, Mrs Warwick?' He looked at her helplessly.

'He didn't know you, Hitolo. And he wouldn't expect you to come back. He thought you were afraid.'

'I was afraid,' he said. 'I go mad. I run away. Then I remember.' She gave him a long glance of admiration, seeing how magnificently he had acted, defying the accumulative force of panic, and returning like this, dressed for vengeance.

'I called to him,' said Hitolo, 'and waved my hands.'

She was beginning to see how it had happened. 'And he shot at you and missed you?'

'Yes.'

'And so you came on, calling and waving your hands? He did not expect you,' she murmured. 'He did not expect anyone. There is nobody here, everyone is dead. He knew that. He *knew* that everyone was dead. They died at a festival dressed up as you are now, for dancing.'

Hitolo blinked at her. He did not understand. 'Poor Philip,' she said.

'They are all dead,' he repeated stupidly.

'Yes, there's nobody now. I expect some got away, but they would never come back. The rest died of food poisoning. Bad tins, the same that killed Sereva. He ate a bad tin. It was an accident, Hitolo. It was not meant for him.'

There was no reading his encrusted, birdlike face. I wonder how he feels, she thought. I wonder if it pains him that there is no murderer to chase, no Jobe to hate, no justice to pursue.

The ground around them was soft and spongy, and they managed to dig a shallow grave. It seemed a pointless courtesy to pay him in such a place, but Stella, remembering the clot of ants on the side of a skull and the fat grey rat, could not bear to leave him uncovered. They worked with sticks but could not dig deep – the floor of the jungle was laced with the roots of trees. They covered his body with soil and heaped the mound with leaves and branches.

It was about four when they left. Stella was exhausted. She yearned to lie down and sleep but felt that if she slept here she would never wake again.

Stella had very little recollection of the journey back to Maiola. She felt that if it had been a hundred yards further away she would not have reached it. As it was, Hitolo all but carried her during the last day's march. She was not in pain but she was weak and at times hardly aware of her surroundings. They always seemed to be walking through the same stretch of jungle. The trees were the same, the path was the same and turned round corners to reveal jungle that had just been crossed. They might have been marking time.

When they reached Maiola her strength gave way and she could no longer stand. She remembered vaguely stumbling up some steps into an empty hut. She remembered, too, looking down and seeing with surprise Hitolo's shadowy fingers gripping her arms.

Then she slept a long, uneasy, broken sleep. Occasionally she could hear voices outside. Someone brought her food, but she could not remember if she ate it. Once she opened her eyes and looked into a long, rectangular strip of sky lit with enormous stars. She felt a yearning, for something, someone, she did not know what – perhaps her father – and lay for a long time with tears welling up in her eyes and running down her cheeks. She did not move. Her body might have been weighed down with chains. At last she opened her eyes and saw Thomas Seaton's lean face peering over her.

He asked her some questions, but she could not remember having answered him, or even what the questions were. She went to sleep again, and while she slept she was carried outside on to the station launch. When she awoke she was in bed at Seaton's house at Kairipi.

She knew immediately where she was, though she had never seen the room before. She could look out through an open louvre down a pathway lined with hibiscus bushes. Two boys were cutting the lawn with pieces of bent hoop-iron. Her fever had gone. Her head was clear and her skin dry, but she felt she would never move again.

As she lay there a Papuan girl in a blue calico frock with a cross around her neck crept forward from a corner of the room and peered into her face, then brought a basin of water and washed her. She slid away out of the door, and a few moments later Seaton came in.

'Washington's dead,' Stella said. 'He shot himself.'

He stood stiffly to attention at the end of her bed and nodded. 'I know, you told me.'

'Did I? Have I been very ill?'

He was obviously not used to sick-rooms, particularly with women in them. His head was drawn back and his expression severe. He nodded again. 'Fever. Shock, too, I should say. Couldn't move you. Risky. Best to stay here. You're all right now.'

'When can I go back to Marapai?'

'Not until you're stronger. Better stay here for a while. I know a bit about fever.'

The yearning that had not left her even in sleep became more urgent. 'Do they know at Marapai?'

'Yes.'

'And did no one ask for me? Has no one been to see me?'

'I got through to Nyall.'

'Anthony?'

'Trevor. Most concerned. Wanted to fly over but there was no point. Better if you stay quiet for a few days. Had a long talk.

No official report till I've been to Eola and had a look around.'

Where is he? Why doesn't he come and see me when I'm alone and ill? If he loved me why doesn't he come and look after me?

'Bad show,' said Seaton stiffly. He looked for a moment straight into her eyes and the gulf between them shrank. 'Bad show. Funny how people break up here. Never know what they'll do next. People you'd least expect.' He straightened his shoulders, lifted his chin and resurrected his impersonal expression. 'Bad for the Territory,' he said sombrely, 'bad for the administration.'

'Bad for the Eolans,' said Stella and started to laugh. She found that once having started she could not stop. Laughter rippled up her limbs and choked out of her lips. She clenched her teeth but she could not stop.

Seaton looked at her and wondered if he should slap her face. She looked too sick to strike, so instead he moved forward, put a hand on her shoulder and shook her sharply. Her laughter stopped instantly, and he drew his hand away.

'Tough on you ... plenty of pluck too. People break out, you know, Washington ... understandable, not the sort of man to come to this country. No principles. But Warwick ... he was a good fellow. Can't understand it.'

'*Was* he a good fellow?' said Stella, looking up with large feverish eyes.

Embarrassed, Seaton glanced away. 'Oh, yes,' he said gruffly. 'One of the very best.'

'Was it my fault or would it have happened anyway?' said Stella.

Not following her fleeting, disconnected thoughts he gave her a puzzled glance. 'What?'

'Washington? Was he mad? He would have killed himself, wouldn't he, like David? They did something that was far outside their natures and then couldn't live with it.'

Where was Anthony? He knew about Philip, he understood. Why didn't he come and tell her that it wasn't her fault, that he was mad and wanted to die?

'It wasn't my fault?'

He gripped her shoulder again and gently shook her. 'Go to sleep. Plenty of rest, that's what you need. Nasty experience. Try not to think about it.'

'He killed my father,' said Stella and turned her head into the pillow.

A fortnight later she returned to Marapai. The flying boat came to rest on the ruffled blue bay at about 3.30 in the afternoon. There ahead was the town with its white roofs straggling up the slopes of the hills. The trees, their flowering nearly over, were breaking into violent green leaf. Her eyes turned to the wharf where a group of white figures stood waiting.

One of them would be there, she felt sure. But which? She did not know which emotion was strongest. Dread that it might be one, or hope that it might be the other.

The hostess, who knew she had been ill, helped her into the boat. The wharf drew nearer. The brown faces under topees and straw hats gradually acquired features. Then she saw him. It was Anthony, and Janet was with him.

He came half way down the steps to help her up from the boat. They did not speak or smile. The rush of feeling towards him died away as she looked into his face. She walked up the steps beside him thinking, He won't help me, he won't even comfort me. I am on my own.

She realised that throughout her sickness she had been wanting him to cling to and rest against, that the picture of him as she had reconstructed it had seen her through those terrible weeks. But it was not a true picture; she had forgotten what he was like. For he would fulfil none of these supporting and protective functions. He was even more lost and bewildered than she. The weight of twelve deaths hung around his neck; she only bore the weight of one. His dark, unhappy eyes looked into hers only for an instant and then he turned away.

Janet stood above them on the wharf. The wind blew her dress about her tiny body. Stella pressed her hand and smiled. She no longer shrank from Janet, knowing what it was she had shrunk from before.

'You're to come and stay with us,' said Janet, as they moved off down the wharf. 'Trevor insisted. And you're not to work until you're stronger.'

Stella thought she was less vague and stupid than she remembered her, but perhaps this was only because her husband was not there.

She glanced at Anthony. 'Do you think it's all right?'

He did not meet her eye but shrugged his shoulders. 'You'll need a rest. I see no reason why not. It's up to you.'

I see no reason why not. She continued to stare at him, wondering if this meant that they were to lie to each other. But he would not be drawn by her glance and gazed ahead.

'Trevor couldn't come to meet you,' said Janet. 'So I came instead. He was kept back late. But I expect he'll be home when we get there.'

Stella watched her face with its large, unfocused eyes. She doesn't know, she thought. And Anthony...? Yes, Anthony knew. 'Why didn't you come and see me,' she said quietly.

'At Kairipi?' he glanced at her and glanced quickly away. 'I didn't know what was best. I thought of going, but I didn't know what you would want. Seaton said you were all right. I didn't know what to do.'

'So you did nothing.'

His lips tightened. 'This was your show,' he said. 'I thought it was best for you to be on your own until the end.'

'Here we are,' said Janet as they approached Trevor's large, expensive and thoroughly unsuitable car. 'Tony, will you drive?'

She looked up and blinked her big, drained eyes. He

moved forward. But she held up a hand and her face crumpled with uncertainty. 'No, perhaps I should drive. He doesn't like you driving this car, does he, because of your eyes and not being able to see out of the sides of your glasses.'

Anthony opened the back door. 'I'll drive.'

Janet was looking up and down the street as if hoping that Trevor might arrive to resolve the problem. An argument followed that ended with her getting into the back and then leaning out again to entreat Anthony to drive carefully.

Stella was not listening. A woman was standing on the opposite side of the road looking at her. She wore no hat and the sun blazed down on her shining black head. She stood with her hands at her sides and her feet together, and something about her suggested that she had been there for a long time, waiting. It was Sylvia.

Their eyes met. Instinctively Stella moved forward and put out a hand. A car drove between them and when it had passed Sylvia was walking swiftly down the road away from the town. Stella stood gazing after her. Sickness had pulled a protective skin from her senses and any emotion that she experienced was sharp and intense. Her eyes filled with tears.

She got into the car and shut the door. They drove off towards the town. It was four, the stores were just closing and the streets were filled with people. Trevor was already at home, waiting for them. As they entered Janet and Anthony dropped behind her, and she found herself walking ahead as if they had accepted her leadership against a common adversary.

It was a shock to see him standing there, his hand held out to her – tall, handsome, smiling. During the past few weeks her memory of him had changed, and it was a face altogether different from this that she had expected. Then she looked closer and thought, No this is just the sort of face he should have.

He felt for her hand, for she had not held it out to him,

and gripped her fingers. Because she had been ill and her senses were more responsive than at anytime since her father's death, she almost shuddered.

'Well, and so you're back with us, thank God!' he said.

She had intended to be calm and natural, but anger and loathing swept her resolution away. She could not help saying, 'It must surprise you, you couldn't have been expecting it.'

She stared at him, and because his eyes were clear and guiltless there was no need for him to look away. She began to understand just how much beyond David and Philip he was in the scope of his capabilities.

He put out a hand and patted her shoulder. 'I'm afraid later on you'll have to answer some questions, but for the moment we don't want you to even mention it. We want you to forget the whole affair.'

'Yes, you would want that,' she said, drawing away. She heard an uneasy movement behind her and saw that her words were not touching Trevor, only tormenting Anthony. Janet fluttered away murmuring, 'I'll see about tea.'

That evening she spoke to Anthony alone. Janet was playing bridge and Trevor had gone to a meeting. It was very hot so they sat on the verandah overlooking the town to catch the breeze. They sat for some moments in silence. It was taut and wretched, and there was no feeling of communion between them. At last Stella said, 'What are we going to do?'

He did not answer, but turned to look at her. The light flashed on his glasses and intensified an air he had of nursing secrets.

'About Trevor,' she said.

'What about him?'

She remembered the night outside Washington's hut when he had abruptly changed his attitude and had appeared to approve of what she was doing. He had permitted her actions, had even encouraged them, and now feared to face the consequence. He had reason to fear. 'Don't let *us* be dishonest,' she said quietly. 'He was behind it, he began it. It was his idea.'

He looked away from her over the town. His voice was unsurprised but still guarded. 'Did Washington tell you that?'

'Not exactly. He was too muddled and frightened to be lucid. But he let it out – in several ways. I *knew*. When he told me about it, he said "we all" and one doesn't say "we all" for two. But of course he's behind it; it's so obvious. They could never think it up; it wouldn't occur to them. They could only do it and then under compulsion.' She shuddered. 'He's loathsome. He's a million times worse than they are. They're children, they're babies compared with him. People can do just about anything when they're actually *there* – and out in the jungle, you can see, when you get there – anything could happen. Anyway I don't believe they meant it to be as wholesale as it was. Perhaps they only wanted to frighten them away, to make a few of them sick. But they misjudged either the strength of the poison they used or the villagers' resistance. I think it got out of hand.'

'You let them off lightly.'

'Not because of anything I feel for David, if that's what you mean. You were right there.'

He knew what it meant to her to say this, and let it pass. 'If you let them off with less terrible intentions,' he said, 'then you have to let him off too.'

'No!' she cried. 'He tried to kill me! He sent me out there to die. He sent Philip to kill me and he hoped it would be the end of Philip. Philip would never have worked out *that* solution; he dreaded the place. It was agony for him to go back. And anyway he was incapable of killing me. They were both of them incapable of the whole thing.'

'They managed to kill off a whole village,' Anthony said tonelessly.

'Yes, they did. But Philip, in spite of all his tolerance, would see that as less terrible than killing one white woman.

Anyway I don't believe they meant to. It was beyond anything they had intended ... and then Sereva, on top of everything. It was beyond Philip even more than David. Suicide wasn't enough for Philip, he wanted to be punished. But Trevor! He wouldn't care, he would see the destruction of the village as an improvement on the plan. And then he quietly arranged another murder to tidy it all up.'

'I think you see him as larger than life,' he murmured.

'He is,' she cried. 'He's a monster.' Her voice trembled. 'He doesn't know what it's like out there. He didn't even see his own victims. He spills blood by remote control. The whole thing to him was as passionless as algebra. He wouldn't go mad or commit suicide; he spares himself from the discomfort of such things. He sits behind his desk and thinks up monstrosities, keeps his hands clean and sleeps at night without dreaming. I'm not even afraid of him, though he knows I know. He wouldn't dirty himself with hurting me. He's so clean.'

For the first time he looked fully at her and smiled. 'Don't you know that most of the world's biggest crimes are committed by men who sit behind desks, keep their hands clean and sleep at night without dreaming? And usually when things blow up in their faces, as they sometimes do, they manage to worm out by a back alley, or, as Trevor has done, walk boldly through the front door.' He paused and there was an ironic twist to his lips. 'Yesterday he made out a detailed report of the whole thing. There's something magnificent in that; you can't help admiring it. I'm afraid you haven't got a shred of evidence against him. He's completely in the clear. The gold's been dug up. Possibly his cut has already been disposed of.'

He paused, and when he spoke again there was a note of anxiety in his voice. 'You could of course invent a confession from Washington, but it would hardly cut much ice. You've suppressed it so far, and it would be argued that you had thought it up to clear your husband. You're known as something of a fanatic in that line,' he added, looking away. 'But it would make things exceedingly uncomfortable for Trevor – and for others.'

'Janet.'

'Janet, for one.'

'But, good God, she can't love him! He treats her like a dog, a fool. She doesn't even know what he's like.' She stopped abruptly.

But he let the opportunity for cheap triumph pass by. 'She's used to him,' he said quietly. 'She'd be completely lost without him. She wouldn't know what to do. She's happy enough, in a way. She gets a lot of pleasure out of doing what she thinks he wants. Without him she'd be terrified. She hasn't made a decision of her own in years.'

Stella waited, hoping that he might say more, but he was silent. At last an overpowering curiosity pressed her to say, 'What was she like when she was younger?'

He did not answer, but turned and looked at her. She understood. 'And that night when I came to dinner you changed your mind. You decided you'd stop it from happening again, you'd let me find out, about David and Trevor, no matter how horrible it was.'

'Perhaps,' he said. 'It was more that I couldn't bear to see someone else being taken in by Trevor.'

She felt a sharp stab of disappointment. 'I don't understand you. One moment you seem to loathe him – I felt it even then – then in the next you protect him.'

'That's what makes it so impossible. You see, in his way he's been good to me. When we were at school there was a little boy whose father owned a sweet shop. Trevor used to make him steal chocolates. And he always gave half of the spoil to me. I don't know what he did, but that little boy was frightened of him. When I found out I stopped taking the chocolates, but I could never tell on Trevor. That was the beginning; it's always been like that. He's hung on to my job for me, he's housed me and fed me.'

'But don't you see that's his line,' said Stella tensely. 'That's how he works. That's what he did to David, helped him to an enormous extent. He gave him money and then suddenly turned round and forced him into this. He strangles with obligations. Look at the position he's got you in. You can't hurt him because you ought to feel gratitude, because you've eaten his chocolate and because you have a dead village of your own. He's ruined your life. He certainly doesn't like you.'

'I don't know what he feels,' said Anthony slowly. 'I didn't know that I hated him until you told me. I disapproved of him, but ... he feels we should stick together.'

'You can't. It's killing you.'

A car was coming up the hill past the house. For a moment its headlights flashed through the trees and glanced off Anthony's face. He looked pale and tired, and gazed at her with fear and longing.

Impulsively she put out both her hands. She saw in the flash the horror of his situation. Her heart went out to him, and in that moment she gave herself completely over to seeing him through it.

'You're right,' she said. 'We can't do anything. It would be quite useless. It would do no good. It would be trouble-making and no more. He'll just have to get away with it.'

His face twisted into a spasm of anxiety. 'Do you think so? Are you sure? I'm not.'

'Well, I am. I'm quite sure,' she said definitely. 'Don't look like that.'

She wrenched her hand away and pressed her palm on his brow. 'It's terrible that he should get away with it, scot free, no scars, no fears, no bad dreams. But we can't do anything about it. So let's just admit it's terrible and forget it. Don't brood on it. Forget it.'

They did not speak again for some time. Stella was watching the long black beans of the flame trees still hanging in the young foliage of the new season. I shall leave too, she thought and go back to the mess. She remembered the little room with the faded bed cover and the lizard in the corner of the ceiling. The memory took her back to her first days in Marapai, and a moment later she said, 'I wonder what happened to Jobe.'

He was at that very moment talking to Trevor Nyall, who had not gone to a meeting but was driving slowly along the sea-front.

'What else could I do?' Nyall was saying sharply. 'Do you think I liked it? Do you imagine it pleased me to see it go?'

Jobe sucked on the damp butt of a cigarette. 'Seems to me it was a mistake to ever let this fellow Washington in on it,' he said. 'Can't think why you did that. Nervous type. You should know about people. You should have picked him.'

'We had to have him,' Nyall said. 'I never dreamed Washington would fall down on it – he's too greedy.'

'I'm glad she got back,' Jobe said mildly. 'Nice little thing, pretty as paint.'

'You're glad!' Trevor threw him a brief glance, making no attempt to disguise both surprise and revulsion. The smell of Jobe's body filled the car. The need to be even moderately polite to such a creature was irksome to Trevor. 'Then don't complain about losing the gold. It's unfortunate, but it was the only thing to do. We're lucky to be out of it. We're clear; let's thank our stars for that.'

Jobe sucked on the damp brown butt of his cigarette, then dropped it on the floor of the car and crushed it out with his toe. 'I haven't lost it, Mr Nyall, you have.'

'Well, it amounts to the same thing. If you can think of some way of getting it back from the administration, you're welcome to it. When I promised you Warwick's share ...'

'You didn't exactly promise it, Mr Nyall. Mr Warwick gave it to me. Handed over his claim as it were.'

Nyall gritted his teeth. He was not given to uncontrollable

anger, but he burned with rage whenever he thought of what Warwick had done – those stupid, blundering, sentimental, repentant acts. The weak, hysterical, troublesome fool who was too squeamish to live with his own deeds – a letter to a sick man that had driven them all to this drastic end, a confession to this crooked rogue beside him. And then the weakest act of all, the taking of his own life.

Jobe was still speaking. 'Now if I should want to get the gold from the administration all I would have to do would be to take along Mr Warwick's letter. That would show them plain enough how it all happened. How the gold was mine and you and Mr Warwick and Mr Washington had hopped in and grabbed it for yourselves. I think the administration would probably see that I'd been hardly done by.'

If Nyall was disturbed by this speech he gave no sign. 'They'll probably give it back to the Papuans or put it into Native Revenue. You can bet your life you wouldn't see any of it.'

Jobe did not appear to be upset by the idea of the natives winning in the end. 'Well, it would be worth trying, wouldn't it?' he said mildly.

'Warwick was mad when he wrote that letter' said Nyall harshly.

'He was a little upset. But I can't help feeling he knew what he was doing. I can't help feeling he knew I'd insist on my rights.' He turned round and gave Nyall a slow smile. His eyes sparkled in their dark sockets. 'I think maybe he didn't like the mess you'd got him into. I don't think he liked you at all. He says in his letter he would never have agreed if he hadn't been so pressed for dough. It was you that was doing the pressing, wasn't it? I can't help feeling he thought it wouldn't hurt much if things was made uncomfortable for you.'

There was no longer any denying the direction he was pointing the conversation. Nyall faced it without further evasion. 'Blackmail,' he said calmly. His eyes did not leave the road ahead. It was empty. They were out of the town and the houses were few and scattered.

'I only want my rights,' said Jobe plaintively. 'I'm only asking for my share.'

'It would take me years to pay you,' said Nyall. His voice was quiet and controlled. His face gave no indication of his feelings.

'I don't mind waiting. You can pay it in instalments.'

'How do I know you'll be satisfied when it's paid off?'

Jobe was still smiling. 'You'll have to take a chance on that, Mr Nyall. On my word. After all I haven't been unreasonable, have I? Another man might have expected the lot. I wouldn't want to be a burden to you, Mr Nyall. But there is a lot you could do without. This car for instance. Bit flashy for this place, don't you reckon? Jeeps are better for the islands. Sydney, that's where this little baby should be.' And he patted the door of the car. 'And when it's paid up I give you my word I'll send back the original of Warwick's letter. In the meantime' – the road was cut into the cliff and he looked pensively over a steep drop to the sea – 'it's in the hands of a friend of mine who has instructions to send it to the administrator in the event of my death.'

Nyall did not speak. He drew the car to a standstill, backed it into the cliff and turned round. He felt he could not bear the stench of the man's body for a moment longer. They say natives stink, he thought. You could at least keep away from natives. The smell seemed to have soaked into his own clothes, and the pores of his skin. He had vague notions of hurrying home and cleansing himself under a shower. Realisation of the larger evil, the more devastating and lasting contact with this man, he still held at arm's length.

'You probably won't place much faith in my word, Mr Nyall,' Jobe was saying cheerfully. He was lighting another cigarette. The big, inappropriate car gathered speed. The road ahead stretched straight into the town.

'You don't like me, Mr Nyall. I know that. I can feel these things. Sort of instinctive, you know. You think I'm not a gentleman and you think I won't keep my word. Well, I'm telling you, Mr Nyall, you can trust me. You'll see.'

His eyes glittered in the headlights of an approaching car. With laughter? With greed? Or merely with high spirits?

'You'll see,' he said again.

ABOUT THE AUTHOR

Geraldine Mary Jay was born in 1919 in Adelaide, Australia where she still lives and works as a novelist and art dealer. She worked as a secretary in Australia and in London during the 1940s and as a court stenographer for the Australian Court of Papua New Guinea in 1949. She and her husband, John Halls, who worked for UNESCO, traveled widely during the 1950s. He died in 1982.

Charlotte Jay is the name under which she has published most of her nine mystery novels, all of which appeared between 1951 and 1964 except for one, *The Voice of the Crab*, which was published in 1974. Only her first, *The Knife is Feminine*, takes place in Australia. The others are set in Pakistan, Japan, Thailand, India and Lebanon. *The Fugitive Eye* was made into a movie starring Charlton Heston.

Soho Crime

Other Titles in this Series

Janwillem van de Wetering

Just a Corpse at Twilight

Outsider in Amsterdam

Tumbleweed

The Corpse on the Dike

Death of a Hawker

Seichō Matsumoto

Inspector Imanishi Investigates

Martin Limón

Jade Lady Burning

Jim Cirni

The Kiss Off

The Come On

Timothy Watts

Cons

Money Lovers